meet me on Lilac Lane

praise for
Meet Me on Lilac Lane

"This novel about second chances and building resilience after a traumatic event is one you won't want to miss. It's everything I am looking for in a contemporary romance. I closed my Kindle, realizing that I'd just experienced a supremely satisfying read and given my emotions a real workout."

—The Literate Leprechaun, GOODREADS

"I am loving this series on Jonathon Island! I couldn't wait to read more about Mia and Cody."

—Laura, GOODREADS

"The story is heartwarming and emotional, and the setting is colorful and gorgeous. Many background characters shine and the sense of community leaps off the pages. You'll want to relocate to Jonathan Island—I guarantee it!"

—Deena, GOODREADS

"*Meet Me on Lilac Lane* is an awesome read with realistic characters, a chance at love, and overcoming fears."

—Allyson, GOODREADS

meet me on Lilac Lane

ANDREA CHRISTENSON

SUNRISE PUBLISHING

To anyone brave enough to find love.

"When the cares of my heart are many, your consolations cheer my soul."

PSALM 94:19 ESV

Jonathon Island

Meet Me on Jonathon Island (prequel novella)
Meet Me at the Grand
Meet Me on Lilac Lane
Meet Me at the Fudge Shop
Meet Me on Blueberry Hill
Meet Me at Sunset Cove
Meet Me at the Christmas Cottage

JONATHON ISLAND
N W E S
Jonathon Family Home
Sullivan Pumpkin Farm
Lake Shore Drive
State Park
Sullivan Way
MacBride Resort
Airport
Jonathon Blvd
Quinn Ranch
Sunset Cove
Maple Ln
Sugar
Blueberry Hills Neighborhood
LAKE HURON
Barrett House
Partridge Ln
Blueberry Blvd
Dahlia Dr
Lilac Ln
Zinnia Blvd
Poppy Place
Rose Rd
Pinnacle Dr
Blueberry Hills Park
GRAND HOTEL
Main Street
Downtown
Marina Way
Marina

One

UNDER THE BEAUTY OF THE SUN BANK-ing to the west in a brilliant May sky, Mia Franklin could almost, almost believe her life wasn't about to fall apart. She grimaced and pushed harder on the pedals of her bike, the colorful two-child trailer attachment bouncing empty behind her.

In between the shops dotting Main Street on Jonathon Island, Mia caught glimpses of Lake Huron sparkling in the sun. If only each sparkle were a diamond, then her problems would be solved. She knew better though. Knew just how deadly that deceptive lake could be.

Patrick Kelley waved at her from the doorway of his bar and grill. "Hi, Mia." The fifty-something's wiry mustache curved up as he smiled. "Got Finn and Maggie back there? I just got a shipment of peanuts in the shell, and I know how much they like them."

"Nope, sorry." She slowed to a stop in front of Kelley's. "I dropped them off at Mom and Dad's."

"Come by anytime. I'll give them a bag. My treat." He waved again before disappearing back into his building.

Sometimes her life felt like an art piece. She pictured a museum curator explaining to a tour group, "Observe this portrait of Mia Jonathon Franklin. Widowed two years ago at twenty-two, mother of two children . . ."

Everyone on this island had their own way of showing their pity for her plight.

Too bad pity didn't pay the bills.

Her phone alarm buzzed; five minutes until her meeting at the bank.

A chilly breeze floated in off the water and between the buildings as she biked her way down the cobblestone street, ending up at a graying clapboard structure.

Her belly rumbled as she pushed her way into the bank. Crammed into the handbag slung over her shoulder were three months' worth of overdue notice letters sent to her from Great Lakes National Bank. Three months where she'd needed to choose between paying the mortgage or clothing her growing kids. Three months of keeping the heat on. Three months of avoiding Mr. Michaelson on Sundays at church.

She hated that she even needed to make these choices. She shifted the bag on her shoulder, the strap rubbing her through her jacket. Dark paneling lined the walls of the bank's interior.

"Mia, come on back." Mr. Michaelson poked his head out of the office bearing his name.

Gray-haired, tall, and slim, he hadn't changed much in the almost fifteen years she'd known him. His thin lips didn't curve into his normal, cheerful smile. Kyle, her sister's husband, worked for this bank too. For a fleeting moment, Mia wished she'd scheduled this meeting with him at his branch in Port Joseph, but ferrying there and back would add so much extra time away from her kids. Not to mention the expense of the ferry ticket.

She hung her jacket on a coat hook in the corner and then settled into a chair in front of Mr. Michaelson's desk. The cold plastic seat sent another shiver through her. The clean desk, organized within an inch of its life, contrasted sharply with the ratty, thrifted crossbody bag she set on it. Across from her, Mr. Michaelson tented his fingers.

"Look, Mia, let me just cut to the chase here. The board is pressuring me to foreclose on your loan."

Mia sucked in a breath. It was one thing to know what was coming. Another thing altogether to have it said aloud. Her stomach clenched. "Please. You can't do that." She sat on the edge of her chair. Reaching into her bag, her fingers closed around a tattered envelope. Her last lifeline. She handed it to him. "Here, it's not much, but I've been saving some back from my tips." After Troy's life insurance dipped into a four-digit number from the six it had started at, she'd taken a few shifts at Martha's on Main. They hadn't been able to give her regular hours, just some shift work when others had to be off island.

Mr. Michaelson flipped through the meager notes in the envelope. "This isn't even enough to cover half a month."

"You know how slow things have been around here since the pandemic." Of course, things had never really recovered after the Grand Sullivan Hotel fire ten years ago. Mia's heart squeezed as an image of that once majestic hotel flashed in her mind. They'd just recently broken ground on the project, and her cousin and best friend, Dani, had high hopes for a revitalized economy. But until then . . . "Martha has barely been able to give any of us hours. There's just not enough tourists to support the work. Plus, it's been so hard since my husband died. Now, the life insurance is running out—" She cut herself off, hating the whine that started to creep into her tone. She would not whine. Beg if she had to—she had her kids to think about after all—but never whine. This was her lot in life. She'd chosen it. She would live with it.

Mr. Michaelson nodded. "I'm so sorry again for your loss. I really liked Troy. He was on the track team with my son." He fiddled with the envelope in front of him. "I certainly don't want to be turning a widow out of her home. Especially one with little kids."

She pictured Finn and Maggie's sweet faces. Four-year-old Finn's serious look, with his blond curls and brown eyes so like his father's. And Maggie, two years younger, born just after Troy died, pixie-like with her darker blonde hair and blue eyes. She would do anything for them. Even beg.

"Just give me a few more weeks. Now that tourism season has started . . ." But what hope did she have, really?

Please, God. Let something come up. She thought back to the email she'd received from a friend in Traverse City offering her a job. She shoved the thought away. Last resort only. She wouldn't tear her children from their home until it was her only option.

"Maybe you could ask your dad for help," Mr. Michaelson said.

She stood abruptly; the chair rocked on its legs. "No. That is out of the question." She hadn't asked him for help since she'd arrived home, pregnant and unmarried at nineteen years old, determined to show him that she and Troy could make it as teenagers with a child.

Even after marrying Troy, buying a house, and having two beautiful children, she couldn't shake the disappointment that seemed to linger from him.

Mr. Michaelson held up a hand, palm forward. "Okay. Just a suggestion." He rubbed his hand through his thinning hair. "Fine. I'll give you one more month. I'll hold off the board until . . ." He flipped a few pages on his desk calendar, "June 15th. Let's plan to meet again then and see where you're at."

A wave of relief washed over her. "Thank you so much," she said and turned to grab her jacket. Behind her, she heard the scratching of a pen across paper. She kept her back to the banker for a moment, blinking back tears.

After composing herself, she shoved her arms into her jacket then turned back to the desk. "Your kindness means the world to me." She picked up her purse and slung it onto her shoulder.

He shook her hand and she hurried out of the building. She put her purse into the bike trailer, then flung a leg over her bicycle and rode slowly down Main Street. So many of the storefronts closed and shuttered. Abandoned by their owners, the deterioration beginning to show. Some of the buildings had cracked windows, siding sagged, one even had plywood where plate glass used to be. Martha's on Main was still open though, as was Good Day Coffee and Kelley's Bar & Grill. The Kelley siblings—Frank, Patrick, and Jill—had pretty much a monopoly on the restaurants in town.

After dodging a few tourists, she paused outside a small storefront. Gray clapboard siding rose to a peak at the top of the structure. Large windowpanes let in the light. Closed now, the store once held Sampson's, a small art studio and gift shop. If she squinted, she could almost picture her teenage self at the till, ringing up a customer and dreaming of the day she owned her own gallery.

A cold wet sensation in her hand startled her, and she looked down to see a scruffy Jack Russell terrier nuzzling her palm. "Hello, Jack."

The dog lived on the streets of Jonathon Island. He belonged to no one and to everyone. Everyone fed him, and some gave him a place to stay overnight when he deigned to let them. Sometimes Mia thought he should run for mayor—the dog would definitely win.

She scratched behind his ears. "Do you have any idea how to raise enough money to pay a mortgage?" The dog gave a soft roo-roo and then trotted off. "Some help you are."

Her phone buzzed with a text from her mom's number.

<u>Mom</u>

Can you bring a loaf of bread? I forgot to pick one up.

<u>Mia</u>

Sure. Be there soon.

Better quit daydreaming and get back to Finn and Maggie. She pedaled through town and turned into the neighboring street until she came to her own. Hanging a right, she headed halfway down, then turned into the front yard of her little house on Lilac Lane.

The small two-bedroom, one-and-a-half-floor Craftsman sat nested between two much larger houses. The white siding was flaking off near the bottom of the walls. And one shutter hung askew alongside the living room window. These imperfections didn't stop the rush of tenderness deep in her core every time she spotted the home she and Troy had worked so hard on.

They'd gotten plenty done on the inside, including updating the bedrooms and bathroom, but other than painting the front door, they hadn't managed to spruce up the outside before the boating accident.

And now she might lose it.

She shoved the thought into a far corner of her brain—it was getting crowded back there—as she ran past the lilac at the front door and then inside to grab a loaf of French bread from the kitchen at the back of the house. In the kitchen sink, dishes from the morning's breakfast sat waiting for her to scrub the dried-on scrambled eggs. She ignored the urge to move the laundry into the dryer.

Being late for supper wasn't an option. Back outside, she tucked the bread next to her purse and took off again.

A few miles of hard biking gave her time to bury the past hour deep into her heart before the weekly family dinner with her parents.

Her parents' grand house with its sweeping porch and turrets came into view at the northern tip of the island. Jonathon Island had been named for her great-great something grandfather, Jacob Jonathon, who had established the first settlement in the early 1800s.

Kicking down the bike's kickstand, she parked on the lawn. Along the front porch, Adirondack chairs waited for lounging guests. Near each support beam hung the baskets of flowers she and her siblings had chipped in on for Mother's Day a few days before—a Mother's Day she had spent at home with Finn because he had a fever.

She reached into her bag for a Kleenex and her hand brushed a ragged piece of paper. What the . . . ? She pulled out her tattered envelope still stuffed full of cash. Across the front in a slanted script, Mr. Michaelson had written "for the children." She pressed a hand to her mouth for a heartbeat then straightened her shoulders and walked up to the porch.

Following her nose, tickled with the scent of her mother's signature spaghetti sauce, she headed straight for the kitchen.

Finn chased Maggie around the butcher block center island, and her dad, Liam, and Dani were talking over in the far right corner. At the stove her mom stirred a pot, and her big sister, Evie, was pulling plates out of the green-paneled cabinets on the other side of the kitchen.

Mia crossed the room and kissed her mother on the cheek. Her mom's gray-streaked, dark, bobbed hair brushed her cheek, and the scent of her gardenia perfume wafted over Mia.

"Hi, honey." Her mom didn't look up from the pot. "We're almost ready here. Can you take care of the bread?"

"No problem." Mia took a place at the island, slicing the bread and giving it a generous coating of butter before adding some garlic salt, wrapping the whole thing in foil and slipping it into the oven.

Dani crossed the kitchen and gave Mia a hug. "Good to see you, cuz." She pulled back a bit. "What's wrong?" A crease formed between Dani's green eyes.

Mia pasted on a smile. "What do you mean? I'm fine."

Dani raised one eyebrow. "I'm not buying it. We'll talk later." Her cousin moved to the silverware drawer and scooped up a handful of forks before heading to the dining room.

I'll give you one more month. The banker's words swirled through her head. She closed her eyes and took a deep breath, releasing it with a burst when someone ran into the back of her legs.

Her eyes flew open. Finn blinked up at her. "Finn!"

"Sorry, Mommy." He moved around her and dashed three steps before her dad swooped him up into his arms.

"He's just full of energy today." Her dad, every piece of his salt and pepper hair neatly in place, leaned over to pat her on the shoulder, but the timer for the bread began chiming and she whirled away. Behind her she heard her dad sigh and then set Finn on the floor. "Almost time to eat?" His deep voice cut through the chaos.

She nodded and then pulled the bread out of the oven and turned. Finn scampered away, chasing Maggie again.

Nora, her fifteen-year-old sister, slouched into the room, dressed in her standard uniform of leggings and a hoodie. Her dark hair hung loose around her face. "When are we going to eat?"

Evie's three kids joined Finn and Maggie in squealing around the middle of the kitchen.

"Hi, Nora." Her mom turned from the stove and bussed her cheek. "Done with schoolwork? Can you take these kids to the table? We're almost ready." Her mom pulled the pan of spaghetti sauce off the stove. Hopefully she missed the eye roll from Nora before the teen began obeying her mother.

The kitchen fell to near silence after Nora played Pied Piper to the kids.

Soon, they'd all moved to the dining room table.

After saying grace, they began dishing up. Mia tended to her kids' plates while Evie helped fill five-year-old Cora's plate. Eight-year-old twins Chloe and Chase didn't need any help. At the end of the table, Dani and Mia's dad continued deep in conversation.

"Where's Kyle?" Mia asked as she cut Maggie's noodles into small pieces. The toddler shoved the pasta into her mouth almost as fast as Mia cut it. "Slow down, baby. You're going to get sick."

"He had something come up at work, so he told us to

come over without him." Evie reached for a slice of bread. In her L.L.Bean top and her dark hair just brushing her shoulders, she looked like a cookie cutter version of their mom. Minus a few gray hairs, of course. "Mom, have you heard from Bash lately?" Their older brother, a lawyer, lived in New York City. He didn't come home nearly as often as her mother liked, but that was the price he paid for being successful.

"He called on Wednesday just to check in," Elise said. "He said to tell everyone hello."

"We should find out if the town council is fully on board with your plan by the end of the day tomorrow." Her dad's voice boomed over the table.

Mia forked a bite of spaghetti into her mouth and glanced at Dani. Her best friend and cousin lit up at her dad's words.

"What plan?" Evie asked.

Mia missed Dani's reply because Maggie chose that moment to lift her plate off the table.

"All done," the toddler said. Then she tipped the last of her spaghetti into her lap.

The table erupted into chaos. Evie's kids took this as permission to resume their game of chase with Finn, her dad chose to continue his conversation with Dani, only louder, and her mom jumped up right away to catch the pasta before it all went onto her dining room rug.

"Kids, if you're done eating come back and clear your plates!" Evie called.

Mia swooped her daughter out of the seat and took her to the bathroom. Even the cool blues of the room's walls failed to calm her as she wiped Maggie off. Her daughter's eyes lit with a sparkle, and her mouth turned up in a crooked grin.

"I messy."

Mia's chest loosened. Maggie looked so much like Troy. Her dark blonde curls flopped over her forehead, nearly covering her blue eyes. "Yes. You messy. You can't dump your plate when you're finished eating. We've talked about this."

"Okay, Mommy." Her daughter pushed her lip out in a fake pout. Mia laughed and kissed the top of her head. Fatigue tugged at every one of her muscles.

"Let's go get Finn. Time to head home." Hand in hand, they walked back to the dining room. Most of the others had finished eating, and her mom was stacking the dirty plates.

After corralling Finn and herding him and Maggie outside, she paused in the doorway.

Her mom tucked a Tupperware into her hands. "Some leftovers for later. You didn't get much before cleaning up Maggie."

"Thanks, Mom. Thanks for watching them today too."

"I always like having them, you know that." Her mom reached out and squeezed her shoulder. "How did it go at the bank?"

Overhead, dark clouds piled up in the sky. "They're giving me a little time to catch up on my mortgage. So, you can pray that I find something steadier for work." Just like she'd been praying for the past several months.

Maybe she should start to listen to that voice in her heart that had started to whisper that God had abandoned her.

"I wish Troy had planned better." Her mom pursed her lips.

A churning started in her stomach. The little spaghetti she'd managed to eat rolled over. "He was twenty-two years old, Mom. We thought we had plenty of time for things like mortgages. At least he had life insurance."

Her mom sighed. "You're right, of course. Let me know if you need help covering your next payment. Dad and I can write you a check."

Not gonna happen. "Not necessary." She began backing off the porch. "Please don't say anything to Dad. At least not yet."

"Okay, but—"

"I gotta go, Mom." The clouds covered what was left of the late evening sunshine.

A storm was coming. The kind that this time might just take what was left of everything she loved.

And she had less than a month to stop it.

There was nothing better than putting in a full day of honest work. It was one of the reasons Cody Hart used to love fishing so much. Check that. *Still* loved fishing. Even if he hadn't been truly out on the water since his best friend, Troy, had died along with Troy's dad, Steve.

He wiped oil off his hand with a shop rag he found lying on his workbench. Silence echoed in the pole shed that doubled as his home and shop. Situated next to the waters of Lake Huron on a small cove, the building had once housed his dad's fishing business. After the accident that had sunk their boat and shuttered the business, his dad reluctantly allowed him to take over the building, at least until he sold the business. His dad kept most of their old equipment in a shed on the mainland where it had been closer to the places they'd sold their catch. Now Cody lived in the small office, which he'd converted to a bedroom and a small bathroom. Out on the large shop floor, he worked on restoring a commercial fishing boat.

Living in a shop made him feel a kinship with Dirk Pitt, hero of those old Clive Cussler books. Except instead of a shed full of classic cars, he had a beached whale of a fishing boat.

He clenched and unclenched his fist a few times to ease the ache in his fingers. Some days, he operated more like a surgeon than an ex-fisherman. The pieces he worked with could be minuscule. He contemplated the patient in front of him. Along the ten-foot length of the metal workbench spanning one wall of the shop, a John Deere inboard engine lay in pieces waiting for him to reassemble it and reinstall it into his boat.

If he could find the parts he needed.

A wave of cool air washed over him as the shop door opened and closed. For a split second, he thought he would see Troy come around the boat currently occupying the majority of the shop room floor. But, of course, he would not see Troy again. Not on this side of eternity.

"Hey, Cody. How's it going?" Liam Stone—recent transplant to the island and current rebuilder of the Grand

Hotel—appeared. "Whoa. Looks like quite a project you have there."

"Yeah, when I bought this boat, I didn't know it would take so much work to get it back into shape or that parts would be nearly impossible to find." He had been confident he could rebuild the engine in his own shop and save himself some cash. He shouldn't have been surprised that it didn't turn out that way. Bad things always seemed to happen to him. "I waited weeks for a new overhaul kit. Then another two months for the fuel pump."

Two years had passed since he'd stood at Troy's grave and vowed to reopen the fishing business. He'd almost gotten the funds together for the extra gear and the boat parts. If he didn't get back on the water soon, he'd lose all credibility with the restaurants Hart Fishing Company used to sell to. He couldn't keep stringing them along. If he didn't open during this fishing season, he would never open at all.

"I think I diagnosed the problem though," Cody said. He pointed at the piston sleeve. "It's cracked along there."

Liam came closer. "Even I can see that. Will you replace it?"

"I'll have to see if I can find the part on eBay. It's not something they have down at any old hardware store. I don't think they'd have it at the marine store over in Port Joseph either."

"Might be easier to just replace the engine." Liam shoved his hands into his pockets. The guy might wear jeans and T-shirts instead of a full-on suit now, but his expertly tapered brown hair and the high quality of his clothing still spoke of his former executive lifestyle.

Cody had only known the builder for a few months, but he'd come to respect him as someone who knew what he wanted and went after it. "They cost between ten and twenty thousand." He shifted a few of the parts on the long workbench. Keeping them organized meant less of a headache later when he put the whole thing back together again.

"Probably not easier, then." Liam's wry grin matched his own.

"If I can't find the part, I might be screwed." Cody reached up to rub his hair, but remembered his grease-covered fingers just in time. "I'll have to order a custom-made part and that can take weeks."

"Remind me again why you're doing this?" Liam turned and looked at the boat high and dry in the middle of the shop. "I mean, I'm not against hard work, but this seems over the top. Will this thing even float?"

Cody looked at the boat too, all thirty-one feet of her. A Radon commercial class with diesel engine—currently on his operating table—outfitted for trap or long line fishing. The paint was peeling off the hull in several places, and the deck needed a serious scrub down. Inside, the single bunk needed a new mattress, but the cockpit and cabin were clean and had been updated just before he bought it. "She needs a lot of work, but her bones are solid. And I need her if I hope to reopen my dad's fishing business."

"Why reopen? It seems to me you're making a good living as the island's favorite handyman. And there's definitely enough of that kind of work around here to keep you busy."

The trouble was, he couldn't say exactly what it was that gave him this drive to move forward with the fishing business plan. "I guess it's just that Troy and I had dreamed about taking over the company for so long. I can't imagine doing anything else." He paused. Swallowed. "Plus, being out on the water used to fill me up like nothing else. So, yeah, I could keep being a handyman, but I don't love it."

"I get that." Liam ran a hand over the hull of the boat. "So, being a handyman pays the bills, but you're looking for more."

"Yep. I've been putting aside as much as I can spare each paycheck to buy Dad's business and equipment. The money's one issue. The boat's another. But the biggest is getting my dad to transfer his fishing license to me."

"Why wouldn't he? You'd think he'd be glad for the retirement funds."

"You'd think. But my dad's one of the stubborn ones. He's decided that the Hart Fishing Company is dead in the water—took the accident as a sign of sorts—and won't even discuss it." He shrugged a shoulder. "I'm hoping that waving the actual money in his face when the time comes will change his mind though."

"Wow. Why's he being so stubborn about it? You'd think he'd be proud his son was taking over for him." Liam knocked a knuckle against the boat. The *thunk* echoed through the high-ceilinged space.

Cody lifted a shoulder. "Honestly? I think he blames me for the accident."

"No way. From what I've heard it was just that—an accident. A storm. Right?"

"Slightly more to it than that. I don't know. Maybe Dad's right. Maybe it was my fault." Cody braced his hands on the workbench. "But either way, the only way to really move on with my life . . . to honor Troy's memory . . . is to make sure our dream of owning the company comes to life."

"I think that's really great, man. But why can't you go out and get a license if your dad won't sell you his? And a loan for equipment?"

"I already tried that. No one wants to take a chance on a twenty-four-year-old whose last boat sank. And commercial fishing licenses are hard to come by in Michigan. There's a wait list." He shook his head. "I'm going to keep hacking away at this dream a little while longer. I don't want to see another thing I love die."

Liam was quiet a moment. "I get that," he said. Then, "Listen, I mentioned to Dani that I was stopping by and she said she'd meet me here. She's got something to talk to you about."

Dani Sullivan, Liam's girlfriend, worked as the head of tourism on Jonathon Island.

Great. "What does she want? She's not going to hassle me about taking tourists charter fishing again, is she?" She'd mentioned it once before, wondering aloud if it could be a big draw. No thanks. Too much risk. Besides, he wasn't sure how soon this boat would be up and running.

Liam cracked a smile. "No idea. Something about

sprucing up some houses and some buildings in town, I think."

Sprucing up sounded much better than taking drunk, seasick frat boys out to catch fish all summer. "You never said what you came for. Did you just come here to hassle me?"

"I hassle because I love you, you know that." Liam had only been on the island a few months. He'd come to help Dani plan the renovations on the Grand Hotel. Already the islanders had accepted him as one of their own.

"Doesn't answer my question."

Liam crossed his arms. "I was debating whether to do this . . . I need your advice on something. I wondered if you would help me pick out a gift for Dani."

Cody stared at him. "I'm sorry. Did you just say you want me to help you pick out a gift for your girlfriend? You can't be serious." He spread his hands wide. "I'm not exactly the person to ask for romance advice."

"Oh, come on. You're probably a secret romantic."

"As evidenced by the girls lined up, knocking down my door." Above their heads, the shop fan turned on, its huge blades stirring up the oily scent of the building.

"The right girl is out there for you. I know it."

A flash of a smile, brown curls, green eyes. She'd been out there since he'd first met her in elementary school. He shrugged it away. *That* girl was off limits.

"You'll be glad to know there is no romance involved anyway. I just wanted to buy Dani and myself a pair of fishing rods. I thought fishing could be a fun activity for us."

Cody pictured Dani and Liam out on the water, Liam

getting sprayed by fish guts. "You seriously want to do that? Aren't you supposed to be a city kid?"

Liam uncrossed his arms. "Yeah, well, I'm trying to do better. This is a first step."

"I don't know, man, fishing rods are kind of romantic." The newest Bass Pro Shop catalog featured a few that had made his heart skip a beat. Shoot. He really needed to get out more.

Liam laughed. "Maybe for you. What do you say, can you help me find a good starter rod and some tackle?"

"Sure, it's no problem. I'll text you a few links."

"Hello!" Dani's voice echoed through the cavernous shop.

"We're on the other side of the boat," Cody called back.

A moment later and Dani came into view. Cody had known the willowy blonde all their lives. She walked to Liam's side, and he put his arm around her. She smiled up at him, and Cody glanced away, a pinch forming under his breastbone.

"I've got to get going," Liam said. He dropped a kiss on the top of Dani's head. "See you both later."

"I need your help with something." Dani clasped her hands.

A laugh burst out of him. "No warm-up? Just straight to the punch? I already told you I don't want to take out any tourists on charters."

She held up a hand to stop him. "No. It's nothing like that. You know about the revitalization project, right?"

"I was at the town hall meeting, yeah." Cody pulled a stool out from under the bench and placed it in front of

Dani before grabbing one for himself. "We may as well sit, and you can explain. Want a Coke?"

She shook her head and sat. "Okay, so you know that step one of our plan is to rebuild and reopen the hotel so we have a place for guests and seasonal workers to stay, right?"

Cody nodded. The work on the hotel had already begun. Everyone in town knew about that. He crossed his arms and leaned against the workbench, the metal cool through his T-shirt. A tang of engine oil hung in the air.

"Step two is all about opening the businesses themselves. You know how we have all these open storefronts on Main Street?" Dani's gestures grew more expansive as she warmed to her topic. "Uncle Seb owns those, obviously, but as part of our revitalization plan, he's willing to majorly lower the rent for the first several years to attract new owners."

"Sounds reasonable." Cody cocked his head. "But is that really enough to get people here?"

She shifted on her stool, leaned forward. "Not on its own, no. Recently I saw a Travel Channel documentary about a tiny town in Italy. After the pandemic, this town had all of these empty homes and offered to sell them for the equivalent of a dollar just to get people there."

Oh. Wow. He sat up straight. "So, you're going to do the same thing?"

"Basically. So many of the older homes behind Main Street were left abandoned over the last decade. People moved away and couldn't pay their mortgages, so the town pretty much claimed ownership."

"Right." So many families had left over the years. Jonathon Island was still amazing, but to think about what it used to be . . . the comparison ached. "And those are the ones you're going to offer for a dollar?"

"Yes, but not just to anyone. To business owners who apply—and are vetted and approved by the town council. We have fourteen available storefronts and at least that many empty homes. Here's hoping we have a lot of applicants." Dani chewed her bottom lip. "That's the part I'm most worried about." She stared up at the vaulted ceiling for a moment.

In the silence, Cody heard the ticking of the clock mounted on the far wall. Overhead, the fluorescent lights buzzed. Finally, he cleared his throat. "So, what exactly are you wanting me to do?"

Dani's smile flashed again as she looked at him. "I want to hire you to make sure the buildings and houses are move-in ready. We want people to be able to see how charming Jonathon Island really is." She named the amount she'd been authorized to pay him. "Uncle Seb is chipping in a lot of the money, since he owns the buildings, but the town promised to put some up too. We'd like you to start right away."

His shoulders relaxed and a grin spread across his face. "I think I can help with that." He mentally reviewed the list of handyman projects he had going—not too many right now. He'd cleared his calendar when he'd bought the boat, hoping to be back on the water soon. Even this small salary would go a long way toward the parts he needed. And it would be more regular work than the odd jobs he'd been taking around town. "Just tell me which places we're talking about."

Dani hopped off her stool. "Thank you. Come by my office tomorrow and I can get you the list and a bunch of master keys."

He could make that work. "I planned to check Mia's lawnmower in the morning. It shouldn't take long, so I can be there by ten or so."

A strange look passed over Dani's face. She opened her mouth then clapped it shut.

"What?" He pushed off his stool. Dani started walking for the door, and he went with her.

"It's just that I think—never mind." She waved a hand in the air. They rounded the boat. Straight ahead, a line of light shone through the gap in the bottom of the door leading out of the shed.

"At the risk of repeating myself, what?" He reached for the doorknob and twisted it open. The warmth of the May sunlight streaming in chased away the chill always present in the metal building.

Dani gave a little shrug. "I know it's not the same without your third musketeer, you and Mia and Troy were always inseparable, but I don't think Troy would want you hiding away."

"I'm not hiding away." He gazed out toward the boardwalk running past his place, not really seeing it. "I'm keeping my head down. Working toward getting this business back."

"I'm probably way out of line here, but maybe it's time to ask her out."

He whipped his gaze to her. "Ask who out?"

She speared him with a look. "I think you know who I'm talking about."

Of course he did. But . . . "We're just friends." The words felt wrong in his mouth, but honestly, it didn't matter how he felt about Mia. It mattered how she felt about *him*.

And the fact that Troy would always be between them. "Not gonna happen."

Dani lifted a shoulder and let it fall. "Okay, maybe I imagined it. But Mia could use someone like you in her corner."

His heart squeezed. "I'm in her corner. I'll always be in her corner. As a *friend*."

"My mistake." She waved as she walked into the sunlight. "See you tomorrow, Cody."

After Dani left, Cody plugged in the sander fitted with a heavy grit paper and began attacking the peeling paint along the boat's midsection. The rhythmic motions soothed his nerves. Dani knew Mia best. If she thought he was good enough for Mia then . . . Maybe . . . No. He couldn't go there.

He popped his earbuds in, donned a pair of safety glasses, and tugged a mask over his nose and mouth. In his ears, the rap artist Flame sang about joy in Christ. Maybe if he listened long enough, some of the truth would sink into his heart.

He soon fell into a rhythm, the sander in his hand swishing across the surface of the boat until he could make out the fiberglass hull underneath. He needed to take off a layer of paint and all of the barnacles and other accumulated biofouling before he could hit the whole thing with a blast of primer. If everything went well, he could be putting the second coat of marine paint on by the end of the week.

After two feet more of the hull gleamed in the harsh light of the shop, he stepped back to admire his progress. Between all the interruptions, he'd finished four measly feet this afternoon. So much for his personal timeline. So much for this part of the project getting done anytime soon.

His smart watch buzzed with a text from his mom.

Mom
____

Can you stop by the house? Dad needs a hand clearing that branch that fell during the storm last week.

He unplugged the sander, gave the boat a hard stare, then pushed the safety glasses up onto his forehead.

This boat had waited a long time for this paint to be stripped. It wouldn't hurt for it to wait another day.

Now that he had some guaranteed income, it wouldn't be long before he'd be back on the water for good.

And maybe, just maybe, keep his last promise to Troy.

Two

I T WAS HARD TO PANIC WHEN THERE WAS mac and cheese to make and bath time and books before bed, but Mia felt the edges of it creeping in during the few quiet moments.

It had been two days since that meeting at the bank. Two days of job searching on the island. Two days of pushing off the anxiety eating a hole through her stomach. She stood at the stove in her kitchen, its chipped white surface a contrast to the brown faux stone of her Formica countertops. Noodles boiled in a large pot.

A loud bang echoed from the backyard. What in the . . . ? She turned and looked out the window over the sink. Someone was in her shed. The door hung ajar, and a gust of wind slammed it against the wall with another bang.

"Finn, Maggie, stay put." The kids would be safe playing in the living room a minute on their own. She'd deal with whatever was going on in the backyard and be back before the macaroni was overcooked.

Tightening her grip on the wooden spoon in her hand, she pushed open the back door. She walked on the balls of her feet the ten steps to the shed. Her lawnmower roared to life, and she yelped.

The engine cut out immediately, and a man leaned out of the shed. His dark blond hair caught the last of the evening sunshine.

"Cody?" Her heart still raced. *Settle down, it's just Cody. Breathe, girl.* "What are you doing in my shed?"

"Sorry. I should have messaged you." Cody came fully out of the shed and wiped his hands on a tattered towel. "I didn't mean to scare you."

"I wasn't scared." Lie.

His blue eyes lit with mischief. "I don't know if I believe you." He nodded at her hand, still raised to her shoulder. "That's some weapon you have there."

The laugh that escaped was part relief and part humor. Mia lowered her hand. "What are you doing here?"

"I wanted to make sure your lawnmower is tuned up for the summer. We might actually start getting grass now that the weather is warmer." He shut one of the shed doors. "I hoped to come this morning, but my mom needed help, and then I had to meet Dani."

"You've been working all day, you must be exhausted. You really didn't have to do this."

Cody studied the rag in his hands. "I'll always be here when you need me." He raised an eyebrow and looked at her. "But next time, I'll text first. Don't want to get hit with any cooking utensils."

"Har, har." She rolled her eyes.

"Any new leads on jobs?" He stuffed the rag into the back pocket of his jeans.

She sighed. "I was looking at postings earlier today." Her gut churned. "There's nothing really on island."

"If there were any way I could help you, I would." The blue of his eyes deepened.

"I appreciate all you've done around here since Troy died." She gestured toward the house. Cody had come almost every week, sometimes more, to do things around the house. "But even you aren't a miracle worker. I'll figure something out for work. I have to."

"I believe in you." Cody's gaze drifted to the darkening sky. The rays of the setting sun purpling the heavy clouds on the horizon. "I'd better get home before that rain hits. Unless you'd like me to stay, wait out the storm?"

Have another adult around to help ride out the storm? Tempting. But she couldn't rely on him forever, despite his words. "Nah. I'm good. See you later, Cody. I'd better get back inside. Make sure my kids aren't killing each other."

Cody gave her a long look. Then he shrugged and smiled. "Okay. See you. Text me if you need anything."

An hour later, after mac and cheese and bath time, her thoughts kept skittering back to the problem of how to pay her mortgage.

"One more story, Mommy," Finn's pleading voice broke through. The three of them sat in the kids' bedroom off the kitchen. Now that Maggie had graduated from the crib, both Finn and Maggie had a twin bed pushed to opposite walls in the small room, Finn's bed covered with a space themed quilt and Maggie's with a unicorn one. Mia could sit on the floor between them and put one hand on each child. She found herself in that position more and more these days.

On the wall, a clock with a sun for its face ticked past a few seconds. The house creaked and settled. The familiar nighttime noises sank deep into Mia's heart. How could she take her kids from this place?

She sat on the floor, blue shag rug underneath her, a pile of books on her lap. "Another story? We've already gone through six tonight."

Maggie clambered off her bed and crawled into Mia's lap, pushing the books to the floor. Her little body warm against Mia's chest and smelling of baby shampoo. "One mo-ah, peas."

And who could argue with that? "Just one more, and then it's definitely bedtime." And time for her to check the job listings board on the Jonathon Island community website. Again.

Maggie picked a book from the bookshelf nested between the beds, and soon they were lost in the antics of an alligator who goes to school.

Many kisses and giggles later, the kids were tucked into bed. Mia fixed herself a cup of tea before heading to her own bedroom, set it down on a bedside table, and plopped down on top of the covers of her four-poster bed.

Mia's bedroom rested at the back of the house, just beyond the shared bathroom, close enough to hear if either of the kids cried out in the night, but far enough she didn't have to be totally silent when they were sleeping. Troy had talked about making the small dormer attic rooms upstairs into a master suite when the kids were old enough to stay on the ground floor on their own. Another project he would never be able to complete.

Shaking off the thought, she propped a pillow behind her back and picked up her notebook from where she'd left it the night before. "Job Ideas" was scrawled across the top. The rest of the page was blank. She doodled a line of roses along the bottom.

Picking up the laptop her parents had given her when she graduated from high school, she navigated to the Jonathon Island website. Plans for the renovations of the Grand Sullivan Hotel scrolled past. Her cousin, Dani, along with Liam Stone, was working on a remodel and rebuild of the once beautiful structure. The building had partially burned down ten years ago or so, leaving few housing options for tourists and seasonal staff. When the hotel reopened, so would Jonathon Island. Or so everyone hoped.

Too bad it might be too late to matter for her.

She clicked the "Jobs" tab. Waited as the laptop whirred and stalled as it loaded the page. A message bearing the words "Opportunities Await on Jonathon Island" popped up on the screen. But, below that, no opportunities awaited. The job listings remained as blank as the day before, and the day before that.

Maybe it was time to face facts. She only had two options. Move in with her parents, or move off island.

Despite her parents' offers, she just couldn't burden them with so much. Not with Dad still recovering from his last near-heart attack. He was failing all his attempts at retirement. Her mother thought he was barely trying.

No. Her eyes burned as she entered Port Joseph into the search bar. Outside, the wind kicked up, rattling the windows. Sounded like the weatherman was right. Springtime in Michigan went hand in hand with stormy weather.

The job offer from her friend in Traverse City was unthinkable. *It would be fun to have you around,* her friend had written. *We could go out together. Maybe meet some guys . . .* Yeah, maybe other people her age were out having fun, but she had responsibilities. Like keeping her kids near their family. Troy's mom, Constance, still lived on the island, just a few doors away, actually. Recently Constance had taken over the care of her mother, who had fallen and broken a hip. No, Traverse City wasn't an option, but Port Joseph was closer. A lot closer. Plus, Evie lived there. At least her kids would have their cousins nearby.

A knit blanket lay at the foot of her bed. She pulled it up and over her as the Port Joseph Chamber of Commerce website blinked to life on her computer.

A banging sound started outside, followed by the *shhh-ing* noise unique to sleet falling in waves against the siding of the house. Her gut churned with the noise, unable to escape the memories of another night.

Another storm.

"Mommy?" Finn's voice came warbling from the doorway to his bedroom. "Mommy, I need you."

She untangled herself from the blanket and raced to

him, thoughts of the storm hovering at the edges of her mind. She'd gotten within two steps of Finn when he opened his mouth and threw up directly in her path. She skidded to a halt before she stepped in the muck. Leaning over the mess, she picked up Finn.

"It's okay, honey. I've got you." She took him into the bathroom and set him on the toilet seat, lid down. "Does your tummy feel yucky?" She felt his forehead. No fever.

Finn nodded.

"If you need to do it again, just lean into the garbage can." The toilet would be better, but she didn't want to leave him sitting on the cold tiles. She opened the cabinet under the sink. Empty. "I'll go grab a washcloth." She dashed to the alcove where they had managed to fit a stackable washer and dryer and then rummaged through the dryer, praying she'd remembered to put the load of towels in to dry that morning as she had planned. Triumphant, she pulled out a dry washcloth then grabbed a few clean towels too. Might come in handy.

Retching noises echoed from the bathroom. *Please let him be hitting the garbage can and not the floor.* She didn't know if it was a prayer or just a fervent hope. Outside, the wind screamed louder. Another crack of thunder boomed, and she resisted the urge to wrap her arms around her head. Barely.

The broken shutter banged against the wall. One problem at a time. Rounding the corner to the hall, she almost stepped on Maggie.

"Hey, baby." She put her hand on Maggie's head. Hot and sweaty.

"I frewed up." Maggie's eyes welled with tears as she held up her stuffed bunny. "Trixie is all yucky." Trixie, dilapidated by being excessively loved, looked even worse now. Mia didn't want to think about what might be waiting in Maggie's bed. Her stomach rolled over. She took three deep breaths, willing the bile to stay in place.

"Oh, Mags." Mia picked up the bunny by the one place on its right ear that seemed cleanest and dropped it onto one of the towels. She wrapped the bundle up and set it next to the wall. "We'll get Trixie cleaned up in a little bit. Let's go help your brother." Fatigue pulled at her bones as she picked up Maggie.

A tiny spark of warmth lit her heart as Maggie wrapped her arms around her neck and buried her head on top of her shoulder. Thunder boomed directly above them, and they both yelped. Mia jumped and clutched Maggie tighter. Her heart raced.

Yeah, she knew that storms were a normal part of a Michigan spring and summer—she even used to enjoy them. Now, all she could hear in the thunder was the groan of a ship against rocks. The rain was the waters of Lake Huron swamping a boat, dragging down the only boy she'd ever kissed.

Maggie convulsed once. Something warm and wet made its way through the hair tucked behind Mia's ear and down her neck. She knew even before Maggie spoke.

"Mama, I frewed up again."

A heat prickled in her eyes. She would not break down. She didn't have time for that.

In the bathroom, Finn sat on the toilet, legs pulled tight

to his chest, chin between his knees, hair tousled. Vomit filled the garbage can and spotted the floor. "I'm sorry, Mommy," Finn said to his knees.

The wind found its way through a crack in the attic and began moaning. Finn looked up, his eyes wide. "Is that a monster?"

"No, honey, it's just the wind." She set Maggie in the empty tub. The loose shutter began banging again.

"The monster wants to get in," Maggie said and began sobbing. "I don't want any monsters." The two-year-old shivered.

Enough. Mia squared her shoulders. She wrapped one of the clean towels around Maggie. No need to dirty up a blanket, the towel would do for now. "Stay here, Mags. Finn, watch your sister. Stay in here. I'll go get the monster."

She marched out of the bathroom and toward the front door. Something cold slid down her back. Not stopping for her jacket hanging on its hook—no sense getting the sick all over it—she opened the door, and a gust of wind almost tore it from her grip.

A wet spray of sleet hit her in the face as she stepped onto the cold front step. In defiance, the broken shutter banged a few more times. She grabbed the edges of it and began tugging. If it could bang around so much, surely it was loose enough to come off the side of the house.

It held tight.

A bolt of lightning streaked the sky, followed by a rumble. Mia could taste the sleet streaming down her face. It tasted salty. Oh wait. Maybe she was crying. She pulled again at the shutter, twisting it this time.

It came loose. A shocking pain ran through her hand and she fell backward, shutter still gripped tightly. The cold feeling of wet mud bit into her pajama pants. Another bolt of lightning—no, a flashlight this time.

Over the roar of the storm, she could hear someone calling her name.

"Mia?" Evie's voice. She almost cried in relief. Mia felt Evie grasp the shutter and move it away. "Mia, what are you doing out here?"

"Monsters." Mia couldn't stop shaking. Evie put her arm under Mia's armpits and lifted her up. Evie's rain jacket crinkled. Mia cupped her sore hand to her chest.

"Let's get you inside," Evie said. "Mia, are you bleeding?"

"What are you doing here?" Mia clung to her sister's arm, slip sliding in the mud to the front door.

"I was visiting Mom and Dad when the storm came up. They canceled the ferry service, so we'll be spending the night." Evie shrugged. "I know how these storms freak you out. I thought I would come by and check on you."

"Across the island? How could you even see in this downpour?" Mia scrubbed a hair out of her eye.

"It wasn't raining this hard when I left. Besides, why are you always surprised when people show up for you?" Evie held open the door for Mia. "Never mind, don't answer that. You're dripping blood on the floor. And is that vomit in your hair?"

"It's been a long night." Mia reached up to push her hair

back but then remembered the cut on her hand. "The kids are in the bathroom. Watch out in the hall. I haven't had time to clean up."

"I see. It's that kind of night." She squeezed Mia's arm. "I got this." Then she headed down the hallway.

Later, after the kids had quick baths, Evie volunteered to put them back to bed while Mia showered. She lingered under the spray until the water turned cold, then put on some old flannel pjs and went to find Evie.

"Show me your hand." Evie reached out and gently examined Mia's cut. "I don't think this is too deep. Are you up to date on your tetanus shots?"

Mia nodded.

Evie bandaged her hand and then made them both a cup of Earl Grey. Mia followed her sister into the living room and plopped down on the couch.

The room had been the first she and Troy finished. Original hardwood flooring shone after they refinished it. They'd found the couch and loveseat on Craigslist. Troy's favorite recliner sat empty in the other corner. Mia never could bring herself to sit in it.

The fatigue from earlier threatened to eat Mia whole. The Earl Grey had steeped too long, bitter orange on her tongue. "Thank you, sis. You're a lifesaver." Mia closed her eyes and leaned her head back against the couch.

Evie patted her on the knee. "I was going to come even without the storm. I hope you don't mind, but Mom told me about your meeting at the bank."

Mia kept her eyes closed. "Whatever. The whole island

probably knows by now. The widow who will lose her house."

"Stop. It's not like that. People care about you."

Mia opened her eyes and sat up. "Sorry, I didn't mean to sound so bitter. But how can I be twenty-four and already a stereotype?"

"Honestly, Mia. You are too hard on yourself." At thirty-two, with a banker husband and mother to three great kids, Evie was a different sort of stereotype. One who would never understand Mia's predicament.

She leaned forward to take a gulp of her tea. The heat of Evie's stare bored into her. "Okay. Fine. You're right. It's just been a long two years, I guess. I thought I'd be more put together by now." It didn't help that the ghost of Troy was all over this island. She couldn't go anywhere without being reminded of him or of people looking at her with pity. Maybe she *should* move to the mainland.

And yet, this was still her home. Even when she'd gone away to art school for a year, she'd missed this place something fierce.

"And I get that, I really do. As much as I can anyway," Evie said. "Just remember you don't have to do things solo."

"Evie, I'm a single mother. Of course I'm doing things solo. The only person I can rely on is myself." She gripped her cup tight.

"You need a plan."

Mia slumped lower on the couch. "Do you think I don't know that? I've thought about leaving the island, but I hate to take the kids away from the only home they know.

Plus, it's nice for them to be able to see their grandparents anytime."

"Move away? You need a plan, but let's not do anything so drastic." Evie pulled a blanket out of the basket.

"I don't know what else to do. There aren't any jobs here. But, I admit, moving away feels like giving up." Mia tucked her feet up under her. "And I don't want my kids to see me as a quitter. I want to be strong and resilient for them." She took a deep breath. "Plus, what marketable skills do I even have? An artist who quit school after a year. Yeah, that would look great on a résumé."

"It's not quitting to try and find a better life for yourself," Evie said.

"I was looking at jobs in Port Joseph." Mia pushed a wet strand of hair off her forehead. "At least I'd be near you."

"Don't move to Port Joseph on my account. You know I want to move back on island."

A lump sat firmly in Mia's chest. "I don't know what else to do."

They sat silent for a moment. The wind from earlier had died down.

"You know . . ." Evie seemed to be choosing her words carefully. "I was talking to Dad—"

"Stop." She put up her hand like a traffic cop. "Don't even suggest I ask him for help."

"I still don't understand this wall you have put up between you." A line formed between Evie's eyebrows.

"It's just that whenever I talk to him, all I can remember is his disappointment when I came home pregnant and unmarried." Mia tugged a blanket tight around her torso.

The memory jumped into her mind. *What do you mean you're pregnant?* Her dad's face had fallen, shoulders slumped. *I thought your mom and I taught you better values.* And then he'd sighed.

The kind of sigh that had shattered her heart.

Then he'd turned away and called for her mom.

He didn't have to say anything more for her to feel the disappointment falling like a wall between them.

Now she looked at Evie, the perfect daughter, married *before* getting pregnant. "Dad will never see me the way he sees you. I'm a disappointment, and now . . . now I'm even more so. He told me to invest the insurance money, but I didn't. There wasn't much to begin with. And now it's down to nothing."

"Listen. You did what you had to after Troy's death. I would have taken the kids away on a trip too. And helping out his mom . . . You did the right thing." Evie leaned forward. "You know that Dad loves you. And he loves Finn and Maggie, of course. This all sounds like a you problem."

Her head began to pound. "Anyway. It's all awkward. I don't know how to make him proud of me again. And I don't have the bandwidth for dealing with that right now."

"And you won't be able to until you sit down and have a real conversation with him," Evie said and then readjusted her position on the couch. "Don't bother to argue with me, I'm done doing the older sister thing. I wasn't going to say you should ask him for help."

"Okay . . ." Fine. She'd let it go. Evie would never be able to understand. "What then?"

"I was just remembering that conversation he and Dani

were having the other night at dinner. The one with attracting new businesses to the island?"

Mia nodded. She vaguely recalled them talking about it while she cleaned spaghetti off Maggie's face and kept Finn from continuing a kicking game he'd started with his cousin.

"Right. They're giving away housing for a dollar. Pretty crazy." She watched the steam off her tea swirl away and evaporate. "I wonder how that works exactly."

"You'd have to ask Dani for details. Which is what I was going to suggest—that you talk to Dani. She seemed stressed the other night. Excited but overwhelmed, you know? Maybe she needs some help."

Mia eyed her sister over the edge of her cup. "Ha. That's funny. How would I help? I don't have any marketable skills. Unless you count refereeing children and cleaning up messes."

Evie laughed and rolled her eyes. "What about that realtor license Dad encouraged you to get right out of high school? You could put that to good use."

"You mean the real estate license that has gotten dusty from unuse? That license?" At the time, it had seemed like a great way to hold down a job and work on her education at the same time. Part-time, weekend work.

Then Finn came along and changed everything.

Still. "I have kept renewing it . . ."

"So, dust it off and use it. Maybe it was a God thing. He kept prompting you to keep up with it for just this opportunity," Evie said. "I don't know if you will need it or not, all I'm saying is that you should call her."

Later, after Evie had left, her *maybe it was a God thing* still echoing in Mia's ears, Mia wrote *Call Dani* on her list of job ideas. She added another row of roses.

Then she wrapped herself in the blanket, listened to the storm roar, and wondered if, maybe, God hadn't completely abandoned her.

At least, not yet.

With only a few weeks to get fourteen businesses and fourteen houses ready, he needed to work fast. No distractions.

Cody tightened the last screw and stepped back to check his work. The new light-switch plates gleamed against the fresh coat of paint he'd applied. He'd picked up the keys from Dani a few days earlier and gone straight to work. Today, he was finishing up with a small storefront on the corner of Main and Ferry.

His phone buzzed with a text from Mia's number.

Mia
Are you in town? We're out for a walk. Maybe we'll see you.

So much for no distractions.

Cody
I'm at Sampson's. See you soon.

He hadn't been back to Mia's since that night a few days ago. He'd checked in with her the next day, and she assured him she was fine.

He looked around the space. Floor-to-ceiling windows

flanked the front door, bringing great views of Main Street. The building used to house Sampson's Gallery, but it had stood empty for many years now. After cleaning up the accumulated dust and animal droppings, he'd refinished the wood floor and repainted the walls—three off-white and one a bright golden color. The finishing touches he'd made today were the icing on the cake.

He checked his phone for the time. It was still early enough that, once he finished the light-switch covers, he could check the next building on his list and maybe finish that one too. If everything went well, he could even fix the swollen door at the back of this building.

The spring sunshine invited him outside for a breath of fresh air.

He took two steps out the front when he spotted Mia and her kids walking toward him. His breath hitched. A smile spread across his face before the survivor's guilt swept in to drown it away. The trio stopped in front of him.

Mia brushed a stray brown curl off her face and tucked it into the deep red handkerchief she'd tied around her dark hair. The color brought out the flush of her cheeks. Next to her, Finn and Maggie were dressed in matching rain boots. Maggie wore a fuzzy purple hat topped with a bobble that swayed with her every step.

"Hi, Cody." Mia's smile lit her face.

Keep it casual. "Hey, Mia." He bent down to shake Finn's hand. "Hi, buddy."

"Me too." Maggie clutched a stuffed rabbit under her arm. She reached out and grabbed his left hand with her right and shook it vigorously. Her purple bobble and the rabbit's ears kept time. "Hi-hi."

"Hello, to you too, Little Miss." He winked at her. "What brings you guys into town on this beautiful morning?"

"I have a coffee date with Dani in fifteen minutes," Mia replied. "But we were all going stir-crazy in the house, so I thought I would take these guys for a walk first."

Finn chased Maggie around and around his mother's legs.

"Looks like that was a good plan."

"Are you working here?" Mia turned to look in the window of the store. "Someone painted."

"Yeah, Dani asked me to spruce up a few places downtown. I started with this one." He gestured at the door. "Want to come in?"

"Sure. C'mon, kids." Mia corralled her charging steeds and ushered them into the unit. "Is the paint still wet?"

"No. I finished that yesterday. They can run around if they want."

Mia shot him a grateful look and let the kids go. They scampered off to the cabinets at the back of the space. "I remember when this was Sampson's Gallery. It was so sad to watch it decay over the past few years." She spun in a slow circle. "They used to display art over there to the left and the gift items to the right. I used to love to come in here."

"You even showed a few pieces here, right?" He'd never forget the expression on her face when she'd told Troy and him about the showing in their senior year. Excitement had lit her up from the inside.

"I can't believe you remember that." Mia brushed another stray hair back into her handkerchief.

Cody pushed his hands into his pockets. "How could I forget? You made Troy and me call you Madame Monet for a week straight. Even though Monet painted with—"

"—oil paints and not watercolors, which are clearly superior," they said together.

Mia laughed. "I guess I did say that a lot. It seems like so long ago now." Mia strolled around the small space, ending up in the center of the room. "We were just babies back then. So much has happened in the last six years."

He tried to see it through her eyes. He'd cleaned up the flooring and painted the walls, and now the seven hundred fifty square foot retail unit looked almost brand new.

"I hardly think seniors in high school are babies. But I know what you mean." Cody picked up the paint brush he'd been using to touch up a few places on the walls and wrapped it in plastic to clean later. "Troy and I thought you were brilliant. We knew you'd make it big with your art someday."

"Yeah, well, see how well that turned out." Mia kept her back to him. "As much as I love Finn and was thrilled to be married to Troy, leaving art school was the death of that dream."

"Sorry. I didn't mean to bring up a sore subject." Cody reached to touch her shoulder but let his hand fall back to his side. "There's still time though, right?"

"Sometimes I feel the old spark of inspiration and think

about getting my supplies out, but I don't have time for that right now." She turned to him, lifted her palms in the air. "My kids need me."

"Your kids need you at your best. Maybe your art is part of that."

"I suppose."

But he could see her shrug off his words. "Do you still have any of your pieces?"

"When the Sampsons closed up shop, they gave me back my paintings. Those must be somewhere at Mom's house along with the things I painted at Kendall." Mia spun in a slow circle again. "You did a good job in here. I like how this gold wall warms up the space."

Okay then. If she didn't want to talk about it, he wouldn't push.

He took another look around the room. "It was Dani's idea. She's hoping to sell someone on using this as a gallery again." The gold wall contrasted with the creamy off-white on the other walls and drew out the golden hues of the wood trim around the windows and doors.

"Mom! There's a hidden room in here!" Finn yelled, his voice echoing from behind the cabinetry.

Mia looked to Cody. "Yep," he said. "I found a small door and a tiny room back there. I cleaned it up but didn't do anything else to it. I think it got created through a remodel between this store and the one it's connected to."

"Be careful," she called out. "Watch your sister. We're leaving in a minute."

"They'll be fine back there. There isn't anything to get hurt on."

"I think you underestimate a small child's ability to find danger." Her smile warmed the room.

"We're right here. This place isn't big enough for them to get into any trouble. Come and see the cool doorknobs I found for the front door." He gestured at the glass door. "They're practically a work of art."

"Knobs? Seriously?" She raised her right eyebrow.

"What? I like antique hardware." He shrugged. "I found a pair of cut-glass knobs a while back and thought they would work well here."

"Okay, but then I need to go." She checked her phone in a quick gesture. "Dani is expecting us in less than five minutes."

They walked to the front door. The fluted doorknobs shone crystal clear in their brass setting. "A lot of these antique knobs get cloudy after a while. I'm surprised these ones still look so great." The back of his neck prickled with the heat of her gaze.

"Doorknobs." She reached out to touch the knob. "You know, Troy would have given you such a ribbing about this."

He gave a short laugh, no humor in it. "Why do you think I never brought it up?"

"Um, Cody?" She gave the knob a twist. A thunk sounded, but not the corresponding click of the latch being opened. "I think there's something wrong here. The knob is turning, but the door won't open."

Strange. "Maybe you have to jiggle it. The knob worked fine when I came in this morning."

"I am jiggling it." She gave a twist and a pull, and the

glass piece came off in her hand. She held it up to him like a child presenting the baseball that just flew through the front window. "Oops."

"Seriously, Madame Monet? Breaking my stuff?" He put his hands to his hips in mock anger.

"Don't call me that. And, if you had a more practical knob this wouldn't have happened." She glared at him. Hopefully he wasn't imagining the glint of humor in her eyes.

"A more practical knob is way less fun."

"Fun isn't all there is to life. Now we're stuck in here." She popped a hand to her hip.

"Wait, are you mad at me?" Weren't they just having fun a second ago? He took a deep breath. The scent of paint and cleaning fluid tickled his nose. Come to think of it, if they were trapped here, he wouldn't have time to finish that next building. He really needed that money.

"I'm supposed to be meeting Dani." She didn't yell, but it was close. She checked her phone again. "I'm already late."

Great, more guilt. "I'm sorry. I didn't mean to make you late. Let me see what I can do."

She sighed. "No, I'm sorry. I'm just on edge. I've got a lot going on right now. I was going to ask Dani if she needs help with the new initiative. I need something more steady than occasional shifts at Martha's."

He got a flashlight from his toolbox. "Here, point this toward the door." The light jiggled. He glanced up and saw her looking toward the hidden room. "Hey. Keep it steady." The room echoed with Finn and Maggie's laughter. Mia readjusted, bringing her gaze and the light back to him. After several attempts to reattach the glass piece, he could see there wasn't anything he could do while the set was still attached. "Someone will have to open it from the other side."

"Isn't there a back door to this place?" Mia clicked the flashlight off and swung toward the back.

He sighed. "Yes, it's code to have two doors, but the other one is swollen shut."

"So we are stuck in here."

He watched her shoulders creep toward her ears and scrambled for a way to fix this. "I can possibly take the door off its hinges, but that will take a while."

"I'll text Dani. Maybe she can come and free us." She swiped at her phone then tapped out a message. A moment later he heard an answering ding. "She'll be over in a minute."

A heartbeat passed.

The silence was broken by a chuckle from Mia.

"What's so funny?"

"I was just thinking about the story Troy would have told about this. He would have made it long and complicated and full of danger." Mia swiped at her eye. Sad, or just from the laugh? A pang seized his heart. He was the cause either way.

"His storytelling was part of what made him such a great fisherman; he fit straight into the stereotype," Cody agreed. "His tall tales made every sunfish into a five-foot sturgeon."

"It sure was." Mia's mouth curved into a small smile. "Thank you."

"Thank you for what? Locking you in here and making you late?"

She laughed. "No, thank you for keeping me calm when I freak out for no reason. For being a good friend to me all these years, especially the last few."

Friend. The word held the same taste it always did when applied to Mia. Not quite right, a bit sour, but still sweet. Because if friendship was all he could ever have with her, he'd take it just to have her in his life.

"Always."

She lifted her gaze to him, fully meeting his eyes. His mouth dried.

Two small bodies barreled into them at the same time as Dani opened the door from the outside.

"Auntie Dani!" Finn pushed past them and grabbed Dani around the knees. "We found a secret room!"

"Did you?" Dani looked from Cody to Mia and back again. "Why didn't you guys just use the back door?"

"It's swollen shut," they spoke at the same time. Mia swallowed.

"It's still on my list to fix," Cody said. And he would be doing that in a minute, once everyone cleared out.

"You know how to do that?" Mia looked surprised. Her statement jabbed him like a fishing spear straight through the heart. He'd been doing odd jobs at her house for the past two years. Did she really not notice his skills? "My front door sometimes swells shut at home," Mia said. "I have no idea what to do about it."

How had he missed that? "I can come take a look at it, if you want."

Mia moved past him and out to the sidewalk. She laid a hand on Maggie's head. "Would you? That would be amazing. It seems to get stuck whenever I have my hands full of everything." The tilt of her head toward her kids at the word "everything" and the wry smile made him chuckle.

He leaned against the doorway and crossed his arms. "Sure, I'll stop by later this week."

The group headed away from him. He watched them walk away for a minute, trying to swallow back the longing. Overhead, a cloud passed over the sun and he shivered.

He turned back to finish his tasks in the empty gallery. The sooner he finished, the sooner he'd get paid. Time to focus on a dream he actually had a chance at achieving.

Three

WAS THERE MORE AIR OUTSIDE THAN normal?

Mia's relief at being freed from the store with Cody seemed all out of proportion. After all, she knew it was only a few moments before rescue, and she knew that Dani wouldn't really mind if she was a few minutes late for their coffee date. And finally, she knew that Cody was a safe person to be stuck with.

Then why the sense of being able to breathe so much easier once the door was unstuck? She shook off the thought. Right now, she needed to concentrate on her kids and her conversation with Dani.

And somehow work up the courage to ask for a job.

Because Dani was her last hope.

Finn and Maggie skipped down the sidewalk in front of her and Dani. Well, Finn skipped. Maggie performed a little stumble hop on her chubby toddler legs. The bobble on her fuzzy purple hat danced with her antics. Even after the snow melted, Mia hadn't been able to convince her toddler to put the winter hat away.

"Still want to grab that coffee?" Dani asked. Black jeans and a T-shirt featuring a picture of Jonathon Island draped her tall, willowy frame.

Did she still want to follow through on her plan to beg her best friend for a job? No. Did she want to leave the island? Also no. The lesser of two evils it was, then. "Yes. I need more caffeine as soon as possible. Especially if it comes with an extra helping of caramel and whip."

Inside Good Day Coffee, the sun made the white walls glow. The twin scents of sweet syrups and bitter coffee surrounded them the moment they stepped inside. She could practically taste the caramel already.

Tara Chamberlain, the pastor's wife, bent her silvery blonde head toward Henrietta Hudson, a retired baker, at a table near the door, coffees steaming between them. Mia gave them a quick wave. Jill Kelley stood behind the counter with her red hair tied back in a ponytail and apron over her thin frame.

Mia's son was currently spinning the greeting card display. "Finn, stop that." He barely looked at her, but thankfully stopped what he was doing. She approached the counter and spoke to Jill. "I'll take a tall caramel latte with extra whip, please. And hopefully extra caffeine." She smiled, or maybe grimaced, at Jill as she inclined her head toward her kids.

"Latte coming right up," Jill said with a wink. "I'll toss in an extra shot of espresso. On the house."

Finn had now found a stack of ceramic coffee mugs and was adjusting each one so their handles faced outward. "Finn, knock it off!" Finn looked up at her from under his dark lashes. Mia sighed. "Sorry, Jill. Maybe we'd better take these coffees to go."

Dani laughed. "He sure is full of energy today."

"That makes one of us." She fixed the coffee mugs then grabbed her own to-go cup.

"At least he's not being naughty. He's not harming anything." Dani ruffled Finn's hair. He gave her a goofy grin.

"All the same, it's probably better if we let him burn off some of that energy outdoors and keep this coffee mug display out of danger."

A few minutes later they headed down the sidewalk, Finn and Maggie scampering around them.

"So, you and Cody?"

"What do you mean?"

Dani looked at her from over the rim of her cup. "You looked pretty cozy when I showed up today."

"I think you need your eyes checked. Cozy?" Mia made a face at Dani. Her cousin was seeing things.

"That's what I said."

"It was no big deal." A fizzy sensation worked its way through Mia. "I was walking past with the kids, and he invited me in. He remembered that I used to have some paintings hung in that studio."

Finn chased Maggie between her and Dani, her son bumping her at the last moment. She clutched at her coffee to avoid dropping it. "I haven't seen as much of him lately. He's been so busy. I hear he's doing some work for you."

They walked past Doug's Market, the only place on the island to get groceries. In a few weeks, the flower boxes lining the front windows would be spilling out with colorful blooms. If they could talk anyone into planting some.

"Technically, he's doing some work for your dad, since he's the one who owns practically all the downtown buildings." Dani waved her hand in the direction of a derelict storefront, a sharp contrast to the quaint and tidy Doug's Market. "And he works for the town because they own the houses. We need them all looking move-in ready if this scheme is going to work."

Ahead of them, Finn and Maggie had stopped to pet Jack. The island pet sat on his haunches accepting their love as if it was his due.

Oh, to be a dog.

They reached Finn and Maggie and stood in silence for a moment.

Mia's heart stirred. Dani's idea could work. It would have to for the town to survive. They needed to rekindle tourism to the island. She imagined the people and places it would take—a few tchotchke shops, a new fudge place, maybe some more restaurants.

And maybe a new art gallery would fill the place where the old one stood empty.

They paused and looked out over the harbor, the kids mercifully quiet for the moment. Only a few boats bobbed at the marina, most of the slips empty and waiting for the full return of summer.

Mia willed her pulse to stop jumping. "I actually wondered if you needed help with all of that."

"The town council is helping. They want to be able to vet all the applicants for the venture." Dani took a long drink of her coffee. "They've been pretty hands-on so far."

Mia's body grew heavy. "Oh."

"But what I could use help with is advertising the opportunity. As well as making listings for each of the houses and business spaces available." She dropped Mia's arm and pulled a step away, her eyes hooded. "I keep thinking I can do that, but helping Liam with the Grand Hotel repairs and renovations and planning how to keep the tourists here once we get them to come back . . . it's a lot suddenly dropped on my plate."

"Maybe I could help with that." The words hung between them for a minute.

"I'd appreciate that, really I would." Dani twisted the cup in her hands. "And honestly, I was thinking the same thing. With your realtor skills . . . But here's the thing. I can't pay you. I know you need a job, but I can't ask you to work for free. Thanks for the thought though."

Her heart sank faster than an anchor. "I understand. I'm disappointed, but I understand." Now what was she going to do?

Across the bay, Mia could see the Grand Hotel. For the past two weeks, workers had been chipping away at the burnt portions of the once great hotel. The renovation work had begun in earnest. Hopefully, Mia would still be on the island to see the finished product.

"I just really need . . ." She sucked in breath. "I'm going

to lose the house, Dani. I've got a month to get my late payments made on my mortgage or . . ."

"Oh, Mia. I didn't know." Dani reached a hand to her shoulder.

"I didn't want you to know. I'm so embarrassed." She dropped her gaze to the ground.

"You don't have to be embarrassed. You've gone through so much. More than any twenty-four-year-old should have to. Wait. What if . . ." Dani stopped, seeming to collect her thoughts. "We really don't have the money to pay you a salary, but what if I could convince the board to include your house in the deal they're making to the others? Maybe in exchange for helping us out full-time, you could pay off your mortgage for a dollar."

"You could do that? That would be amazing!" If she didn't have a mortgage, she wouldn't need as much to make ends meet. Her eyes welled up at the thought.

"I can't make any promises, but I can certainly try. I don't know why they would do it for the new people but not for someone who has proven she wants to live on the island." Dani gave her shoulder a squeeze before dropping her hand. "I can't tell you how much it would help me out to pass some of this to you."

"Now is the time my mom would say 'this is a God thing.'" And maybe Mom was onto something. This moment had a definite miracle feel to it.

Dani looked at her, concern written in her eyes. "But I have to ask. Will this be too much for you? Two little kids, no money coming in, and a job that doesn't pay?"

"I still have Troy's social security checks. I think I could make it all work if I didn't have a mortgage to worry about." Could she do it? A fifty-pound bag of bricks lifted off her shoulders at the thought of not having a mortgage. "It'll be tricky with the kids, especially with Constance tied up with Grandma Harmon. But maybe Mom can help out, and Evie sometimes too." Not to mention, this kind of work could be done after the kids were in bed at night. She squared her shoulders. "I'm sure it won't be a problem."

"Okay. I'll make some calls." Dani smiled at her, excitement shining in her eyes. "I really think this plan could work." She checked her phone. "I should get back to work. I'll give you a call later."

Mia gave her cousin a hug and waved goodbye.

"Come on, Finn. Maggie, you too. Time to head home."

Home. And now she might never have to leave.

If only he could clear away his thoughts as easily as this tree. Cody wiped a line of sweat from his hairline before reaching down to grab another section of the paper birch lying in his parents' backyard. After he and his dad had cleaned up those branches a few days ago, they'd had another storm, snapping this birch in half. The tree had narrowly missed taking out the rickety swings Cody and his sister, Lily, played on as kids.

"Your dad could use your help," his mom said on the phone that morning.

"I don't think Dad wants my help, Mom." Last week his dad had said a total of six words to him during their cleanup efforts. *I've got it from here, Cody.* No "thank you," no "good to see you, son." Not that Cody needed the thanks, but this cold shoulder rubbed vinegar right into his stinging wounds.

"Nonsense. He's just going through some stuff right now." Mom plowed right over his concern. "This will give you two a chance to talk about the business."

"Mom." His mom knew how much Cody wanted to take over the business his dad had quit after the accident. "He doesn't want my help, and he definitely doesn't want to talk about the business. I know he blames me for the accident."

"Pssh. He doesn't blame you. There was a sudden storm. You're both just being stubborn. I'm tired of my two favorite guys not speaking to each other." He heard some pans clanking together on his mom's side of the phone. "Come over and we can have supper together after."

So, here he was. Schlepping this tree from point A to point B, Dad silent beside him.

He glanced at his dad. When had he gotten so much older? At 61, he'd spent more than forty years working on the water. His face, leathery and tanned, bore more gray in his stubbled beard, the thinning hair on top of his head also more gray than the full dark it used to be. His dad wore his usual uniform of khaki work pants and a black T-shirt.

His mind drifted to an image from earlier in the day. The one near the entry of Sampson's when he and Mia discovered they were locked in. Mia's laugh washed over his memory.

"Look out!" Dad's shout interrupted his thoughts.

A log landed on Cody's foot. The pain hit a moment later, even though the steel-toed boot kept the log from breaking something. He grimaced.

"You've got your head in the clouds today."

Wow, Dad. A whole ten words. But he had a point. Cody needed to wrangle his thoughts. He was working with power tools here. He shook out the pain in his foot. Could've been a lot worse.

"Sorry."

His dad grunted in reply.

"Where do you want these bigger logs?" Cody followed his dad's pointing finger and started a stack of firewood near the back of the house.

The mid-May sun pushed its way through the cloud cover, mottling the ground where it fell. Cody's work boots squished through the muddy grass, sending up the musky, earthy scent of spring. The yard probably would have dried out by now if they hadn't had a rash of storms for the past week.

His parents had lived in the single-story rambler since before he and his sister, Lily, were born. The house in the north end of the Driftwood Hills neighborhood had been the first big purchase his parents had made after getting married. His dad always talked about buying one that was bigger, fancier, but Cody's mom resisted, insisting that she loved the house and the quiet neighborhood.

He dragged another branch from the downed tree and laid it on the pile next to the firepit. That pit hadn't seen much use in the past few years, but before that, they'd had a bonfire party every weekend. Those parties saw the whole neighborhood turning up at one point or another, adults and teens and kids.

Some of the best times of Cody's life happened right here by the firepit, laughing with Troy, teasing Mia, and horsing around with their other classmates. Usually around ten, the adults would drift off, back to their homes and beds, but the teens stayed much longer until they too followed their parents home. Then it was just the three musketeers: Troy, Mia, and him. "Hey, Dad, remember those bonfires we used to have?" But before he could finish his thought, the chainsaw revved and whined as Dad chopped another piece off the fallen log. The smell of sawdust lingered in the air.

A breeze picked up, sending a shiver down his spine.

The back door opened and his mom came out, wrapping a sweater tightly across her chest. Her salt and pepper hair was held back from her face with a pair of clips, softening the fine lines around her eyes. Picking her way around the tree debris, she halted next to Dad.

"You're making good progress out here," she said during a break in the chainsaw's activity. His dad grunted again. She turned to Cody. *Talk to him*, she mouthed. "I'll leave you to it." She leaned over and kissed Dad on the cheek then rubbed a circle on his back. He gave her a swift smile before turning back to his task. She gave him one last pat before returning to the house.

Cody rubbed at the sudden ache in his chest. For all his dad's faults, Cody never doubted his love for his wife. The two of them shared a bond that seemed to get even stronger after almost thirty years of marriage.

"Mom says Lily is coming home in a couple of weeks," Cody said to his father's back.

"Yep." His dad tossed a log aside.

Cody picked it up and moved it to the pile. "Will you be picking her up at the airport here?" The island boasted a small airport, mainly used as an air ferry stop.

"Yep."

"Is she staying long?"

"A week."

Okay, then. *I tried, Mom.* How was he supposed to talk to his dad about buying the business if his dad wouldn't even talk to him about something as mundane as his sister coming home?

The back door opened again. Mom came out carrying two steaming mugs. "I brought coffee!" She handed them each a cup. "And I have a request. Can you cut me some pieces like this?" She pulled her phone from her pocket and swiped to the internet browser. Pictured were several pieces of paper birch, each with a small hole cut in the top. "It's a candle holder," she explained. "I thought it would look cute on the mantel. I'll take care of the details, but if you could cut a few pieces of different lengths and sizes? I need a creative outlet since I'm not doing as many cakes or any fudge right now." She put her phone away then massaged a few knuckles on her left hand.

"Will do," Dad said. "How many you want? There's five in that picture."

"You should probably cut some extra in case I mess up the first ones. Maybe nine or ten."

Dad nodded and the group fell silent.

"How is your boat project coming, Cody?" Mom asked, her eyes wide with innocence. Dad stiffened. Cody could almost feel the cool breeze coming off his dad's cold shoulder.

"Slow but steady." Cody resisted the urge to run his hand through his hair. That nervous habit would scream his lack of confidence.

"It worked for the tortoise." His mom winked at him. Then she inclined her head toward Dad in a short, swift motion. If Cody had blinked, he would have missed it.

What did he have to lose? It seemed like it was now or never. Dad already wasn't speaking to him. "Have you given any more thought to me buying you out, Dad? With the money I'm earning from the town, I'll have the full amount by the end of the summer."

The wind chose that moment to quit blowing, and everything around them stilled.

"I told you no before, and that's still my answer. Nothing to think about. It was never about the money." Dad handed his empty cup back to Mom and picked up the chainsaw again.

"But why? I don't understand."

"Why are you so all-fired ready to get back out on that water?" His dad's bark made Cody catch his breath. "No means no."

"But—"

"But nothing. Besides, I have an offer for the last of the gear from an outfit on the mainland. They're wanting the license too."

Cody took a step back. The state of Michigan only issued fifty commercial licenses for the whole state. If his dad sold the license he'd held for almost thirty years, there was no guarantee Cody would be able to obtain one.

Dad tossed a log onto the stack Cody had made. Several pieces fell off the top of the pile and onto the ground, scattering like a school of fish when startled.

"Randy!" Mom's face had paled. "That license is older than our marriage. Are you sure? You didn't tell me that part."

"I'm sorry." Dad reached out a hand to her but let it fall before touching her arm. "I thought you understood that I was finished. Selling it all. I just wish it hadn't taken this long to get it done."

"And I support you in that, but I never thought you'd let the license go." Mom groped behind her until her hand hit the railing along the stairs. She gripped it until Cody saw her knuckles turn white. "I never thought . . ." The words hung between them.

"Why, Dad?" Cody's words ground out of him. "Can you at least tell me that?"

"You of all people should know." His dad pulled on the cord of the chainsaw. It roared to life, drowning out any other sound. He lowered the saw to the tree in front of him, and the chain ripped through the bark.

So. It was true then. His dad blamed him for the accident. He remembered his dad's face at Steve's funeral, and then Troy's a few days later. The sorrow in his eyes accompanied by the small shake of his head when he looked at Cody told Cody everything he needed to know.

Cody handed his mug to his mom. "I'm going to take off."

Mom opened her mouth. Shut it. Then, "What about supper?"

"Sorry, Mom. I'm not hungry anymore."

Forget getting the parts for the boat. If his dad wouldn't sell him that license, his dreams drifted dead in the water.

Four

THIS PLAN HAD TO WORK.

Because Mia was staking everything on it.

She looked around at the members of the town council seated at the table in the conference room of the Tourism Bureau. She knew them all, of course. The island was small enough that people who lived here permanently all knew each other.

Dani had called a day after their chat by the water and said the town was willing to work with the bank to pay off her mortgage. Hallelujah. Today they were meeting to hammer out the details.

Martha Kelley, owner of Martha's on Main, stood up at the end of the table. She brushed a gray-streaked hair behind her ear. "Let's get this thing started."

They all quieted down.

"I think you all know that I have reservations about this plan," Martha said.

Mia wanted to sink under the table. Dani shot her an apologetic look. She hadn't mentioned that the council wasn't a hundred percent on board.

"Martha, we all agreed this was a good idea," Tara Chamberlain said. As the pastor's wife, Tara was often called the "island mom." Her silver-blonde hair brushed her shoulders as she turned her head to look each one in the eye. "Mia has skills we need to make this work. And she's willing to put in the hours."

Around the table, Patrick Kelley, brother-in-law to Martha—although they were more like enemies—and Historical Society president, Janine Dirks, nodded along with what Tara said.

Dani had also invited Cody. Although he wasn't officially on the town council, she'd told Mia that she wanted him to know how much work there was to do on the houses. He and Mia would work together on some of those details in the coming weeks. She glanced at him now. He sat at the back of the room, a neutral expression on his face. She turned back to the discussion.

Martha crossed her arms. "Fine. But we need some ground rules. How much is this town willing to shell out for this project?"

Everyone began talking at once. Finally, Mia's dad boomed over them all.

"People. Enough of this." He stood up, his crisp dress shirt a contrast to the casual outfits everyone else wore. The room quieted as everyone looked at him. "Mia needs clear guidelines on how to do this job."

Wow, Dad. Thanks for that. Mia shrank even further into her chair.

"I think we need to set up a goal for her to reach in order to move forward with plans." Dad used a raised finger to punctuate his point.

A general murmur of assent arose.

Mia glanced across the table. Cody sat back in his chair, face serene. He walked a pen through his fingers. Looking up, he caught her gaze and smiled. Then he winked.

Good old Code. Always on her side.

After almost two hours of grueling debate, they'd settled on the details.

"Okay, to recap," Tara said, reading off a legal pad, "for the next two weeks, we will gather applications from people who want to move here. Mia, you will take point on that. The applications will come to the email already set up on the town website. Then you can spend a week narrowing those down to a manageable number. Let's see if Mia and Dani can set up phone and video interviews for the first week of June. I suggest as many of us as possible attend those interviews." She tapped a pen on the paper as she listed each item. "Near the beginning of June, we will have an on-island event where everyone can come and tour the island."

"Who knows, they might not like us," Janine said.

"Or we won't like them," Patrick grumbled.

"Hush." Martha gave her brother-in-law a glare. "Of course they will like us." She dusted her hands together. "Final decisions about who we will approve will be made as a group. Hopefully, we can make our final decisions by mid-June, then they can start moving in. Cody, will you have everything ready by then?"

Cody snapped to attention. "I'll know more after I go through the houses, but I don't foresee a problem."

"Okay. I've got to get back to the restaurant." Martha stood again. "If Mia can fill fourteen houses and fourteen businesses, we'll pay off her mortgage. If not?" She shrugged then gathered her purse from the table and left the room, the door banging behind her.

Um. What? Mia hadn't thought the deal was contingent on a certain number of filled houses.

No pressure there.

She looked around the room. Everyone beamed at her. Except Cody. A line appeared between his eyebrows. Did he think she couldn't do it? She stiffened her spine.

She'd save her kids' home. Just watch her.

The rest of the meeting broke up a few minutes later.

Call me. Dani had motioned to her as Patrick cornered her behind the table.

Mia walked out of the conference room and down the tiny hallway. The opposite end of the building opened up into a large room housing the Jonathon Island Museum. She pushed out of the front door and into the morning sunshine.

"Mia, wait," Cody called from behind her. He caught up and tugged a ball cap over his hair. "How are you?"

She scrubbed a hand over her face. "I don't know why Dad put Martha and Patrick on a team together. A recipe for arguments, if you ask me."

Cody shrugged. "He probably knew that no one could accuse him of favoritism."

"True." She'd give him that much. She looked down the street. Her heart wrenched. So many businesses still looked forlorn. The old Great Lakes Memorabilia shop had a broken window, and so did a few others. Peeling paint and listing window boxes decorated others. The dark and empty storefronts echoed the emptiness of the streets. Well, she would change that.

"Will you be able to meet this quota?" Cody stood at her shoulder, gaze steady on her.

"I don't have much choice." She pulled herself to full height. "I'll make it work. This is the miracle I've been hoping for. My only shot at keeping my home."

Cody opened his mouth. Closed it. Then, "I know you can do it, Mia. You'll figure it out. I can come by in a little bit to check out that door."

"That'd be great. Thanks. See ya later."

After a brisk walk home and collecting her kids from Constance's house, Mia sat at her dining room table. Finn played with a truck at her feet, and Maggie sat next to her scribbling in a coloring book. She looked down at the list that she was making.

Develop social media profiles.

Create a website for applications.

Advertise?

Take photos of prospective businesses and houses.

Network?

Mia didn't know how to do some of those things. How was she supposed to network with businesses when she didn't even know who might be interested? But she did have a few contacts left from her art college days and the business school connected with that college. She could start there. She jotted down a few notes before composing a paragraph to send as an email. She could also send the info to a few realtors she knew from when she first got her license.

"Mama, what color dis?" Maggie held up a reddish crayon.

"Let me see." When Maggie passed over the crayon, Mia took the opportunity to give her warm little hand a squeeze. "It says, plum." She handed the crayon back.

"What pwum?"

"It's a little fruit. It grows on trees."

"We have a pwum tee?"

"Nope. Sorry, baby. We don't have any fruit trees." She and Troy had hoped to plant fruit trees, but everything else was always more urgent. Now it looked possible that there never would be any fruit trees for them.

Mia turned back to her list. She would need Dani to provide her with the house addresses that were being included in the incentive program. Then she'd need someone with keys to let her in so she could update the real estate listings as needed.

A knock at the door interrupted her concentration. She hurried down the hall, the kids trailing behind. The door held fast as she tugged at it. She braced her feet and tugged again. It flew open and out of her hand, the doorknob hitting the wall with a smack.

"I can see why you needed me." Cody stood framed in

the doorway, the bright sunshine highlighting gold flecks in his blond hair poking out from under a Detroit Tigers cap. His teasing smile hovered on his lips a moment before he spoke again. Then his eyes darted away. "Good thing I know what to do about a sticky door. But I'm gonna need a helper. You don't happen to have anyone who is four years old here, do you?"

Biting back a smile, Mia played along. "I don't know," she said. "There is Finn, but I don't think he's four yet."

"I am too four!" Finn stuck his head between her legs, knocking her off balance.

"Whoa there." Cody reached out a hand and grasped her upper arm to steady her. He let go then bent down to Finn. "Which is it? Are you two or are you four?"

Finn pushed his way through Mia's legs. "I'm four. But on my next birthday, I'll be five."

"Good. You're just the person I need to help me." Cody raised an eyebrow at Mia. "If it's okay with your mom."

"Of course it is. I trust you. Are you okay if I go back to working, or do you need me to stay and help?" She pointed a thumb over her shoulder toward the dining room where she'd left her list.

"We can do it, Mama." Finn flexed his arm and patted his bicep. "We're strong," he growled. "Right, Cody?"

Cody laughed and flexed too. And wow . . . had his muscles always looked like that? He'd been such a lanky kid in high school. Troy had been the football star. But it made sense—Cody was a fisherman, after all. And now a handyman doing all sorts of manual labor. Of course he had muscles.

But those muscles, combined with his tan skin and that teasing glint in his eyes . . .

"Mia?" Cody asked, blinking at her.

Oh, goodness. He'd caught her staring at his muscles. "What?" Mia leaned against the doorway, pretending nonchalance while also gripping it tight with her fingertips.

He gave her a strange look. "I said we've got this. You okay?"

"Mm-hmm. Why wouldn't I be?"

"I don't know. You just look a little pale."

"Do I? Must just be the stress. I've gotta get back to work. A website won't create itself."

"Okay." He smiled at her, and it was a quick shot to her chest.

Holy cow. What was happening? Did she actually find Cody—her oldest friend—attractive?

But that would be . . .

No.

"Okay, bye." Heart pounding in her chest, Mia spun on her heel to get back to her notes.

Cody and Finn's voices carried down the hall. "I'll need you to hold the door still, buddy." Cody's deeper voice contrasting with Finn's higher, excited tone.

"Like this?"

"Yep. Just like that. I'm going to run this planer across the sticky spot in the wood, and I need the door to stay just like this."

Over the sound of metal moving across wood, she heard Finn. "Am I a good helper?"

Her heart squeezed at Finn's little voice—the boy who didn't remember his daddy. The boy who longed for a strong male influence in his life, for approval. Her serious boy, who always wanted to do everything right.

"You are the best helper I've had all day."

Oh, man. Her heart couldn't take the swelling at the praise he'd given her son. Praise that probably meant more to him because a man gave it—not just his mom, but a capable guy Finn looked up to.

"Mia, do you want me to replace this shutter?" Cody called down the hall.

Her palm throbbed at the memory of the scrape she'd gotten fighting off the "monster." "That would be amazing. Thank you." She'd just left the shutter lying in the muddy grass after the drama of that stormy night earlier in the week. "I think Troy had some long black screws left over. They're in the shed."

She listened as Cody called for Finn to lead the way to the shed. For a moment, she thought about joining them. Maybe catching another glimpse of Cody's muscles. But she pushed the desire away. If she was going to save this house, she needed to focus on the work in front of her.

Aside from getting the fishing business off the ground, helping Mia was the best way he knew to honor Troy's memory.

Cody tightened the last screw on the shutter. He'd gone around the house, making sure each one was secure. Finn had grown bored after they'd finished the door, and now he was playing in the muddy grass. Cody gathered up his tools and headed toward the front of the house. A movement inside the dining room window caught his eye and he paused. At the dining room table, Mia sat with her head buried in her hands.

Looked like she needed some outdoor time too.

"C'mon, Finn," he said. "Let's put these things away and then talk to your mom about some lunch."

"Lunch!" Finn scrambled up from the ground, knees dirty from the damp soil. Cody's heart pinched. If he could make life better for Mia and her kids, he would. He just needed to step up his game. He handed Finn a hammer to carry, and they made their way into the house.

"We've come to take you girls on a picnic," Cody said. The dark wood on the walls of the dining room absorbed all the light. Mia definitely needed some sunshine. "I'll buy us sandwiches from Martha's on Main."

"Seriously? A picnic?" She hit a key on her computer and then closed the lid. "I don't think so, Code."

"C'mon. Where's your sense of adventure? It'll be fun."

"It'll be muddy is what it'll be. It just rained again." She crossed her arms and arched her brow at him.

He mimicked her pose. "Bah. Mud, shmud. The clouds are clearing off. The sun is sparkling on the water. Down by the shore it will be beautiful. Who cares about a little mud?"

"I care about the mud." She thumbed her chest. "I'm the one doing laundry later."

"Fair point. What if I promise to help?"

"You do laundry?"

"I've even been known to cook for myself. A bachelor's lot." He winked at her. "C'mon, Mia. It'll be fun. What happened to the spontaneous girl I used to know?"

"She grew up. Got married. Had kids. Not, of course, in that order." Mia ducked her chin.

Aw.

"Hey." Cody touched her hand and drew back just as quickly. "You know you're forgiven for that, right? Last I checked, the blood of Jesus covers that too."

"Yeah. But sometimes it just gets to me, you know?"

"Trust me. I know about guilt." His chest tightened, and he drew in a long breath to loosen it. Then he tossed her a grin. "You know what's a good cure for guilt?" She shook her head. He nodded his once. "Picnics."

A laugh bubbled out of her. "Fine. You win. We'll go on the muddiest picnic known to man."

"What, you don't think they have picnics in pigpens?"

She just rolled her eyes at him. "Kids! Get your rubber boots on and your jackets. We're going on an adventure. I'll grab some juice boxes and chips."

A few minutes later, after wrestling Maggie into her jacket while Mia helped Finn step into his tall rubber boots, they set off down the street. Cody reached for the insulated bag Mia carried full of juice and chips.

Martha's on Main stood just across the street from the shop where his mom used to make fudge. His heart pinched as they passed the empty storefront and walked over the cobblestone street. Just imagine how great it would be when someone made it into a thriving shop again.

In front of Martha's, he handed Mia the insulated bag. "I'll run in and see if they'll make up some sandwiches to go."

At his knee, Maggie tipped her face up to him. "Me go too." He lifted her up into his arms.

"Sounds good to me." In the street, Finn was banging his stick against the cobblestones and counting. Cody met Mia's eye.

"Go ahead," she said. "I don't think we need to bring Sir Count and his stick into the restaurant. I'll wait out here. Besides, I want to take a few photos of downtown for the new Jonathon Island social media pages."

Inside, the high-backed booths were empty. Must have gotten here before the lunch rush. The smell of something peppery filled the air. Vera Graves, the gray-and-dark-haired waitress, stood behind the counter.

"Hey there, Vera." He set Maggie on one of the stools lining the counter. "Can we get some sandwiches to go?"

"Sure, sugar." Vera flipped open an order sheet. "What can I get for you?"

He put in the order then played Pat-A-Cake with Maggie until Vera brought him a paper sack bulging with food. "Thanks, Vera."

Soon, he and Maggie stepped back into the sunlight. Mia stood a few steps away, watching Finn. Sunlight glinted off her soft curls. The look of pride on her face turned his heart over. *Don't worry, Troy, I'll take care of them for you.*

"I've got sustenance." He held the paper bag aloft. Mia

turned to him, her smile making his heart flop like a fish out of water.

They made their way through town to a small strip of land near the water, situated next to the ferry landing. While not really a park, the area had a picnic table used sometimes by people in the nearby businesses for lunch breaks. The sun glinted off the choppy waves, sending sparkles through the air. A light, fishy scent permeated the air, crisp in the spring afternoon. They claimed the picnic table and laid out their sandwiches.

"You were right," Mia said around a bite of her sandwich. "This was a good idea. I needed a break from the computer screen."

"I'm sorry, did you say I was right?" Cody opened his eyes wide, feigning shock.

"I'll freely admit when you have a good idea, Codes." Mia waved off his words with a flip of her hand, her mouth turned up in a half smile. She finished her sandwich, and they cleaned up the remains of the lunch. "I'm gonna snap a few more photos." She pulled out her phone before spinning in a slow circle.

Cody took a minute to look around. What would make a good photo? The harbor lay to the left and the town to the right. With the muddy ground, their picnic space wasn't too pretty, but there were some views of the town where each unique building held its own charm.

Jack came trotting past, disappearing between two buildings.

"Drat. He was too fast," Mia said. "Jack would make a cute feature. I'll have to keep an eye out for him." She studied her phone for a minute, swiping at the screen. "Hey. I just had an idea. I'm gonna shoot a quick video for my first post."

"Great idea." Cody cleared up the paper wrappings from their sandwiches. "What do you want me to do?"

"Nothing. Just be natural. And maybe make sure Maggie doesn't wander off?" She dropped a quick kiss on the heads of her kids. "Mommy is going to make a movie. Everybody look cute."

Maggie immediately began heading for the water. Suppressing an amused eyeroll, Cody swooped her up onto his shoulders.

A few paces away, Mia began filming and narrating.

"It's a beautiful late spring day here on Jonathon Island. A place where you can find your dreams coming true." She turned the camera and panned across the marina. "As you can see, there are many things to attract you to our little island. Boating, fishing, a charming downtown without traffic congestion."

Maggie held tight to Cody's forehead as he bent down and picked up Finn. Turning the boy over, he held him by his ankles. The kids giggled. Mia began turning toward them. "Make a funny face," he whispered as she fully faced them, narrating the whole time.

"And here, you can see another local attraction, Cody Hart. Say 'hi' Cody."

Their eyes met. Hers danced with a merriment that shot electricity straight down to his toes.

He grinned. "Hi, Cody."

"Hi, Cody," Finn echoed.

"Hi, Cody," Maggie said. She patted Cody on his head.

"Anyway. This is our home. We welcome you to come and check it out." Mia fumbled her phone. Her cheeks pinked. She turned away from them. "I'll, uh, just get this posted."

Local attraction, eh? He liked the sound of that. He spun in a circle, the kids squealing.

"Faster!" Finn put his arms out like an airplane. Cody spun around again then collapsed to the ground, cradling Finn and Maggie to him on the way down.

"You two are wearing me out." Cody sprawled on the ground. Finn climbed to his feet and ran around, arms outstretched, making airplane noises. Maggie snuggled into Cody's shoulder. "Come join us, Mia!" He snagged Finn and pulled him back with a mock growl.

"Join you on the ground? No thanks." She turned back to him. "Besides, I have to get these things posted."

"Let's make a deal. If you come over here and play for a minute, I'll help you with anything you want today."

"You've already helped enough."

"What can I say," he said. "I like helping."

"Thanks, but no thanks, Code." She sat down on a bench nearby.

He didn't know the first thing about social media. He preferred to work with his hands over spending time online. What had he been thinking, offering his help? Of course, Mia said no thanks. Cody lay in the cold grass, mud seeping into his shoulder, Maggie still snuggled up to him, the bobble of her fuzzy hat tickling his nose.

But then again, how could he not offer to help? The

widow of his dead best friend was hurting, and he couldn't stand by and watch.

Maybe she didn't want any help from the guy who lived through the accident that stole her husband's life.

Or maybe she blamed him, even just a little.

Kind of like he did himself every day.

Beside him, Mia got up from the bench and brushed herself off.

"Thank you for inviting us out here," she said. "It was nice."

Yeah, that was him. The nice guy. He clambered to his feet, Maggie sticking to him like a barnacle clinging to a boat's hull. "We should do this again."

"Sure," she said. "Another time." She reached for Maggie, and the little girl went into her arms. "C'mon, Mags. We'd better get home."

Cody felt a sudden chill. He reached out a hand to Mia, but she'd already moved toward the remains of their picnic.

"Finn, time to get going." Her call to Finn appeared as though it went in one ear and out the other as the boy continued playing airplane. "Finn!" Mia's shoulders slumped.

"I'll get him." Cody ran the few steps to where Finn made his circles. "Time to go, bud. You heard your mom."

"Will you walk us home?" The airplane stopped mid-flight and looked up at him. Cody looked to Mia and raised an eyebrow. She nodded. "Yep. I can walk you home."

They retraced their steps from earlier, the fishy and wet scent of the harbor replaced by the loamy aroma of the damp lawns they passed. The silence drew long between them. Even the kids were quieter, though he suspected fatigue in their case. Mia carried Maggie the whole way while Finn scampered ahead.

This quiet was too much.

"I'll keep you posted about the places I'm working on," he said. "You can get some footage for your reels or whatever. Of the updates I make."

"Thank you." Her quiet reply kept him from saying anything more. The chatter of the kids the only sound on their walk.

They turned down Lilac Lane. He could see her house partway down the street. The gray Craftsman looked wholesome, surrounded by its white picket fence. He remembered replacing the shingles with Troy just three summers ago. It felt like a lifetime. A few branches had come down from the elm in the backyard. He'd have time this week to come and clean that up.

They passed Constance Franklin's house. She was standing on her front step, sifting through some mail. "Hi, Grandma," the kids called to her.

"Hi guys!" Her smile died as she saw Cody walking with them. He raised his hand to her, but she looked back to her stack of mail. A sharp ache buried itself in his chest.

"Is Grandma Harmon all settled in?" Mia paused at the end of the short sidewalk leading up to Constance's front porch.

Constance's face brightened again. "She's doing remarkably well. Come by sometime to say hi."

"Will do." Mia gave a last wave and started on again.

"Troy's Grandma Harmon, Constance's mom, fell and had to have a hip replaced. Since she doesn't have any other family, Constance brought her here. I think it's nice for her to have someone to share her house with again. It must get quiet there at night."

They walked past the Franklins' place.

"Hey, remember when Troy and I ran over that sugar maple with a four-wheeler?" In the corner of the yard clung the bent tree.

"I still can't believe the tree stayed bent like that." Mia moved her hand in an elongated, sideways s-pattern mimicking the shape of the tree. "I used to love sitting on that tree."

He remembered. If he closed his eyes, he could see Mia sitting on that trunk holding court over him and Troy as they both vied for her attention, wrestling in the grass, telling fish stories, and goofing around.

Cody had been friends with Mia first when she came to the island, and then when Troy moved to the island in sixth grade, they'd all been best friends. He didn't know when Mia had fallen for Troy, but after Troy asked her to the junior prom, well, that was that. For a long time he had kicked himself for not speaking up when they first started high school. He should have told Mia how he felt about her, but then it was too late. Anyone with eyeballs could see she and Troy were head over heels for each other.

So, he'd done the right thing and buried his feelings, going all in on supporting their relationship.

When Mia had gotten pregnant, there was no doubt about who the father was. He walked with Troy through his feelings of guilt. Then he stood as best man at their wedding.

At least, despite his many failings, Cody had done something right—he'd let Mia go.

Not that she or Troy ever knew it. And Cody had never admitted it to a soul.

Finn bobbed ahead of them, returning to them once in a while to comment on something he'd seen.

A few steps later, they reached the sidewalk up to Mia's front step. Cody put one hand on the white picket fence. It wobbled. "I'll come by and fix this," he said.

"Thanks for walking us home." Mia's voice was subdued. She shifted Maggie on her hip. He longed to ask her what she was thinking, but she turned away from him and was walking toward the house. Maggie waved at him before burying her face in Mia's neck. At the front step, Finn had pushed the door open.

"Thanks for the picnic," he called to her retreating back. "Let's do it again."

She looked back over her shoulder, a slight smile on her lips. It didn't make it all the way up her face to her eyes. "I'm going to be pretty busy with the job for Dani, but today was nice. I'm sorry, Code." She turned back to him. "I know you mean well, but I just . . . It's hard for me to accept help. I need to prove that I can take care of things on my own." She shrugged as if each word wasn't a knife to his heart. Then she went into the house and shut the door.

And, sure, she didn't slam it shut, but Cody felt the impact.

He spun on his heel and headed back to his place. The walk would be twice as long without company.

"Cody!"

He glanced over his shoulder. Liam raised a hand in greeting from down the block as he jogged to catch up to him. Cody had helped him update a house near Mia's on Lilac Lane when Liam had decided to move to the island. Liam had moved in a week or so ago.

"I was going to text you, but when I saw you walking, I thought I'd shout instead." Liam clapped him on the shoulder.

"You caught me heading home." And now he had company, but it wasn't the same.

"What's wrong, man?" Liam peered at him.

"What do you mean?" Cody turned and started walking. Liam fell into rhythm beside him.

"I don't think I've seen you this solemn since, well, ever, really. Of course, I haven't known you very long." Liam raised an eyebrow. "If I didn't know better, I'd guess woman trouble."

Cody snorted. "Gotta have a woman for that."

"No, actually, you don't. In fact, I made that face plenty when Dani and I were first getting to know each other. But if it's not a woman . . ."

"No. You were right the first time. It was a woman, but not in a romantic way. I mean Mia and the kids and I just had a picnic. It was great. For a while. We had sandwiches and hung around near the water." They passed by a house on Cody's fix-it list. Grass was getting long. He added mowing to his list.

"Uh huh." Liam was still frowning.

"She laughed and had a good time." He hadn't imagined that, right? "She even said it was a good idea. But then, I don't know. I must have said or done something wrong, because all of a sudden it was time to pack up the kids and go home." He ran a hand over his face.

Liam's face had cleared. "Women," he said. "They are unknowable. But usually there's a clue. What happened right before that?"

He thought back. "The kids and I were horsing around, and then I offered to help her with some projects she has going on."

"Did she want your help?"

"I guess not." They turned off Jonathon Boulevard and started walking down Main. Down the way, he could see that Good Day Coffee had hung a new, bright blue awning. It added a cheery vibe to the rundown appearance of the rest of the street.

"Well, there you go. She's a strong, independent woman, and she wants to make it on her own."

"I know she's strong and independent. I don't want to take that away from her. I just want her to know that she doesn't have to do everything on her own all the time." He wanted to be there for her, especially now that Troy couldn't.

"You want to be the big, strong rescuer."

"No." Or, maybe it was yes. Didn't all guys want that? "Okay, but it's not just that. It's just . . ." Cody tugged at his ball cap.

"Just what?"

"Our relationship is super complicated." A piece of trash drifted over his foot, and he bent to pick it up.

"I hate to break it to you, but all relationships are complicated, man." Liam put his hands up in a what-are-you-going-to-do gesture.

"Complicated like, I've been half in love with her since middle school but then she married my best friend who then died on my boat complicated?" Yeah, he hadn't meant to say all of that, but now his chest was lighter. Freer.

Liam grinned at him. "Okay. You've probably got everyone beat on that level of complication. But it's not a competition, so I suggest you simplify things a bit in the future. You like her. She tolerates you. Sounds like the foundation for something great."

Cody laughed at Liam's teasing. "I guess. I'm just trying to help her out. You know, honoring Troy's memory."

"Seriously though, I've seen the two of you together, there's some chemistry there. Look. I don't know much about love—we've already established that. But I think you need to stop thinking about yourself as her husband's best friend and just try to be her friend." Liam shrugged. "She probably senses you are trying to be a rescuer, and she doesn't need that right now, but I'd bet she could use a friend."

A friend. Right. He could do that. After all, they'd been friends a long time. Since before Troy moved to the island. "Thanks for the pep talk." He paused on the sidewalk in front of his property.

"Anytime." Liam clapped him on the shoulder. "Hey, have you had time to look up that fishing gear for me?"

Shoot! "Aw. I'm sorry. I got busy and—"

Liam squeezed his shoulder. "No worries. I know you've got a lot going on."

"I'll get it to you tonight. I have to search for that engine part anyway." And try his hardest to figure out how to be just a friend to Mia.

Five

COULD SOMEONE PLEASE REMIND HER why she'd thought taking this job was a good idea?

Mia sat in Dani's office, the two of them surrounded by piles of papers. Mia's eye strayed to the poster of a hillside in Tuscany Dani had on her wall. Taking an extended vacation there sounded pretty good right about now.

"I can't believe we had this much response in such a short time, Mia." Dani's words broke through her thoughts, and she shifted her gaze back to the papers in front of her. Each stack represented a business owner who had seen her call for applications and were eager to move to Jonathon Island. Dani had printed the applications off the online portal, and now the two of them were sorting through the piles on Dani's desk.

"I can't believe it either." Mia reached up and retied the bandanna she'd wrapped around her hair this morning.

Hopefully it covered the fact that she hadn't had time to wash her hair during her five-minute shower this morning.

"I can't believe how many of these mention your video reel. Or how many of them are just wondering if Cody is available." Dani thumbed through a few sheets of paper. "I think if we eliminate the ones who are only looking to date Cody, we should have a good starting point." She raised an eyebrow at Mia. "Unless you think we should set him up with one of them."

Mia's chest went hot. "What? No. He would hate that." She shifted in her chair. The cushion in the seat must have been mashed flat, she could feel every spring.

"*He* would hate it?" Now Dani raised the other eyebrow.

"What?" Mia furrowed her brow. Cody wouldn't be interested in a blind date, would he?

"It's just that every time we come across one of these, you huff a little and then throw it on the floor." Dani smirked at her. *Smirked!*

Mia arched her back. "I do not."

Dani crossed her arms and sat back in the chair. She didn't say anything, just gestured to Mia's side of the room. Mia looked around. Scattered around her chair, lay dozens of crumpled papers.

Her cousin leaned forward again and picked up an application off the desk. "In that case, maybe you will approve of this one. Look at this, she is an artist. She makes sculptures out of driftwood. She likes long walks by the shore and would love to live in a maintenance shed. She would make a great fisherman's wife."

No. Her heart thudded to a stop. She reached over the desk. "It doesn't say that." She snatched the paper out of Dani's hand. She scanned the lines of text. It was an application from an older couple who wanted to open a pizzeria. "You little sneak."

Dani laughed. "It was worth it to see the look on your face."

Mia's shoulders fell to a reasonable level. "Fine. You're right. I guess I am being a little protective of my friend."

"Mm-hmm." Dani crossed her arms again.

"What?"

"It's just that I don't think you think of Cody as a friend." Dani gave her an intense look. "And I know he has feelings for you."

That couldn't be true. "I do think of Cody as a friend. And don't be silly, he doesn't think of me as anything other than Troy's widow." But why did that thought sting a little?

Mia's phone buzzed. A text from her mom popped up.

Mom

Want me to start some lunch?

Shoot! Was it that late already? Her stomach plummeted. When her mom had arrived that morning to watch the kids, Mia had promised to be back in two hours. It was now bordering on three.

Mia

That would be great. Thanks. I'll be home in a
few.

"I'm sorry, Dani, I've gotta go." She gathered up the

piles into a haphazard stack and shoved them into her messenger bag.

As she rushed out the door, she almost missed Dani's parting words. "Call me when you've narrowed down the list."

The beauty of the May sky beckoned to her, almost begging to be set to canvas. She pushed away thoughts of the perfect watercolor shade and hurried on toward home.

After she'd sent her mom on her way and the kids had been fed, Mia spread the papers back out on the dining room table.

She should be ecstatic, but instead, a wave of nausea threatened to take her under. She swallowed it down, took a few long breaths to slow her heart rate. Could she even do this job? If she failed, she would have no choice but to move.

Around her, the room embraced her. The dark wainscoting lapping the bottom of the walls, with a light gray around the top had been the first house compromise she and Troy had made. He wanted more wood in their home, but she thought it was too dark. He proposed the wainscoting, and she countered with the gray above. When they'd finished that part of the remodel, Troy had danced her around the room, laughing. *We make a good team,* he'd said.

Funny how that memory didn't hold a sting anymore. In fact, all memories of Troy had faded into sepia-toned photos she took out more and more rarely every day.

Maggie climbed onto a chair next to her, a purple crayon clutched in her hand. "Hi, Mama."

"Hi, baby."

Something crashed in the kids' bedroom. "Don't come in here." Finn's voice sounded pinched.

"Well, that's never a good sign," she said to Maggie. The toddler nodded even though Mia knew she had no idea what her mother was talking about. "Stay here."

In the bedroom, the table lamp, normally on the bookshelf, lay on the ground. The crescent moon stem was in pieces. Nearby, lay the ball Finn had been repeatedly told not to throw in the house.

Finn sat on his bed, studying his fingers.

"Are you hurt? Did you cut yourself?"

A quick shake of his head told her he was fine.

"What happened here?"

"I was holding the ball and it slipped." Finn wiped his hand across his face.

She put her hands on her hips, tried for a casual tone. "Slipped, eh?"

"I only threw it a little."

"You aren't supposed to throw it at all." She knelt by the bed and raised Finn's chin until he looked her in the eye. "What did I tell you about throwing things in the house?"

"I'm sorry, Mommy." He sniffed.

"I forgive you." Finn reached out his arms and she pulled him into a hug. "I'm glad you weren't hurt. Go get a trash bag. We'll get this cleaned up." He ran off and was back a minute later, white garbage bag held around his neck like a cape. They carefully placed all the broken pieces into the bag before Mia scoured the carpet looking for stray shards. When she was satisfied there were none left to cut anyone's feet, she tied the bag shut.

"We've left your sister alone too long." They walked hand in hand the few steps to the dining room. "Maggie! No!" At the table, her cherub daughter drooled purple crayon, the half which was not in her mouth was dancing all over the application papers spread before her.

"Cowor, Mama." Maggie grinned wide. Bits of purple crayon stained her teeth. Gripping the crayon tight in her chubby fist, she drew a long streak across the page in front of her.

"Oh, Mags." She scooped her daughter out of the chair and carried her to the kitchen. "Those are Mom's papers. You can't color on them." Sitting Maggie next to the sink, she dug the remaining crayon bits from her mouth, then washed her face. "You can't eat the crayons."

"Pwum is fwuit," Maggie informed her, showing her the damp, uneaten end of her plum crayon.

"I—" A knock at the door saved her from having to untangle that one. "Don't eat crayons." She lifted Maggie down from the countertop and went to the door.

Cody.

Her heart rate picked up again, but this time she didn't mind it as much. In his flannel work jacket and worn Levi's, he looked like the cover of Eligible Bachelor's Weekly. If such a magazine existed.

He held up the toolbox in his left hand. "I'm here to fix your fence. I'd have been here sooner, but I got tied up with my remodel of the old Hansen place. Dani wanted to make sure it was ready."

"No problem."

Finn brushed past her. "Cody!" He barreled into Cody's legs.

"Hey, bud." Cody ruffled Finn's dark hair. "Want to help me again?"

"Yes!" He started to run down the steps, but Cody stopped him with a hand on his shoulder.

"Whoa, bud. I think your mom would like you to be wearing shoes." The smile he sent Mia's way made a warmth gather in her belly.

Ridiculous.

Mia helped Finn find his shoes and started to help him put them on, but he ran over to Cody instead. Cody glanced at her, his gaze searching her face. She gave a little shrug. It didn't hurt to have help getting the kids into outdoor gear.

"Be careful, Finn," she said. "Listen to Cody."

"We'll watch out for each other," Cody said. He put a hand on Finn's shoulder. "Won't we?"

Finn nodded, his face serious. "Don't worry, Mommy."

She leaned against the doorframe as they walked over to inspect the fence. Her heart squeezed as Finn slipped his hand into Cody's. She rubbed at her chest before going back into the house to make sure Maggie hadn't turned more of her paperwork into coloring pages.

She found her daughter curled up under the dining room table, fast asleep, the plum crayon stub clutched tightly in her palm. Mia glanced at the clock. No wonder Maggie was sleepy. It was an hour past her normal nap time. She'd been so distracted with the work and with Finn to notice.

Moving at a snail's pace, she picked Maggie off the floor and cradled her to her chest before tucking her into her "big girl bed." She smoothed the damp bangs from Maggie's forehead then left the room on tiptoe. If she kept quiet enough for Maggie to sleep, she could get a good hour's worth of work done uninterrupted.

Her phone rang, and she jumped before grabbing at it to answer. "Hello?"

"Why are you whispering?" Evie's voice came on the line.

"I just put Maggie down, and I need her to sleep while I work." Stepping around the creaky floorboard in the hall, Mia made her way to the dining room. "Cody has Finn outside fixing the fence, so I think I can make some real progress."

"Cody is there again, eh?"

Seriously? Were Dani and Evie conspiring to gang up on her? "I don't think I like the tone of your voice." She shifted a few papers onto the floor.

"What tone? I don't have a tone."

"Yes, you do."

"I saw your video."

Mia held back a groan. Why hadn't she edited that video? The truth was, it was a good shot, and the harbor looked so pretty that day. She couldn't bring herself to cut out Finn's laughter and Maggie's bright smile. Cody was just icing on the cake. "It was just a picnic."

"'A local attraction,' I believe you said."

What had she been thinking? The words just slipped out. But then, his easy smile and the way he didn't give her grief for saying that about him made her feel safe. Just like he always did.

But still. "Evie. C'mon. You know we've only ever been friends." She looked at the sea of paper swamping her table, threatening to tow her under.

"What do you mean? You told me a few weeks ago you were thinking about dating again."

She had said that. They'd had a long conversation after watching *Sleepless in Seattle,* where she'd admitted the barest possibility that she was lonely. But that was before she'd found out that she might lose her house. Now she needed to concentrate on keeping a roof over her kids' heads. She didn't have time for dating anyone. "Yeah, but it's Cody."

"I fail to see the problem. He's single, you're single. What's the issue?"

"The issue is he was Troy's best friend. How weird would it be to date my late husband's best friend? Doesn't that violate some code?" Although, to be fair, Cody was *her* friend first.

No, she must have just been feeling a spark of getting back to her normal self. A feeling she hadn't had in a long time. Maybe ever. At least as an adult.

After all, she'd been an unwed mother, married before she was twenty, then before she'd adjusted to that, Maggie was on the way. And just as she was getting used to the thought of two kids, her husband was killed in that tragic accident.

Besides, she didn't have time for anything except sorting

through these applicants. When she had agreed to do this job . . . check that—when she had begged for this job, she hadn't anticipated this much response.

"Do you really think Troy would mind?" Evie sounded genuinely curious. "I would think he would be happy for you."

She could never make her sister understand how Troy hovered between them every time she and Cody were together. Perhaps if his death had happened in a different way . . . "People would talk."

"Psssht. Since when do you care what people think?"

"I guess I just feel like I need to hold myself to a higher standard, after coming home pregnant at nineteen. People judge me in a different way."

"I get that, but you don't have to punish yourself forever."

The blood of Jesus covers that too. Cody's words rattled through her head again.

"Besides, your voice got lighter in that video when you talked about him. I haven't heard that from you in a long time. You sounded invested."

Was she attracted to Cody? He was attractive, sure. But was she romantically drawn to him? She thought about their picnic, the way he remembered she liked avocado on a sandwich, his quiet words about her guilt, his coaxing her to be her best self. Not to mention the spark of emotion she'd had when he was playing with the kids.

Sure, she appreciated him, but attraction? That couldn't be it.

"He's like a brother to me. Or maybe a cousin." She

stood and moved a stack of papers to the far corner of the room.

Evie laughed. "So, you feel the same way about him as you feel about Bash? I doubt it."

Um. Okay. "Well, when you put it that way." Mia thought again about the sparkle in his eye. "Sure, I can appreciate his many qualities. But, really, we're just friends."

Evie sighed. "Fine. But as your big sister, promise me you'll think about getting out there again. If not Cody, then someone."

She made a noncommittal noise and hung up the phone before taking in the papers spread out in front of her. If anything, they were a bigger disaster than before.

She heard a rustle at the door, and then it opened. Through the dining room entryway, she glimpsed Cody duck through, Finn on his shoulders. They both belted out the lyrics to "Baby Shark." Cody caught her eye, and she put her finger to her mouth.

"Maggie. Nap." She mouthed. Hopefully he could read lips. Cody swung Finn down and shushed him. She watched as Cody helped Finn remove his shoes before toeing off his own. Then they both came through the living room and into the dining room.

"What happened in here?" Cody tucked a hand into his pocket. She caught the scent of wood shavings and fresh air.

Resisting the urge to clutch her head in despair like an old-time movie heroine, Mia waved at the papers. "Oh, these? Just a little light afternoon reading." Her attempt at nonchalance fell flat as her throat tightened.

"Is this something for your job?"

She nodded. "Can you believe we have over a hundred applications for the housing initiative?"

"Wow! That's amazing. Congratulations." His eyes opened wide. Sincere.

Something loosened in her chest when he didn't tease her. "I'm not sure if it's congratulations or *Good Luck Charlie*."

"Your work paid off big time. That's definitely congratulations territory."

She couldn't help but shoot him a wink. "I'd say it was your face that paid off big time. An even half mention you specifically in their paperwork."

His face turned red. "You can't be serious."

"Wait, are you blushing?" She plucked a paper from one of the stacks, began to read aloud. "'Your island is pretty and would be a great place for me to launch my pottery business. Especially if Cody is around to inspire me.'" Goodness the man was turning an even brighter red. She found another one. "'A friend forwarded your video to me saying I would appreciate the attractions on Jonathon Island. She was right!'"

Cody rubbed at the back of his neck. "Maybe she means the kids?"

Oh, she liked making him uncomfortable. "This one will prove it to you. 'Is Cody single? If not, does he have a brother?'"

"It doesn't say that." Cody snatched the paper out of her hand. She laughed at his growl as his eyes found the sentence she'd read.

"C'mon, Code. You have to know you're bachelor-of-the-month material. No wonder these girls are interested." An itchy sensation began in her chest. What if one of these women came to the island and fell for Cody for real?

Finn tugged on her hand. "Can I watch a show?"

"Sure, bud."

She got Finn settled in front of the TV, his favorite program turned low. "Just one, Finn, and then it's quiet reading time." He didn't even look up at her as the opening music began.

She stood in the doorway of the dining room and surveyed the paper tornado. A long sigh from the bottom of her feet burst out of her.

"Mia." Cody's voice was pitched low. "Let me help."

"What? No. You've already done too much for me."

"Untrue. Nothing will ever be enough."

"What does *that* mean?" She glanced up at him.

"Nothing." His gaze searched her face. He looked so earnest. "Come on. You're overwhelmed, and rightly so. You carry the weight of the world on your shoulders all the time. I'd love to share the load." Cody held up his hands. "It's not because I don't think you're capable. It's just what friends do. And we're friends, right?"

She blinked against a sudden wetness in her eyes. Sweet man. "Yes, of course we're friends." Surely it wasn't giving up if she let him help her for an hour. Just until she could get a handle on things. She nodded once. "All right, come on." Then she led the way into the room.

Mia pointed at the stack of papers. "I think if we weed

out the last of the ones that are just looking for love, we'll have around sixty to go through."

"Do you want to sort them by business type?"

"Good idea. We want a mixture of dining, service-related businesses, and gift shops."

They sifted through the papers in silence a few minutes, Finn's program punctuating the air between them. Cody let out a grunt and tossed a paper on the floor. Must have been another application listing him as the reason to do business on Jonathon Island.

Soon, the papers were in a better order. "I think that's the last one." Mia laid an application for another souvenir shop on top of the stack.

Cody leaned his elbow onto the table. "Not bad. There are some great candidates here."

She surveyed the piles. "I think I might have another problem though."

"Uh oh. That doesn't sound good."

"Count the piles. We only have five unique categories. I don't think the council is going to be happy with me if I present them with six pottery shops. They will want variety, not competing pizza parlors or whatever."

They'd rejected a few things outright, like the gun shop with a racial slur in its tagline, a boutique that only sold mountain-themed tchotchke, and of course any that were only applying as an excuse to meet Cody. They were left with the six pottery shops, eleven pizzeria and pizza-related restaurants, seven art galleries, four bike rental possibilities, and twenty-five applicants who wanted to open some sort of a souvenir shop.

"Okay. So, why don't you make another video? The last one was so popular. This time you could pitch exactly what we would need to fill out the businesses with a better variety. I'm sure there are others out there who would be interested in the opportunity. They just don't know it yet."

It all seemed so overwhelming. But then she looked at Cody. His open and earnest face gave her a boost of confidence. "I guess you're right. In the meantime, I need to organize these into some sort of list, so I know who to contact first."

She glanced over at Cody. His brow creased as he sorted through the stack of pizzeria candidates. A warmth spread through her chest. With Cody on her side, maybe she could pull this off after all.

She was going to get all the applicants she needed. She simply didn't have any other options.

Cody was Mia's friend.

Just her friend. He could convince his head, but his heart stubbornly refused to follow.

Walking this path to town was beginning to feel as natural as breathing. Cody walked alongside Mia, Maggie on his shoulders, Finn's hand tucked into his. Maggie had woken from her nap shortly after he and Mia finished sorting the applications, whittling down the number to a more manageable size. He'd once again coaxed Mia out of the house and toward town for a walk. Nothing like a little evening sunshine to boost your mood. When Mia had cracked her neck and rolled her shoulders for the seventh time, he knew she needed some fresh air.

And he definitely did. His fingers twitched to rub the obvious tension out of her shoulders.

Fresh air. Put some space between them.

At least she'd allowed him to help her. Progress.

"C'mon. It's almost golden hour. A perfect time to shoot some more video and grab some still shots for your social media." Hopefully she hadn't noticed the pleading in his voice. Spending time with Mia had become a lifeline. He hadn't realized how lonely he'd been since Troy died and their friend group splintered.

"What do you know about golden hour?" She'd put her hands on her hips and stared him down.

"I had to take a few charters out last summer on my speedboat to make ends meet. Those groups cared more about mugging for the camera than catching any trout." They'd stiffed him on tips too.

"I really should get started on filling Dani in about our top picks from this afternoon."

She'd hesitated and he jumped in. "You need a break, and the kids need some fresh air. It's a beautiful afternoon."

Soon, they were easing the kids into their shoes, and debating whether everyone needed a light jacket.

Except the fresh air wasn't exactly working. Every step they took, the heat of Mia's hand near his own nearly scorched him.

He took a deep breath and looked around. Flowers, ready to burst into full bloom, lined several homes they passed. A few of Mia's neighbors were out mowing the grass and waved as they walked past. They turned onto Jonathon Boulevard, the road running straight into downtown. When they came to Poppy Place, he pointed down the block. "There are several of the houses in Dani's plan down that block. Did you want to see any of them? Maybe take some pictures?"

"Sure. I'm game."

Cody led her to the second house on the right. A blue single-story home he now knew contained two bedrooms, two bathrooms, and a newly renovated front room, complete with a gas fireplace. "I think this place has been empty since the Hansons moved out just before the pandemic. Last I heard, they live in Minneapolis now." He put Maggie down and opened the door.

The strong scent of paint hit them as they walked through the front door. He showed Mia around while she took notes on her phone, pointing out the new mantle he'd installed over the fireplace. They walked through the newly painted bedrooms, the kids scampering ahead of them.

"Thanks again for helping today," Mia said. "I know you've got your own stuff going on."

"I'm always happy to help you." It was the understatement of the year, but he would never tire of trying to convince her he was there for her.

"Still. You're trying to earn enough for your boat parts. I hate to keep you from making money for that. How's it going?" She pointed her phone camera at the fireplace and took a shot.

Cody ran a hand over the wood panel on a doorway

he'd replaced, the wood smooth under his fingers. "I've not been able to find the parts I need, but it won't matter if Dad won't let me have his license."

She searched his face with her gaze. "He's not going to give it to you? Why not?"

The knot in the pit of his stomach he'd been ignoring tightened. "I really don't know."

"You'll just have to convince him." She reached up and retied the bandanna holding her curls back. "What's your plan?"

"Right now, the only thing I can do is pray."

"Probably the best plan. I'll pray too." She walked a few steps. "Show me what else you've done here."

Her excitement when he showed her the new wood floors in the kitchen filled him with pride.

"I think I've got everything," she said. "These paint fumes are making me lightheaded."

Once everyone was out, he locked the door. "Want to see some of the others?"

Mia squinted up at the sun and shook her head. "Not tonight. Let's keep the plan to head into town while the light is good. It makes more sense to have the business locations take center stage. I'll write up the housing info another time."

Swinging Maggie back up onto his shoulders while Finn ran on ahead, they continued their walk to town. The air echoed with the sound of the construction equipment working at the Grand.

A few minutes later, they passed the old fudge shop.

"I miss your family's fudge." Mia bumped his shoulder

and pointed at it with her chin. "I wonder why that store-front isn't on the list of available spaces."

"Technically, Mom still rents it from Seb. The lease isn't quite up yet, and she uses the kitchen for occasional catering orders. Her arthritis won't let her do much more than that these days." A pang hit his chest. "And I miss it too. Mom sure knew how to make magic with sugar and cocoa powder."

"That she did. You know, we don't have any applications for a candy shop. Maybe Lily should come home and reopen it." Lily, his sister, had moved to Florida almost ten years ago to improve on her candy-making trade so she could eventually move home and reclaim their family fame as the Jonathon Island fudge makers. But then the family shop had closed. "Wouldn't make the Kelley family too happy though," Mia added with a chuckle.

"Nothing makes those people happy. It wasn't enough for them to own all the other restaurants on the island. They had to move in on my family's fudge operation too." He threw a hand in the air. "To this day, even years later, my dad and Frank Kelley avoid each other whenever possible. That's not a bad idea about Lily though. I'll call her later and see if she's interested. I know she's coming home for a visit at the end of the month. Maybe she'll want to take a look around."

"If she applies, she could even have her own house for a dollar. I know there are more foreclosed houses than available storefronts, so it shouldn't be a problem to assign one of them to the fudge shop," Mia said. "It would be nice to know one of the applicants. I'd feel much better about recommending her to the town council than some random stranger."

"She is strange though." He waggled his eyebrows at her and was rewarded with a laugh.

"Brothers." She rolled her eyes at him. They passed by two more empty buildings. One, a small building covered with green shake siding, boasted small flowers painted along the roofline. "This would be a good one to shoot," she said. At that moment Jack came trotting toward them. "Perfect timing as always, pup. Cody, see if you can get him to sit in front of the building."

Cody snapped his fingers and the dog followed him to the doorway. "Sit. Good boy." He leaned down, mindful of Maggie still perched on his shoulders, and patted the mutt on his head. "Stay."

He shifted back to Mia's side and waited while she snapped several photos.

"These will be great," she said. "I'll bring you a treat next time I'm in town, Jack. Thanks for being such a good subject."

The dog, seeming to understand her, stood, stretched, tongue lolling, and then loped off again.

"Do you want to go inside?" Cody reached into his pocket and held up his key ring. "I can let us in."

"Actually, do you mind waiting outside with Mags and Finn for a minute or two before you come in? I want to take a video, and I don't want my kids in too many of these social posts."

"No problem." He chatted with the kids for a few minutes before Mia came back out.

"Okay! The coast is clear."

They all trooped into the space.

"I really like how you updated this. The white paint makes the whole place light up." She walked to the center of the room, footsteps echoing in the empty building.

Pride swelled his chest again as he saw the room through Mia's eyes. Most of the buildings on Jonathon Island's main drag were small. This one, at four thousand square feet, was one of the bigger ones.

He lifted Maggie down and set her on her feet. "Who knew a tiny tot could weigh so much?"

"She does get heavy after a while. Don't feel like you have to carry her everywhere. She can walk, and I can carry her too. You don't have to do it."

"Mia." He touched her arm. "Carrying her is no burden. I like it. I like spending time with your kids."

Her shoulders loosened. A small smile played around her lips. "Thanks."

"Mommy, can I take some pictures?"

"Sure, bud." She handed Finn her cell phone. "Careful."

He aimed the phone's camera around the room, taking several pictures.

"It'll be interesting to see how those turn out," Mia said quietly.

"It'll be a different angle, that's for sure."

While they waited for Finn, Cody took the opportunity to point out different features of the shop for Mia to include in her descriptions for potential clients.

"Now I will take your picture," Finn said. "Stand together."

Cody moved next to Mia. Heat flared in him as his shoulder rested against her and their hands brushed.

"Get closer. I can't see you." Finn's commanding finger pointed him closer to Mia. She turned an amused face up to him. He slung his arm around her shoulder.

Uh oh. Big mistake.

This photo was going to be ruined because of the sparks that were surely flying off him. He tamped them down. He and Mia were just friends, and he was going to do what he could to maintain that balance.

But try telling that to his traitorous heart. The one that was galloping away this very minute. Spending so much time with Mia was a bad idea.

Suddenly he realized Finn was talking to him. "I got the picture. You can let go of Mommy now." Oops. He dropped his arm from Mia's shoulders.

"Time for us to get home," Mia said. She looked flushed and wouldn't meet his eye.

Was she as flustered as he was?

"I'll lock up behind us." Hopefully she didn't notice how hard his heart had pounded when he was holding her.

He walked them to the corner, parting ways at the fudge shop. Nostalgia hit hard.

Using his master key, he let himself in. Two of the huge copper pots used for making fudge still rested near the front pop-out windows, and the two marble worktables were covered with old blankets. A fine layer of dust coated the shelves on the walls and the long counter near the old register. He and his family practically lived here when his mother ran the place. It looked smaller now, somehow. Like the past five years had pulled the walls closer together.

The scent of chocolate still hung heavy in the air. Cloying and sweet, it made his stomach rumble. Too bad it would be another bachelor supper for him tonight. No company, no laughter. Just a pot pie heated in the microwave while he surfed the net looking for boat parts. If he was lucky, there might be a pint of pistachio ice cream for after.

He grimaced. Since when had he been so dissatisfied? This single life wasn't a new development. He was used to it.

Really.

He spun on his heel and walked out of the shop. After locking up, he dug out his cell phone and called Lily.

"Hey, big brother!" He could practically hear the sunshine in her voice. He wondered if that Florida sun had bleached her already blonde hair any lighter.

"Florida still treating you okay?"

She hesitated, then, "Yeah. It's going fine. Why?"

"Hold on." He tucked his earbuds into his ears and his phone back into his pocket before zipping up his jacket. The evening breeze coming in off the lake bit his exposed hands and nose. "I was just in Hart Family Fudge and was thinking about you."

"What? Why were you thinking about me?"

"I was remembering all the good times we had there. Then I thought, maybe you should come home and re-open the place. There's a push right now to revitalize the businesses downtown—"

"I don't think so, Cody."

"Why not?" To his left, the late sunlight winked off the choppy lake water. He turned around and started walking on the boardwalk toward home.

"I've made a life for myself here. Besides, I'm on the verge of something big at my current company."

"Aren't you a glorified gopher?" Despite completing culinary school with an emphasis in candy making, she'd been an apprentice under the same guy for years without any promotion.

"Hey! I still get to make candy. But yeah, Roger does like to remind us that he's in charge and we are lucky to be in his orbit." She snorted. "But someday soon, I'm gonna knock his socks off with a new recipe, and then it'll be my turn. Just you wait."

"I don't doubt it. You're brilliant in the kitchen, Lil. I'm sorry Roger's failed to see your potential." His footsteps sounded hollow on the boardwalk.

"Everyone has to pay their dues. That's just how it works."

"Okay, but you always talked about being the next great thing in fudge on Jonathon Island."

"Things don't always go the way you think they will when you're in high school. You of all people should know that. Hold on, I'm getting in my car and putting you on speaker."

He heard the rustle of the car door, the grumble of her engine starting, and then the echo of the speakerphone. "Can you hear me now?" he teased.

She laughed. "You're good to go. Sorry, I was just leaving my shift and didn't want to stand in the parking lot having this conversation."

"I get that. And you have a valid point. Plans change after high school." He walked past the ferry dock. Normally the port bustled with activity this close to Memorial Day, but now, it was like a ghost town. Maybe Lily was the smart one. Building a life off this island. But if Dani's plan worked . . .

"I know. I'm always right. Speaking of making a life for ourselves, what's the news on your boat?"

He filled her in on the part he was still waiting for. "I might have a bigger problem though." He hunched his shoulders into the wind that kicked up. "Dad is saying he won't sell me the fishing license. He might sell it to an outfit on the mainland instead."

"What?" A rustle came through the phone line. "Sorry, I almost dropped the phone getting it onto the holder. Dad can't be serious. That license is a big deal. If he gives it up, there's no guarantee you will get one for yourself."

"I know." That thought had kept him up more than one night since the argument.

"You have to get him to give it to you. Or at the least, sell it to you." Her voice had risen an octave.

"Sorry, sis, I don't think anyone has ever gotten Dad to do something he didn't want to do. Maybe not even Mom." He'd reached his shop and reached out to unlock the door.

"Mom! Great idea. Get her on your side. Dad will never have a chance."

"I'm pretty sure she's already on my side. You should

have seen her face when he said he was giving up the license." He'd only ever seen that look once before, shortly after the boating accident when Dad told her that Steve, and then Troy, had succumbed to their wounds. A stark grief.

"Well, when I come home, all three of us can work on him."

He took off his jacket and hung it on the hook next to his front door. It fell to the floor. "I don't think that will work. I'm just going to have to figure something else out."

"Mm-hmm. Hey, you're quite the internet sensation." Lily's teasing tone made a refreshing break from the seriousness of the conversation so far.

"What are you talking about?"

"That video Mia took. Evie forwarded it to me."

He suppressed a groan. It seemed he did that a lot lately. "I can't believe you saw that."

"Based on the view count, over three million of us did. So?" Across the line he could hear her blinker clicking on and off.

"So what?" He poked his head into his dorm-sized fridge. A half-eaten jar of pickles, some mustard, and wilted lettuce stared back. In the freezer, his last potpie boasted a layer of frost. Yum.

"So, you and Mia? She called you a 'local attraction.' Is there something I should know? Spill."

"Nothing to spill." He unwrapped the potpie and popped it into the microwave on top of the fridge.

"Come on, the girl you've pined after for years takes

a video calling you a local attraction and there's nothing to spill?"

"I didn't pine."

"Uh, yeah. You did. Totally pined. Which was too bad because if you'd made a move, you probably would've gotten the girl instead of watching her be swept away by your friend."

"I was happy for them." And he wasn't lying. He had been happy that they were happy. His misery at watching Mia and Troy together was no big deal compared to their joy in their relationship. "Friends support each other. Besides, there's too much between us—Troy being the biggest thing. There's no way anything will happen between us now. And I made peace with that a long time ago." Though lately, his mind and heart had been struggling to remember that . . .

"That's because you won't make anything happen. I don't know what you're afraid of, but I do know you don't have to step aside anymore. You can go for the girl."

"I don't think so." The microwave beeped. Using a towel to protect his hand, he grabbed the hot food. The scent of processed chicken filled the air.

Lily sighed. "Why not? You need to fight for what you want for once."

"It's just not that simple. I don't want to take advantage of her. She's a widow. A single mom. Besides . . ." he stopped next to what passed for his kitchen table, a card table shoved against the wall of the shop. A few pictures lined the back of it. A snapshot of Troy, Mia, and him at their wedding took center stage. In it, Mia had her arms around Troy, pregnant belly round and full, eyes full of love. Troy wore a big, goofy grin, and he himself stood to the side, hands tucked into his pockets. He kind of envied the kids in the photograph—their whole lives stretched before them. It was a good thing they didn't know what was coming. "You know I'm responsible for her even being free."

"Cody Nicolas Hart. Do not even start with me. You are no more responsible for Troy's death than an ant in Timbuktu."

If only he could convince his heart of that. Every time he passed by Mia's house, his chest constricted. "She probably blames me."

"There's no way she blames you. It was just a stupid, horrific accident. Not even Michigan's most talented meteorologists predicted that storm. You couldn't have known."

"And someday, maybe, I will convince myself that is true." Sure, he didn't control the weather and couldn't have known there would be a freak storm that night. But he should have had the experience to know how to keep them off the rocks.

"Dad has been fishing a lot longer than you. If anything, it would've been his fault. But, Cody, I've read all the reports." He heard her car door open, a rustle, then it slammed shut. "Everyone knows the whole thing was just a fluke accident. That's what the insurance report says, that's what the Coast Guard report says, and I bet that's what the old guy coffee club down at Good Day Coffee says. You're not to blame."

Lily knew him best. Knew just what to say to convince

him with her words. A glimmer of hope began to shine. Because if he could believe her words, if he could truly let go of the guilt, maybe he could move forward.

And that would be amazing.

Six

TODAY WAS GOING TO BE HUGE.

As she walked to Dani's office in the Tourism Bureau, Mia allowed the frisson of excitement deep in her belly to spread until her fingertips tingled with it. Memorial Day on Jonathon Island used to be celebrated with parades and speeches and red, white, and blue bunting. The past few years, however, the celebrating had dwindled to a somber half-hour service at the historic fort cemetery. This year, Mia had convinced the town to spend it on cleanup efforts. In an hour, people would be assembling at the Little Stone Church.

Before that, though, Mia had arranged to meet with Dani at her downtown office to go over some of the applications she'd received. Since sorting them with Cody a few days ago, more applicants had submitted their paperwork.

"I think these twenty will make a good start," Dani said. She rested her hand on top of the stack they'd sorted through. Again. If Mia never sorted another stack of papers in her life, she'd be the happiest islander on Jonathon Island. "You can set up video interviews with the council for the end of the week."

"On it, Boss," Mia said. "I'm super excited for some of these. I think your plan could really work." Not to mention her housing hanging in the balance.

"That's the idea," Dani drawled. She pushed the stack toward Mia. "Text me with the times you set up for each one. I think we should plan on thirty minutes each, with a ten-minute break between." They worked out the rest of the details, then Mia stood, gathering the papers together.

"Thanks again for making this happen for me," she said. "I don't know what I would be doing now if it weren't for you."

"Don't get all mushy on me. I needed you too, remember." Dani came around her desk and hugged Mia tight. "Personal question. Do you have enough money for food? Since you're not getting a salary from me . . ."

Mia pulled back. "Dani, you're my best friend. You can feel free to ask me any personal question. You know that. And yes, we have money for food. Like I told you before, the kids and I are getting Troy's social security checks." Troy hadn't worked long enough for social security to be very high, but it covered the essentials of food and heat every month. It just didn't leave much left over for other essentials, like paying the mortgage.

"Okay. Awkwardness over," Dani said. She let go of Mia and picked up the stack of applications. "I'll let you get to your kids. Here." She handed the stack to Mia before moving back around her desk. "See you in a few minutes."

Outside, the sun shone brightly over the placid lake water. Mia smelled someone burning brush somewhere nearby. She made her way down Main Street and then turned right on Blueberry Boulevard. Pulling a notebook out of her shoulder bag, she made a few additional notes on priority items for the cleanup today as she walked down the street.

Pick up trash.

Paint window boxes.

Sweep up leaves and small debris.

Remove tattered bunting and awnings.

Passing a third building with broken windows, she jotted down a note to ask Dani if there was money to replace the windows in some of the buildings. And, if not, she'd brainstorm a solution to make them look better with Cody. If they wanted people to choose to make a life here, they needed to make Main Street as appealing as possible. If people could see the charm she knew lay beneath the crumbling paint, they would love the island as much as she did.

Ahead, several people were walking in the direction of the church.

Hopefully, her plea for help had reached enough ears to make a difference today.

Nancy Hart fell into step beside her. "Mia! It's good to see you." Cody's mom looked casual in her jeans and an old Jonathon Island Apple Blossom Festival T-shirt. "This cleanup day is a great idea. I'm glad you thought of it."

"I hope we can accomplish a lot," Mia said. "There are only a few weeks left before we host a bunch of potential newcomers." She pushed back the shiver of electricity chasing around in her stomach at the thought. Would it all come together in time?

Nancy rubbed at her wrists. "Looks like you've got a good turnout." She jutted her chin at the crowd gathered in front of the stone church.

Mia gaped at the group on the lawn. There were at least a hundred people here.

At the fringe of the group, Patrick Kelley was bickering with his sister-in-law Martha about something. Patrick's wife, Whitney, one of the town's schoolteachers, appeared to be acting as referee. Pastor Arnie, bright red hair hidden under a straw hat, and his wife, Tara, in gardening gloves, stood chatting with Mia's mom and dad. Finn chased Maggie nearby. She spotted Nora fiddling with her phone near the rear of the group.

Liam, Cody, and Mr. Michaelson from the bank clumped together as well. Jack wove between the legs of the gathered crowd, the terrier's tail wagging so fast it was a blur.

Cody looked her way, and his face lit in a smile. He jogged over to her.

"Ready for this?" He slipped his red ball cap off his head and readjusted it before settling it back over his head.

"As I'll ever be, I guess. I've never been one for public speaking." Her mouth dried at the thought.

"You did fine in speech class." Cody laid a hand on

her shoulder. Its weight and warmth chased some of the nerves away.

"Cody, we had seven people in our class. And we'd been in school together for years. I'd hardly call that public speaking." She rolled her eyes.

"You'll do great. I know you're passionate about this project, and that's all that matters. When you used to give presentations about your art projects, it didn't matter how many people were in the room." He patted her once then turned to stand shoulder to shoulder.

She took a deep breath, the scent of cut grass and early flowers and grilled meat filling her senses. "Thanks, Cody. Here goes nothing." She let out the breath and then clapped her hands. "Welcome everyone."

When the murmuring group didn't settle down, Cody put his pinkies in his mouth and whistled loudly. She turned to him, mouth open. "I didn't know you could do that."

"There's a lot about me you don't know." He shot her a wink and then nodded at the crowd, most of whom were turning to face them.

"Okay, everybody, listen up." Mia tried to pitch authority in her voice. As the murmuring died down, she gripped the edges of her notebook. "Thank you so much for giving up your Memorial Day to spruce up the town we all love. I'll divide you into teams and send you off. We have a lot to get done, but with so many people enthusiastically participating, we should finish in plenty of time for the picnic Pastor Arnie and Tara have planned." A whooping cheer went up at the sound of this.

"As you can probably smell, Gary Jacobs stepped away from the cheese counter at Doug's Market today and is already smoking ribs for later. A big thank you to Doug's Market for donating the meat for our supper, and to each of you for bringing the rest."

She walked toward a pile of supplies and the mob shifted with her. "The Department of Public Works has supplied us with trash bags." She nodded at the stacks of black and green plastic bags. "You all know how to keep garbage separate from compostable materials. We've received special dispensation to use the ATV and trailer for garbage cleanup. Once you've filled a bag, the DPW team will come and pick it up."

She continued down the line pointing out the flowers that had been donated for the boxes lining Main Street, and the paint for sprucing up as many places as possible. "If any of these tasks are especially interesting to you, let me know, and I will put you on that team. Otherwise, the assignments are random."

The next several minutes was a blur of getting everyone onto teams and giving them supplies and running interference. When the others had dispersed, she took Finn and Maggie and a black garbage bag, and the three of them joined one of the groups cleaning the sidewalks.

After picking up trash for an hour, she sat down on a bench and let the kids go help Nora near the old Great Lakes Memorabilia shop. Her phone buzzed. A missed call notice came up, and she popped in her earbuds to listen to the voicemail.

"Mia, hi," a man's voice said, somewhat familiar. "This

is Matt Goldfinch. From Kendall College? Anyway, I saw your video and the opportunity there on Jonathon Island and thought I'd get in touch. Give me a call back when you get this." He left his phone number and the voicemail ended.

Matt Goldfinch? Of course she remembered him. Good thing she'd tucked her phone into her pocket, or she would have dropped it hearing this blast from the past.

She dialed Matt's number.

"Hello," a deep voice said. "Matt Goldfinch here."

"Matt? This is Mia Franklin, Mia Jonathon." She paused. "I got your voicemail."

"Mia! Good to hear from you! Thanks for calling me back."

"I couldn't believe it when I heard your voice." Mia shook her head even though she knew Matt couldn't see her.

"I couldn't believe it when I saw your video. Mia Jonathon, back on Jonathon Island." Matt cleared his throat. "You looked good."

Mia swallowed hard. "Thanks." She shook her head. "You wanted to talk about the revitalization initiative?" She glanced down Main Street. The cobblestone street and sidewalk had been cleared of all garbage and leaves and other litter. The whole town looked better already.

"This opportunity comes at an amazing time, actually. I've been looking for a more permanent place for my gallery, so I thought, 'Why not Jonathon Island?'"

Her heart leaped. An art studio being established on Jonathon Island would be . . . amazing. She tamped down the excitement flickering in her belly. Any gallery would have her participation in getting approved, but not her art.

"I can't believe it's you." Her brain still sputtered on the coincidence. Mia and Matt had almost become an item during her freshman—and only—year of college, while she and Troy were on a break. Matt was attractive, dynamic, and super creative. She'd enjoyed sharing classes with him, and they'd both challenged each other to make better art. There was a definite mutual attraction there.

Except, she'd loved Troy. Had never been able to forget about the fisherman she'd left behind.

Matt laughed. "It's me. What's it been now, five years?"

"That sounds about right." She leaned against a nearby wall, its peeling shaker siding warm from the sun.

"How's the fisherman husband? And kid?"

She blinked away the sudden prickle in her eyes. "I lost Troy two years ago in a boating accident."

The silence on the phone lasted a beat. "I'm sorry to hear that. Troy seemed like a great guy."

"My kids keep me going."

"Kids, plural?"

"Yep, Troy and I have a little girl too. Finn is four, almost five now, and Maggie is two." She searched for them in the crowd before seeing the purple bobble on Maggie's ever-present hat bent over a window box full of newly planted flowers.

"Hmm. I bet she looks just like her mother." Matt paused. He cleared his throat. "Listen, Mia, I'm not going to beat around the bush here. I really want to do business on Jonathon Island. I've already booked a trip out there to check things out. Even if I don't get into the program, I'm considering going the traditional route to establish myself there."

Something like interest fluttered in her chest. She pushed away the question of whether Matt was as good looking as he used to be. He certainly was as focused on what he wanted as always. "Oh. Okay. I can show you around. You just need to fill out the application paperwork. And then there will be a video interview."

"Why do video if you can be in person?" Matt chuckled. "I'll be there next week. I can talk to the committee, get a feel for the island. Maybe even reconnect with you."

"Shoot me the dates and times you have available, and I'll let Dani know to schedule a meeting."

"That would be great."

"Okay, well. Great. I guess I'll see you la—"

"It will be really great to see you again, Mia."

"You too, Matt." She hung up the phone and clutched it to her chest for a minute. "You too."

The air buzzed with the laughter and conversation of a hundred of her friends and neighbors, and a warmth lit in her heart that hadn't been there a moment before.

Huh.

Life sure had a way of surprising you sometimes.

Was his dad avoiding him? Throughout the workday, Cody had noticed his father working alongside his mother. Every time he approached the two of them, his dad had seemed to find something to do a few steps farther away.

Whatever was going on, Cody was determined to figure it out at the picnic.

Cody watched as Mia guided Maggie's hand, chubby fingers clutched tight around a paint brush almost as big as the toddler herself. Did she even know how amazing she was? The two of them had joined him after the garbage crew had finished. Finn was occupied with petting Jack just down the block. Cody shook off the thought and forced himself to stop staring at Mia.

He turned and looked at the progress the rest of the townspeople had made. It was as if Main Street had transformed in the space of an afternoon. The old peeling paint covering the window boxes of the store fronts had been sanded off, and fresh new white paint brightened up the street. The garbage and leaf cleanup crew had left Main Street's cobblestones nearly sparkling. And slowly, the newly painted window boxes were being filled in with fresh flowers he couldn't identify, their jaunty red and yellow heads bobbing in the light breeze coming off the lake.

He glanced back at Mia and Maggie. The toddler now had a streak of white along the front of her shirt. He laughed as she grinned up at her mother. He walked over to the two of them and crouched down. "Let me help you with that, little lady." He took the paintbrush from her hands and stood again. "Let's go find a place to wash this out." He took Maggie's hand, and together he and Mia and Maggie walked toward a spigot where people were washing out their brushes. After this was finished, they all began making their way toward the little stone church.

At the church, the scent of smoky barbecue filled the

air. Tables had been arranged all over the lawn, and food was piled high. His stomach grumbled, and Mia laughed. She elbowed him in the ribs. "Sounds like you've worked up an appetite."

He rubbed his stomach. "You know it."

Just as he was about to ask Mia to eat dinner with him, Elise Jonathon walked over. "Want some help with getting the kids' plates, Mia?"

Mia agreed and they headed off. He watched them go, a creeping fatigue stealing over him.

"How long are you going to stand on the sidelines of your own life?" Dani, hand wrapped around a dripping pulled pork sandwich with her plate balanced in the other hand, stood next to him.

"What?" His ears rang as though he'd just been hit with a sucker punch.

She nodded at Mia. "I see the way you look at her. I know you want your friendship to be more. So, why aren't you making it happen?"

"You know why." Hunger had turned to something else. A churning ache.

She shook her head. "I know what you say, but I don't quite believe it. I think something else is holding you back. I just can't figure out what. But, if you wait too long, you're going to lose her." Without another word, Dani took another bite of her sandwich and walked away.

Reeling, Cody looked around for a place to sit. Something solid he could lean on.

Was Dani right? Could he lose Mia altogether? Nah.

She loved the island too much. Whatever happened, they would always be friends.

Over by the dessert table, his dad paused, hand hovering above the choices. Cody jogged over. "You can't go wrong with Tara's blueberry pie."

His dad jumped. "I didn't see you there."

Cody reached for a plate and then served them both a slice of pie. "Are you avoiding me?" May as well jump in with both feet.

"What do you mean?" His dad forked a bite of pie into his mouth.

"Every time I came near, you walked away."

"I was busy, we all were." His dad shrugged and took another bite.

Cody took a bite too. The normally sweet and tart treat tasted like cardboard in his mouth.

Around them the people of Jonathon Island laughed and talked. He heard Jill Kelley complimenting Janine Dirks on the pretty arrangement of flowers in the boxes.

His dad moved a step away and Cody followed him. Up near the blue-gray stone walls of the church sat two empty lawn chairs. "Want to sit a minute?"

His dad nodded in agreement, and they threaded their way through the other picnickers to the chairs.

They sat in silence for a while, finishing their pie, Cody tasting none of it. He put his plate on the ground, and Jack came over to lick the crumbs. He dropped his hand down and scratched the dog's ears.

Beside him, his dad sighed and then rubbed a hand over

his face. A gesture that Cody knew well, had even picked up as a habit himself. "What's bothering you, Dad?"

His dad laid his hands on his knees, the leathery knuckles whitening as he gripped. "I sold some of the equipment. Your mother thought I should tell you."

"What?" Cody rocketed up, the lightweight chair tipping behind him. "Dad, you knew I wanted to buy that from you."

"Sit down, Cody." His dad leaned over and righted the chair. Cody slumped into it, the nylon and aluminum construction groaning in protest. "I only sold a few of the outriggers and a couple of other things. Turns out the place that had made the offer for everything couldn't afford all of it." He scrubbed his hand over his face again. "I wanted a little extra cash to take your mother someplace nice for a vacation. We've never really taken one. I'm taking her to Arizona. It's supposed to be a good climate for arthritis."

And, yeah, this was probably the most words Cody had heard his dad say over the past couple of years, but he could hardly concentrate on what he was saying. He should be happy that his mom would get some relief from the aching that plagued her. He should be a good son. But all he could think about was how his dad had chosen someone else to sell to. He almost didn't want to give voice to the question on his heart, but in the end, he couldn't stop himself.

"And the fishing license?"

In the silence between them, Cody heard the tap-tapping of a pileated woodpecker in a tree nearby. The rapid tapping echoed his own heartbeat.

"I still have it." The words dropped from his dad's mouth and straight into his heart. "Your mom is right. I ought to hang on to that a while longer." His dad stood. "Anyway. Thought you should know." Then he made his way off into the crowd.

A moment later, Mia flopped into the chair next to him then lifted Maggie onto her lap.

"Guess what?" Her eyes sparkled. She'd removed the bandanna that had covered her hair earlier and now it spilled everywhere. Her sun-kissed cheeks glowed. Maggie settled against her mother's chest, and Mia wrapped an arm around her.

"You sold Finn to the circus?" His mind still scrambled over his dad's revelation, but he welcomed the distraction.

"An old friend from college is one of the applicants for our revitalization effort." She patted Maggie's back and the girl's head dropped lower. Wouldn't be long before she was sleeping in her mother's arms. He'd put money on it.

"Mia, that's . . ." But what was it actually? Good? Bad? From the light in Mia's eyes, it must be a good thing. "That's great."

"It really is. He's such a fantastic artist."

"He?" Wow. His voice squeaked like a prepubescent teen.

"Mm-hmm. I think his gallery will be an amazing addition to the island." Mia brushed a hair off her forehead. "He was always pushing all of us to get better. At the time, he seemed so wise, so mature. Some of the girls had huge crushes on him." Her gaze grew distant.

"And you?" Cody could barely speak.

"There was a time . . ." Then she shook her head and laughed. "Anyway, that's all in the past. I can hardly wait to see what his paintings are like now. He'll be coming on the ferry in a few days. Maybe you can meet him." She sighed and leaned her head back on the chair, closing her eyes. "Today was a good day. It's the first time I honestly feel like this can work—like I'm going to save my house."

"I'm so glad. You deserve it."

She gave him a knowing look. "Because of all the bad things that have happened to me?"

"No. Because you're a hard worker and brilliant."

"I wouldn't go that far." She made a face, laughing at herself.

But he could only be serious. "I would. You don't give yourself enough credit, Mia."

She opened her mouth to say something, then closed it. Leaned back against the seat again. "Thanks, Cody. And hey, you're getting closer to achieving your dreams too, right?"

Considering his dad still wasn't budging on the license and the girl of his dreams was excited about an ex-crush and his art gallery potentially moving to town?

Yeah, he was totally living the dream.

But instead of doing what Dani suggested and going after what he wanted—what was seeming more impossible by the day—Cody just gazed across Lake Huron. "Yep."

Seven

MORNINGS HAD A WAY OF COMING earlier lately. Mia stifled a yawn as she waited on the dock of the ferry port. She'd spent the better part of the night before tossing and turning in her bed. Pretty much the past few nights, actually. After the town cleanup day, she'd made a bunch more calls to prospective business owners. Most of them had been positive and excited about the video chats. A few had pulled out of the project altogether.

Would she have enough to meet her quota? She pushed the doubt away. She couldn't dwell on that right now.

Any minute now the ferry would dock. Matt had texted when they left the mainland about twenty minutes before. Mia's mind flitted back to the conversation with her mom from earlier that day.

"So, you're meeting up with Matt?" Mia's mom had raised an eyebrow when Mia had dropped the kids off this morning. "I remember you talking about him. The cute, talented one, right? He took you out for pasta?"

She'd briefly thought he might be the one, but then she'd come home one weekend, and Troy had been there to remind her how much she loved him. The passion of that one weekend had resulted in Finn. She'd finished up her year of college and then come home that summer for good.

"Mom." Mia cut her eyes to where Finn stood next to them on her mother's porch. "Maybe this is a conversation for later?" She couldn't stop the warmth spreading across her face.

"It's okay to think that way again, Mia." Her mom opened the door. "Finn, take Maggie inside. I'll be right in." After the kids had gone, she turned back to Mia. "I get that maybe you're not ready for it yet, and that's okay too. But you're not betraying Troy by thinking about someone new. He would want you to be happy."

Mia had backed down the porch stairs. "I guess. But right now, I have more important things to worry about."

"Something to think about anyway." Mom brushed a hair off her face.

Her mom was right though. Troy would want that for her. She would have wanted it for him, were their situations reversed.

Now, on the dock, a breeze washed over her. She shivered. Not wearing a jacket had seemed like a good idea before leaving the house. Clouds gathered and threatened to block out the sun. She glanced up at them. Light gray and billowing, they could bring a rainstorm or completely blow over. It was too soon to tell.

The ferry pulled into its spot with little fanfare. Soon, the crew had the aluminum gangplank lowered, and a few people straggled off.

Matt walked down the gangplank. Square jaw, blue eyes, tousled hair and all. In his gray sports coat and dark slacks, he looked more confident and put together than Mia remembered. Of course, back at Kendall College they had both been covered in paint and clay most of the time. The only time she'd seen him dressed up was on their one and only date.

Until today.

She waited for him to approach before stretching out a hand in greeting. His palm was warm and dry as he shook her hand.

"You look great," he said, a crooked smile on his face.

She ran a hand down her arm. "I look like a single mother of two kids." Sure, she'd taken extra care with her hair this morning, taming her dark hair into smooth curls, swiping on a bit of makeup, and rejecting three outfits before settling on the dark jeans, bright blue slouchy sweater, and black boots she now wore. But she still felt out of place in her body. She knew she looked different from the last time Matt had seen her. Back then she'd been more youthful, more free. Less bags under her eyes. Less baggage altogether.

"I'd say motherhood suits you."

She'd forgotten Matt's smooth compliments. The way they rang almost true. Like you could almost believe what he was saying. She'd also forgotten the intense way he had of looking directly into her eyes and making her feel like she was the only one in the room. Like he was doing now, with her hand still in his.

She pulled away. Tucked an errant hair behind her ear. "Is that all of your luggage?" She pointed to the small rolling bag resting next to Matt's left knee.

He nodded. "I'm ready to get started on the tour."

Mia led the way to the two bicycles she'd left nearby. "You can put your bag in the kiddie trailer on my bike." She opened the flap for him then secured it again when his luggage was stowed. "Would you like the grand tour first, or would you prefer to freshen up at the Inn?" She knew Matt had booked a few nights at Island House Inn, virtually the only place on island for visitors to stay.

"I'd love to see your town. I've seen pictures, of course, and visited virtually by browsing YouTube videos, but there's nothing like getting the feel of the place when you're in person. Bikes, eh?" He ran a hand along the blue Schwinn she'd borrowed for him.

"No cars or motor vehicles on the island, I'm afraid," she said, swinging a leg over her bike. "They used to have horses and carriages, but most of them are gone now. Word is they'll be back next year, so long as the revitalization efforts go as expected."

"Quaint." They settled into a rhythm biking next to each other. "It's beautiful here."

She glanced at him out of the corner of her eye, but he was looking out over the harbor. "Jonathon Island and Lake Huron can be quite lovely when they want to be." When storms weren't tossing those waves onto shore in a maelstrom of fury, that is.

"I've been looking for a new place to be inspired. This could be it." Matt grunted as he ran over a pothole.

They reached the intersection of Marina Way and Main Street. Mia took a left and headed into town. "Many of the buildings here are old." Playing the part of tour guide made her see things through fresh eyes. These eclectic buildings could really be something if they had the right owner and a little TLC. "We're hoping to fill each of these storefronts with the new revitalization initiative. There are fourteen we're especially interested in filling before the middle of July." Which was just five weeks away now. Her chest tightened, and she breathed deeply to release it. Everything was following her plan. She just had to keep working the plan and everything would be all right. "The place I envision for your studio is on the other end of town."

"Will you be giving everyone a personalized tour?" Matt's crooked grin made another appearance.

"Just you," she said. "The town council and I have been meeting everyone else via video chat. Of course, they will all be here in two weeks for the meet and greet." Mia steered her bike around another pothole. "They will all have a chance to see the island, but there will be too many for me to escort around personally."

Matt nodded. "How many competitors do I have?"

Mia laughed. "I wouldn't call them your competitors. You're already a shoo-in for approval. There is one other artist on the list and a total of about twenty applicants who will be coming over."

"Another artist? I hope that won't be a problem." A muscle jumped in Matt's jaw.

"I don't see why it would be. There is plenty of inspiration to go around." Mia gestured vaguely toward the water. "Plus, he mainly works with sculptures. Pretty soon there will be plenty of tourists too."

They biked the last few blocks without speaking, only the calling of the gulls and the chattering of the people they passed breaking the silence. Beside her, Matt's head swiveled as he took in all of the shops. Thankfully, the cleanup day had Jonathon Island putting its best foot forward. As much as she loved her little town, she wasn't sure if Matt would appreciate its charms.

"Here we are." She kicked down her bike's stand in front of the storefront she'd been trying not to think about since being there with Cody. Beside her, Matt did the same. "This is the one that would be great for an art space. It used to be a gallery."

She led the way into the building, being careful to test the doorknob before pulling it shut behind them.

Matt's head moved as if on a swivel. "I see what you mean. I can see an area for displaying my work over there." He gestured to the golden wall. "And the lighting in the other half here is perfect for painting."

"Are you still primarily using oils?" It had been the thing that drew them to each other initially. They'd both taken to staying late after their oil class and working on their projects. "I remember your style as bold and dynamic."

Actually, now that she thought about it, in college his style was dramatic and edgy, not something you would come to a quaint island village to hone or inspire. Huh.

"I've changed it somewhat. Softened the edges. I like to think I've matured since college." He lifted his chin.

"Trying to say something different now?" The fresh paint smell in the building had diminished.

"More like trying to actually sell my works." He smiled at her, a half smile that implied a bitterness beneath it. "I decided the world wanted something different from what I was trying to offer it. So, I changed my technique, started painting pastoral scenes, and then my work began selling." He looked away. "I really do enjoy painting them, but they're very different from college. Maybe someday I won't feel like such a sellout." He crossed his arms and looked back at her. "Anyway, how about you? What are you working on?"

It was her turn to not meet his eyes. "I've not been doing much art lately." Okay. Try not doing any art at all. "With the kids . . ."

"I get that." Matt nodded once, a sharp movement that indicated he understood. "Wait. No. Actually, I don't get that. With your talent, you could go places."

"I have to be realistic. Keeping food on the table for my kids, single parenting . . . Having two little kids doesn't leave much time for creative pursuits." But still, hearing him remember her work warmed her insides like a cinnamon mocha latte on a winter's day.

"I envy you, you know."

"Envy me?" She held back the sharp laugh.

"Absolutely. You have this quaint life in a small town where everyone knows everyone. You have family nearby, kids, the whole package." He moved closer to her. "Plus, you're beautiful and talented. I'd love to share a life like that with someone."

Her breath caught. Did he mean the two of them? She opened her mouth to respond, but he raised a hand.

"Sorry," he said. "I'm coming on too strong. I'd be lying if I said you weren't part of the draw to Jonathon Island though. When you said you were single again . . ."

She started to speak again, but the jangle of the door opening startled both of them.

"Oh. I didn't know anyone was in here." Cody stood in the open doorway holding a toolbox. Sunshine burnished his hair to gold, and his customary flannel rolled to his elbows was shades of blue, picking out the color of his eyes. Mia's fingers itched to pick up her watercolors and find the exact hue.

"Cody!" She took a step toward him, putting space between herself and Matt. "Come and meet my old college friend, Matt Goldfinch. He's the owner of Goldfinch Gallery in Grand Rapids."

Matt stepped forward too, standing next to her a few feet from Cody. "We were in several classes together. Our Mia was top of the class each time."

Cody's eyes flicked over Matt. They paused on his expensive shoes, his jacket, his hundred-dollar haircut. A muscle flexed in Cody's jaw.

"Any friend of Mia's." Cody thrust his hand out to shake Matt's.

"Thanks." Matt nodded once. A beat later, he stuck out his hand and the men shook, their eyes boring holes in each other.

Probably time to break up this little love fest. "I'm showing Matt around town today." She waved her hand in a circle to encompass the store. "I wanted him to get a feel for where his gallery might go."

"This town is pretty great," Matt said. "Lots of inspiration. This space is good too. It could work for me." He put his hand on the small of Mia's back.

Whoa, there. Sure, she had a remembered attraction to Matt, even had a small spark today. But this was too much too fast. "Care to walk with us?" she blurted to Cody as she scampered toward the door. "There's more tour to give."

Mia wasn't sure how to interpret the look on Cody's face, but his eyes matched the water in Lake Huron right before a storm. She needed him by her side for this one. Maybe he could help her decide if Matt was coming on too strong. Plus, Matt's business could make or break her deal with the town. She didn't know how to play this. She sent a plea through her eyes.

"I've got some time to spare." Cody's grunt did not inspire confidence, but at least he'd caught her message.

They visited a few more places, strolling up and down the main drag. Conversation flowed between Mia and Matt, Cody following behind. But with him as a buffer, Mia was able to relax.

"Mama!" A purple fuzzball propelled itself into her legs. Her daughter grinned up at her. "We walk."

A few steps farther up the sidewalk, her mom held Finn's hand. "Hello," she called.

Finn tugged on his grandma. Mia could practically feel him saying "hurry up."

"We were getting a little stir-crazy." Her mom looked like she'd stepped out of an L.L.Bean catalog in her jeans and French sailor top. "I thought a walk would do us some good." In a lower voice she added, "I'm sorry, I didn't mean to interrupt your business meeting." She raised an eyebrow in Matt's direction.

"It's fine," Mia said. She turned to the others. "Matt, I'd like you to meet my mom, Elise Jonathon, and this purple thing." She hefted Maggie into her arms. "This is my daughter, and that handsome lad is my son, Finn." Finn ducked under Cody's arm and smiled at Matt. "Everyone, this is my friend, Matt."

Matt shook her mom's hand and then greeted both kids.

"Want to join us for a few minutes?" Mia raised an eyebrow at her mom.

"Sure. We're game." Elise set Maggie down to walk on her own for a while. The group moved up the street, Mia playing tour guide and pointing out various things to Matt. Cody swung Finn up onto his shoulders and sang a silly song with Maggie. After a while, the kids got restless.

"I'll take them back to your place," Elise said. "Take your time. See you later."

They ended their walk back at the gallery space. Mia noticed Cody's bike tucked next to the building. "Should we all ride over to Island House Inn? That way, Matt, you can drop off your bag."

"I actually needed to do some work on the gallery," Cody said.

Her heart spasmed. He couldn't be going yet. "Cody, you're welcome to come with us," she blurted.

Cody glanced between Mia and Matt then nodded once. "Guess I wouldn't mind a bit more fresh air." After a silent ride back down Main Street, they pulled up to Island House, a modest, thirty-five room hotel. On the veranda wrapping around the front, rocking chairs waited for visitors.

Mia and Cody waited outside while Matt went to check in.

"Mia," Cody said, voice so low she almost missed it. "Are you okay? You seem uncomfortable around Matt."

"I guess I just don't know how to act around him anymore." She fidgeted with the gears on her bike. "I feel so small-town, and I want to impress him for the sake of Jonathon Island. I really think an art gallery would be good for tourism."

"Just be yourself, that's good enough."

Cody's words spread a warmth through her as Matt walked out of the hotel.

"Let's bike up to the restaurant we passed earlier," Matt said.

Mia found herself agreeing to his proposal.

As they biked back the way they had come, Matt outlined a possible timeline for moving on island.

Matt moving to town. That was a good thing, right?

When Mia had told him an old friend from college was the owner of Goldfinch Galleries, Cody had pictured someone . . . eccentric, maybe even ugly. And, yeah, that was probably wishful thinking, but Cody hadn't expected this. Not a shoo-in for bachelor of the year.

Sure, Matt was nice enough, including Cody in the conversation, asking intelligent questions about the island, and even about Cody himself. Matt had even been nice to Mia's kids, taking Maggie's hand now and then and squatting down to talk to Finn man to man before they'd parted ways earlier. Mia had seemed uncomfortable with him at first, which was why Cody had stuck with them even though he had an insanely long list of to-dos for the day. Turned out she was acting that way because she had the wild notion that she wasn't good enough for Matt.

Yeah. Something about Matt still rubbed Cody the wrong way.

Maybe it was the fact that he always seemed to be touching Mia. Holding her elbow when they stepped off a curb. A hand to her upper back as he held the door for her. Even brushing her shoulder as they laughed at some memory from school.

None of that should bother him. Matt was obviously perfect for Mia. They were interested in the same things, they laughed at the same things, they even shared their love of art.

Maybe it was for the best.

He was happy she was finding someone after the tragedy with Troy.

Really.

But that didn't mean he had to have supper with the guy.

He tuned back in to the conversation happening next to him, in front of Kelley's Bar & Grill.

"Cody, you should join us." Matt extended a hand, gesturing for Cody to proceed them into Kelley's. "Supper will be my treat."

Cody shoved his hands deep into his jacket pockets. "Thanks anyway. I'm going to just head home."

Beside him, Mia shook her head. Her curls bounced, and one escaped its place in her high ponytail. The tip of her nose turned pink from the cold air sweeping in after the sun went down. "Actually, Matt, I have to get home too. Thanks for the dinner offer, but my kids are probably driving my mom crazy right now. They are sticklers for evening routines, and me being there is part of that."

"Let me walk you back," Matt said.

Shoot. Cody had been about to offer that same thing.

"Don't be silly. I live in the opposite direction of Island House," Mia said. "Go in. Have a nice dinner. I'll see you tomorrow."

"If you're sure?" Matt raised an eyebrow. Mia nodded and Matt went into Kelley's. Music spilled out behind him, cutting off abruptly as the door closed again.

"Goodnight, Cody. Thanks for coming with me today." Mia gave him a short wave and spun on her heel before throwing her leg over her bike.

"Wait!"

Mia stopped and twisted back to him.

"I'll go with you."

"You don't need to do that. I'm perfectly fine getting there on my own." Her mouth turned up on one side. "It's not like this island is a hotbed of crime. I can take care of myself."

He wheeled his bike up next to her. "Okay, but I'm going that direction anyway, and it will look funny for me to bike a half a block behind you all the way through town." Although, even that would be better than going home to the echo of his shed. Maybe it was time to look into moving in somewhere with a roommate. Or getting a cat.

She rolled her eyes then softened the response with a smile. "Fine."

They biked in quiet togetherness, the sky purpling into twilight around them. Mia didn't object when they turned up her street and he was still biking with her, so he took that as a good sign. Soon enough they arrived at her house.

"Do you want to come in for supper?" Mia laid her hand on the top of the fence. "It won't be anything fancy, probably spaghetti for me and naked noodles for the kids."

"Naked noodles?" His eyebrows raised.

"Finn calls them that. Noodles with just butter and shaky cheese. Since they aren't 'dressed'"—she put air quotes around the word—"without a sauce, they are naked."

"I'm with Finn. I like butter and shaky cheese. I'm assuming, of course, that you mean parmesan?" He mimed shaking a canister of parmesan cheese.

She nodded. "If you're lucky, we have the fancy kind from Kraft."

"Ohhh, gourmet shaky cheese. I'm definitely in." He followed her up the sidewalk and into the house.

Two steps inside the front door, he caught Finn who was skidding by on stocking feet. The boy's hair stood on end, and he had a juice mustache. Cody reached out and ruffled his hair even more.

Finn looked up, his eyes shining with mischief. "You have to come and see the cars Grandma brought me."

Cody shot Mia a look he hoped conveyed apology as he allowed himself to be led away by the kids. He gave Elise a quick smile as they passed in the short hallway. Mia's mom was wiping her hands on a dish towel. The house smelled like fresh baked banana bread.

Cody and the kids went through to the dining room where Finn had a racetrack set up around the legs of the table. He sat on the floor next to the track while Finn pulled out a box of assorted cars and trucks. Finn chattered on about the makes and models of the small cars, but Cody found it hard to concentrate on him.

"So, that was Matt." Elise must not know how much voices carried from the front door. "I wondered if I would get to meet him."

"Mom." Mia was softer, but he could still hear her. He tried to tune into the kids but darn it if his ears didn't betray him by straining even harder to listen to the women's conversation. "Don't start. Okay? I knew Matt a whole lifetime ago."

"Sure. Things are different now. But maybe that's not a bad thing. You're more available," Elise said. "He's definitely got it all in the looks department."

"Mom!"

"I just mean, it's been a long time since Troy died. You deserve to have some fun. Flirt, even."

A choking noise sounded from the hallway. Cody recognized that as Mia's disbelieving sputter. He'd heard it often enough when he and Troy got her riled up about something.

"I'm just saying have fun, without making everything so serious."

Cody didn't hear Mia's response because Maggie chose that moment to sit down in his lap. She placed a slightly damp blue Mustang into his hand. All mystery about how the car became wet was solved when she raised a red fire truck to her mouth and started chewing it. He pulled her chubby hand down.

"That's not a toy for your mouth, Mags," he said. She tipped her head back and smiled up at him before running the fire truck along the wood floor.

"Mom, I have kids. I can't have fun. Especially if it doesn't work out. I don't want to be stuck on this island with an ex-boyfriend. And the kids would be so confused." Mia's voice echoed down the hall.

Now it was Elise's turn to be muffled.

Enough of this. Cody picked Maggie up off his lap and set her on her bottom on the floor. He stood to his feet. But before he could interrupt the women and, hopefully, stop this interminable conversation, Mia's voice echoed again.

"He was super sweet with the kids. And, I can't believe

how much his talent has grown in the past few years. He showed me a bunch of his paintings on his phone."

Cody stifled the growl that threatened from deep inside. He strode toward the front door, but a small hand in his stopped him in his tracks.

"Can we play Candyland?" Finn's puppy dog look almost convinced him to say yes, but . . .

"Sorry, bud. I'm going to help your mother get supper ready. Want to help too?"

The two of them reached the front door as Elise walked out.

"See you later, Mrs. Jonathon," Cody said.

"Bye, Grandma." Finn grabbed her around her knees. Elise leaned down and gave him a swift kiss on the top of his head.

"I'll see you guys later."

Cody turned to Mia. "How can I help with supper?"

A few minutes later they were all in the kitchen, the kids setting the table, and Mia manning the pasta on the stove. Cody got some milk out of the fridge and then corralled Maggie when she tried to reach for the pan of hot garlic bread.

"Let's go wash up. C'mon, Finn, you too." Cody took the kids into the bathroom and helped them wash their hands.

Soon they were all sitting at the table saying grace. The kids' chatter faded into the background as he stared at Mia. She brushed a hair back behind her ear, and he imagined the silky feel of it between his fingers.

She looked up and caught his eye. A slow smile crossed her face. "What?" she said.

He dropped his gaze. "Nothing. You just look so natural here. Mom to two great kids. Doing a great job working for Dani. I'm proud of you."

She ducked her head. "Thanks."

"So," he said. "That was Matt."

She paused, fork halfway to her mouth. "That was Matt."

He couldn't quite figure out her tone. "He seems nice."

"He's very talented. I couldn't believe some of the pictures he showed me of the paintings he sold."

"Nice and talented, then." He shoved a forkful of pasta into his mouth, the noodles almost choking him. "He was glad to see you." He couldn't quite get a read on how Mia felt about the guy. He didn't dare ask straight up again.

"Honestly, he was a little overwhelming." She shot a glance at the kids, but they were busy making piles of pasta and not paying attention. "I loved seeing him again, but . . ."

"But what?" *Calm down, buddy. She might be choosing another man over you again. But she might also feel something for this guy.*

"I don't know. He felt out of place here. Or maybe I just felt out of place. I'm so different than I was when Matt knew me before." Her attention shifted to Maggie and the parmesan cheese she'd spilled on her lap, and Cody sensed that was all the conversation they were going to have on the matter.

One thing was clear. Mia was going to find someone

to move on with eventually. The thought clawed at his stomach.

He just wanted her to move on with him.

Eight

LAST NIGHT HAD BEEN WEIRD. THIS morning in her front hall, Mia tried to think of a different word for it but kept circling back to weird.

Seeing Matt again after so many years, the obvious tension between him and Cody, then the abrupt way Cody left after supper. Not to mention the way Cody's sweet words of support and friendship had wormed their way straight through her. They played through her mind long after she was in bed. He really believed what he was saying. About her. About her worth.

All very weird.

She shook off those thoughts too and focused on the task in front of her—tying Maggie's shoes. They had one goal for this morning: spend some time with Constance and GG. She'd been so busy lately she'd been neglecting her mother-in-law. They couldn't stay long though; this afternoon she needed to spend time developing descriptions of the houses that were available under the revitalization plan.

"Won't GG Harmon love seeing these pigtails?" She tweaked one of Maggie's curly whale spouts, both of which currently stuck straight up from her head. She finished tying the shoes and helped Maggie stand. "Finn! Are you ready to visit Grandma and GG?" Constance said that GG usually felt better in the mornings and invited them to stop by for a mid-morning coffee, promising apple cake.

Finn ran down the hall, one arm in his shirt, the other swinging behind him as he searched for the other armhole. Mia laughed and helped him pull it over his head.

"Let's go!" They headed out into the sunshine. Mia tipped her face to the sun for a breath before Finn tugged at her hand. "All right, Finn. Lead on."

A few minutes later, they stood in Constance's warm kitchen. The late morning sun streamed through the picture window over the pale wood dining table. The scent of apples and cinnamon filled the air. At the table, GG Harmon sat, hunched and small, her white pixie cut hair framing her face, making her blue eye luminous.

"Hi, GG." Mia pulled out a chair and sat next to her. She took GG's hands in her own. Ice cold. "How are you feeling today?"

The tiny woman had gained a little weight in the time she'd been in Constance's home. Her cheeks held more fullness, and she appeared healthier overall. "I'm having a good day today."

Mia glanced up at Constance who stood behind her mother. "Long night," Constance mouthed. Deep bags hung under her eyes, but the corners crinkled when she smiled.

Mia quirked a grin. "I hear apple cake is good medicine." She stood and got Finn and Maggie situated at the table. Soon, their snack was punctuated with their happy chatter. When the cake had been reduced to crumbs, Constance helped GG to her room for a nap, and Mia let Finn and Maggie run to the toy box in Constance's front room.

Constance came back into the kitchen and began clearing off the table.

"Let me help you with that." Mia stood and started stacking the dirty plates. She carried them to the small counter and sink. "I'll wash if you dry."

"You met up with an old friend yesterday, right?" Constance wiped a plate before putting it in the cupboard.

"Yeah. Matt. It was good seeing him again. Weird, but good." A tug in her belly as she remembered his piercing blue eyes. "He's just as talented as always. He has a gallery in Grand Rapids, near our old college, but he's looking for a new place."

"That must have been difficult, seeing his success."

Her eyes prickled and she blinked. "I gave up that life when I got pregnant with Finn. He is worth it."

Constance touched her arm. "Loads of people have a creative job and families."

"But most of those people have someone else to support them, and maybe I would have gone back to it if Troy hadn't died. I never had a chance to find out." Mia scrubbed at a sticky spot on the plate in her hands. The heat of the soapy water did little to warm her up. "No. I'm happy with my life. Or I will be once I secure the house for the kids. Once more people are on island, I'm sure I can get a steady job to provide for them. Maybe even go into the real estate business full-time." *Where did that thought come from?* But it was a good idea. "If enough people start coming back to the island, we can jump-start the economy and convince more people to want to live here again."

"Sounds lonely, only focusing on the town and your kids like that." A cup went into the cupboard, nestled next to several others of various shapes and sizes.

"I don't have the luxury to think about that. Plus, I have Evie and Dani, and Cody, of course." She grimaced. "Sorry, I shouldn't talk about him."

Constance tightened her lips. "I'm not upset at Cody. Not specifically, anyway. It's just that seeing him reminds me of everything I've lost." She let out a long breath. "I have to ask God for peace every time I see him in town."

"I get that." Swishing the water, Mia found a coffee cup and rubbed at it with her washcloth.

"But I don't begrudge him his happiness. He deserves that. He was always such a good friend to Troy. And to you too." Constance picked up a dish and wiped it dry. "And even if the fact I have trouble greeting him seems like it, I know the accident was never his fault."

"No, of course not." She'd never blamed Cody either. How could she, when the fact that Troy had been on the boat that night was because of her? Something she'd never told a soul.

They worked a few minutes more.

"So, is Matt cute?" Constance kept her eyes on the plate

she was wiping dry, but Mia caught a hint of a smile on her lips.

"Constance!"

"What? It's a simple question." Constance bumped her with her hip.

"Yeah, okay. I don't know if he's going to move here, but yes. He's good looking. Always has been." If a little enthusiastic—but it was nice to know a man was interested in her after everything she'd been through. She wrinkled her nose. "But I don't know if he's the right guy for me. He called Jonathon Island quaint."

"It is quaint." Constance laughed. "As for Matt, you won't know unless you're open to dating again. Are you?"

"Well . . . maybe. But sometimes it feels impossible to think about. Troy was . . ." Heat pricked the back of her eyes, and she scrubbed the plate in her hands extra hard.

"I know, hon. He was your match." Constance's voice softened, and Mia met her gaze. "But that doesn't mean God doesn't have someone else out there for you. A second chance. Moving forward is hard, but it's good."

"You haven't moved forward."

"It's different. You have two kids who need a father figure. Troy'd want a good and honorable man to be there for you and Finn and Maggie. He loved you with every breath and would never be upset." Constance paused. "But maybe you're right. Maybe I should put myself back out there too. My own friends are hounding me to join an online dating site to meet men in Port Joseph . . . Maybe I should do it."

Mia held back a laugh at picturing Constance on a dating app. But then she sobered. If Constance could find the courage to move forward at sixty-three years old, maybe she could too.

Just then her phone pinged with a text message. She rinsed off the plate in her hands and then checked her phone.

Matt

I'm headed off island on the next ferry. Can you meet me at the dock in a few minutes? Want to talk over schedule before I go?

And end this conversation with her mother-in-law? Yes, please.

"Constance, can I leave Finn and Maggie here with you for a few minutes? I'll put on a cartoon for them or something." She held up the phone. "Matt needs to meet for a quick chat."

Constance flapped her hands. "Go. They'll be fine here."

Mia hurried the few chilly blocks to the ferry port.

Matt stood on the dock. A ferry waited, but the area was quiet. In the harbor, a few other boats bobbed in the waves. A light breeze lifted the edge of Matt's jacket. A smile crossed his face and lit up his eyes as Mia approached. He walked to her and grabbed her hand in both of his. His cologne filled the space between them. Something strong and spicy and probably expensive. Suddenly, Mia was very aware of the jeans and ratty T-shirt she'd pulled on today. Was the shirt even clean? She took a deep breath and reminded herself of what Cody had said. *Just be yourself.* Well, couldn't get more herself right now than this half-put-together, possibly food-stained T-shirt and secondhand jeans.

"Thanks for meeting me. I was going to call, but I thought I would take the chance to see you instead." His blue eyes searched hers.

"This worked great. I left the kids at my mother-in-law's for a few minutes. It's a beautiful morning for a walk."

"I have a meeting on the mainland with some potential investors in a few hours, so I checked out of Island Inn. I'll be back for the big meeting at the end of next week."

"Okay." Why did she rush down here for this? And why was he still holding her hand? She let go. "Anything else?"

"That's all. Just wanted to say goodbye for now." Matt's gaze flicked behind her and then he took her hand again. "Hello again, Cody."

She dropped Matt's hand again and spun. Sure enough, Cody stood at the end of the dock, arms crossed. His stormy face a contrast to the sun bursting through the clouds overhead. How long had he been there? Her heart lifted. Had he been looking for her?

A long horn sounded from the ferry. "Okay. Good luck on your trip." Mia schooled her voice into something hopefully professional.

"Thanks." Matt rested a hand on her shoulder briefly, gave her a smile, then nodded at them both. "Cody."

"Matt."

Matt picked up his briefcase before turning on his heel and making his way to the ferry.

Mia looked up at Cody's sour face. "Good morning, Sunshine."

He watched the boat pull away from the dock before turning to her. "It is now." He flashed a smile. "I have a car for Finn that I found at my place." He held up a miniature red Corvette. "I sent you a text that I was heading over to your place, but when you didn't answer, I thought I'd go anyway and leave it on your porch. I need to get to work on a house near yours today. Then I spotted you down here when I was walking past. Where are the kids?"

"At Constance's. I need to get back and pick them up. This meetup with Matt was an impromptu one."

A muscle in his jaw jumped and he grunted.

"Wow. You really don't like Matt, do you?" She took the Corvette from him and stuck it in her jeans pocket.

"He's fine." Cody's eyes were hooded.

"Yes. Those two words are very convincing."

He sighed, ran a hand through his sandy hair. "Matt's great. I like Matt. I'd like him even more if he didn't make you feel less than. Plus, he's a flirt."

"What do you mean less than?" A cloud passed over the sun, casting a shadow over them.

"You know. Making you feel insecure. But then constantly smiling at you. Touching your shoulder. Laughing at your jokes. Playing with your kids."

"I'm sorry? Are you upset because Matt likes my sense of humor?" She put a hand to her hip. "And was nice? And likes my kids? Seriously, Code? Any insecurity on my part was just that, *on my part*."

Cody flexed a fist. He squinted at the ground for a beat before his shoulders dropped. "No. You're right. He's nice. Seems like a good guy." His jaw tightened.

"Code." She reached out a hand to, well she wasn't sure what, but Cody pulled a step away from her.

"Are you heading home?" His voice held false cheer.

"Yep." Okay. She'd drop it for now. "Constance was just watching the kids for a few minutes. She can't keep them long."

"I'll walk you. Like I said, I need to work on a house over there anyway."

They fell into an easy cadence. "Seems like this is becoming our thing." Maybe some light teasing would bring him around.

Cody laughed. "Sometimes it still feels strange walking through town without our third musketeer."

"Seriously?" She stopped, crossed her arms. "Why do you do that?"

Cody stopped a step ahead of her and turned to face her. "Do what?"

"Bring up Troy any time I say something about our friendship?"

"I don't do that."

"Yes. You do." She brushed past him and heard him follow. They walked past an empty storefront with a newly painted flowerbox, but even the beauty of the flowers didn't soothe her irritation.

"Don't you want to talk about Troy?"

"Of course I want to talk about Troy. And after he died, I was desperate to talk about him, but everyone in town avoided the topic. Maybe they thought it would be more painful for me." The cobblestones under her feet tilted and she almost stumbled. Cody grabbed her elbow and held her steady. "Thanks. They didn't realize that talking about him would be helpful. Even Constance didn't talk to me about him much. But you . . . you were the only one who grieved with me. Who would talk about him."

"Okay, then. I don't see the problem." Cody dropped her elbow and drew a half step away.

"The problem is, Troy isn't the only thing we have in common. And yet, you use him as a shield. It's like he's always between us. Sometimes I wonder if you do all of the stuff around my house to help me simply because he's not here to do it . . . or because you're *my* friend—not his."

Okay, then. Hadn't meant to say all of that. She hadn't even known she thought that until the words were out. And yet, she did.

Cody paused. A slight frown line developed between his eyes. "You're right." He shrugged. "It's just that it's always been you and me and Troy."

"That's not true. There was a you and me before Troy moved here. *We* were friends first. Being the middle child, it was easy to feel overlooked in my own house, but you always had time for me. Your friendship meant the world. It was a lifeline." She stopped, looked at him. "It still is."

"I'll always be your friend, Mia."

"And yet . . . once Troy moved here, you and I didn't do much just the two of us, did we? The two of you were thick as thieves, and I was like the third wheel."

"Are you kidding? You were the sun, and we were the planets orbiting around you. Trying to one-up each other to impress you, get you to laugh." He shook his head. "If anyone was the third wheel, it was me. Once you and Troy started dating . . . well, you had eyes only for each other." He started walking again.

She hurried to catch up as he reached Constance's yard. Touched his elbow so he stopped. "I'm sorry, Cody. I had no idea we made you feel that way. I suppose we were pretty obnoxious, weren't we?" Mia searched his eyes and was surprised to find a shuttering of sorts—not humor as she'd expected. But . . . more. Something deeper and sadder than her words warranted. Unless . . .

"Was there another reason you pulled away in high school? Not just because we were annoying, but . . . something else?"

"Something else?" His voice had gone husky, and was it her imagination, or was he leaning in closer? "Like what?"

"I don't know." She tugged on a loose piece of her hair that blew in the breeze. "Dani had this crazy idea that you liked me back then." Oh goodness, now why had she gone and blurted that out? Surely he was going to laugh and give her a friendly tap on the shoulder and they'd smile about this later.

Instead, Cody shifted and looked away from her. "You were smart, funny, and talented. Not to mention beautiful. I guess back then, yeah. I had a thing for you."

She stilled. "A thing? Why didn't you ever say anything?"

"C'mon, Mia. Even if it took him several years to pursue you, you were head over heels for Troy from the minute he stepped on the island. And then he had the courage to speak up when I didn't. My two best friends had found love together. So, what was I supposed to say? I chose to be happy for you and move on."

"Oh, Cody." She reached out and put a hand on his shoulder. Even through his flannel shirt she could feel the tension in his muscles. He spun to face her, just six inches separating them. His eyes flared a brighter blue in the midday sun. Her breath caught.

"You meant everything to me back then." His voice had dropped until she had to lean forward to hear him. "In this tiny town, in our tiny school, you were like, I don't know, a water sprite or some other fantasy creature. You always thought up the most interesting things to do, you were spontaneous and fun. And you could look at any situation and see beauty. I'd see a tree and think 'Oh, a tree,' you'd see the same tree and go home and paint something incredible." He paused and wet his lips. "And I thought . . . Then Troy moved here, and we all became friends. But then your focus shifted to him. Which is fine. Honestly, I don't hold it against you at all. But yeah. Troy is between us, because he's always been between us."

Under her hand his muscle rippled. She swallowed. He thought she was a fantasy creature? When had Cody become so . . . poetic? Also, she didn't feel like that carefree girl anymore. But maybe she could again. In time.

Cody's gaze flicked down to her lips.

Heat flared inside. What—

"Mommy's back!" Finn's high cheer from Constance's doorway broke the whatever it was between them. Mia gulped in a breath before taking a step back and dropping her hand.

"Hi Finn!" She pasted on a smile for her son, pretending that her heart wasn't galloping faster than the time she'd run for the track team. In the doorway, Maggie poked her head under Finn's arm. "Hi Mags. You guys ready to go home?" She made her way up the sidewalk. Before reaching the house, she flicked a glance back at Cody. The look he was giving her in return made her legs feel like jelly.

Their conversation wasn't over.

Cody rubbed his neck. So that's what whiplash felt like. Or at least that's what this morning had been for him.

He'd been eating an omelet and deep into researching a new gasket for his boat when he'd gotten a phone call about a lead on some fishing tackle he'd need now that his dad had sold his.

After the call, he found he couldn't concentrate on his research anymore, so he'd grabbed the car for Finn and texted Mia. Then he saw Matt on that dock, holding Mia's hand. Then Mia asking him to talk about how he felt about her.

Culminating in whatever the heck that was outside her mother-in-law's house. Had he really been about to kiss her before the kids interrupted them?

He'd hotfooted it out of there before Mia had a chance to razz him about it.

Coward.

But then, when she'd called and asked him to come to her house to help with something, he'd had lightning in his sneakers.

And now, he was sitting at her dining room table and supposed to concentrate on helping her with some incredibly boring paperwork.

So. Yeah. Whiplash.

"Are you okay?" Mia's eyes were unreadable.

"Sure am." Keep it light. "Why?"

"You keep rubbing your neck. I thought maybe you'd gotten hurt."

He willed his hands to stay where they were. One rested on the table, and one clutched an application. Mia had asked if they could review them one more time. "I'm fine."

"So, I think we should definitely go with the fifteen there to replace all the ones that dropped out when I started scheduling video interviews. But I'd like to pick one more." Mia fanned out the final applications on the table. "These are our choices. What do you think? I just really need a second opinion. I don't want to present the wrong candidates to the council and look foolish."

Cody held out the application in his hand. "This is the one I would choose. Mrs. Harper. Solid background in sales, she's lived in the same place for a long time, which shows loyalty, but now wants some adventure, which shows she's ready to tackle the challenge of living and working over here. Plus, she sells cheesecake. Win-win."

Mia smiled at him. A tight line of a smile that didn't reach much higher than her lips. Not that he should be looking at her lips. They moved. Shoot. He'd missed her response. "I'm sorry, what?"

She bristled. "You don't like Matt Goldfinch as a candidate?"

"I didn't say that."

"You didn't have to. 'I'm sorry, what?'" She added a slight sarcasm to his response.

"That's not what I—"

"I think we should give him a chance. I'd love to see a real art studio here. Who knows, maybe one day Maggie will work there and be inspired." She glanced away, blinking rapidly.

Aw. Sure, he had a raging, green-eyed monster in his belly every time he saw or thought about Matt Goldfinch, but he wasn't going to admit that to Mia. He certainly wasn't about to let himself and his dumb emotions get in the way of her happiness.

"Mia, look at me." She met his eyes and a heat zinged through him. "If you want Matt for this last slot, and you think he's a good fit, I'm not going to fight you on it. I'm on your team."

Her expression softened. "Thanks. I appreciate that. And I appreciate you thinking through these applications with me. It means a lot."

"Anytime."

Mia tapped the table once. "Okay. I think I'm ready to head over and finalize some of these details with Dani." She gathered her papers together. They shook in her hands. "Kids! Get your shoes." She tucked the papers in a folder then ran her palms down the sides of her pants.

"Hey." He stood and took two steps around the table. "Nervous?"

Her smile wobbled. "A little."

"You have nothing to worry about."

Her mouth dropped open. "Nothing to worry about? Cody, if this goes sideways, I could lose my house. My kids could be homeless." A fire he'd never seen before shot from her eyes. "This is the *only* thing I should be worrying about."

"No, I didn't mean—"

"If I don't nail every single part of this. It's not just my life on the line, it's the town's reputation. It's Dani's job." She flung her arms out. "It's the whole island."

"Okay. You have a lot to worry about. But what I meant was, you're smart. You're prepared. Dani is your best friend. Whatever happens in the next hour or so will be fine. You'll figure it out."

She blew out a breath and smoothed back a section of her hair. "Sorry. I freaked out a little there."

"Just a little." He softened his words with a smile. "Hey, here's a great idea. Why don't you let me take care of the kids while you're gone."

"I can't ask you to do that."

"You're not asking, I'm offering. C'mon, Mia. Let me help you."

"You've already helped me." She gestured at the pile of papers, a small movement that reminded him of the flutter of a hummingbird's wings "Plus, you have your own work to do."

"It's fine. I'll bring the kids over to my place. They can play, and I will get a few things done." He spread his hands wide.

She hooked him with a look and put a hand on her

hip. "Have you met my kids? You won't be getting any work done."

How hard could it be? There were just two of them. "You're going to be late if you stand here arguing with me. I can out-stubborn you any day." He spun her toward the door. "Go. Meet Dani. Have a decaf coffee. Come back a conquering hero. I got the kids."

A scramble of jackets and shoes later and he was looking down at two adorable faces smiling up at him under twin bobble hats. Well, one face was smiling, anyway.

"Where Mama go?" Maggie's chin wobbled.

"Your mom had a meeting to get to." He glanced out the window next to the front door. He could just barely see Mia as she disappeared around the corner of the street. Good for her. She deserved to have some time to herself. Hopefully, she would take him up on the offer to stay out longer than her meeting required.

A fat tear rolled down Maggie's cheek. "I go wif her."

"Maggie's going to cry." Finn's brotherly scorn came through loud and clear.

"We can't have that." He swooped Maggie up into his arms just as the little girl began to wail. "Shh, sweetheart. It's okay. I'll take care of you until your mom gets home."

Maggie buried her head in his neck even as she cried harder. He patted her on the back. He made shushing noises. He bounced her up and down.

"That's not going to work," Finn said.

"Very helpful, buddy." Maybe they all needed a distraction. "Do you guys want to see my boat?"

Maggie lifted her tearstained face from his neck, her crying miraculously cured. "I wike boats."

"Let's go, then." He shot off a quick text to Mia letting her know that he was taking the kids to his place. She responded with a heart emoji. Best not to read too much into that.

"Can we take the wagon?" Finn bounced on the balls of his feet.

"Sure, bud. If you show me where it is."

A few minutes later, they were moving down the sidewalk, Finn and Maggie tucked into a soft-sided wagon. The kids sang a nonsense song about a duck and some grapes. See, no big deal. He could handle this.

When they finally reached his shop, Cody's arms were coming loose at the sockets. No wonder Mia rarely used the wagon. The kids couldn't weigh much more than sixty pounds altogether, but when you bounce those sixty pounds for a half a mile over rough pavement and with no suspension, they may as well have been three hundred and sixty. At least the big wheels rolled better over the cobblestone roads than he'd expected. He parked the wagon near the door and rotated his shoulders a few times. Then he held the wagon steady for Finn to climb out. Maggie raised her arms and he swooped her up, making an airplane noise as he did. She giggled.

Inside the shop, Finn stood and gaped up at the fishing boat. "It's so tall."

Cody laughed. From the perspective of a four-year-old, it probably did seem quite tall. He set Maggie down and helped her take off her jacket. Finn's coat lay on the floor, so Cody picked that up then hung them all on the hooks. He pulled out his phone and noticed that he'd missed a call from Lily. With one eye on the kids, he called her back.

"Hey, sis. You still coming home?"

"Can't get rid of me that easily." Her voice had a lilt.

"You sound good. Florida treating you all right?" Finn disappeared around the front of the boat, Maggie toddling after him.

"I've just made the most gorgeous truffle. Bergamot and caramel."

Cody steadied his voice. "They're letting you make the chocolates now?"

"Just . . . you know . . ." Lily dropped the upbeat tone. "I'm experimenting here and there." Across the room, on the other side of the boat, the kids giggled. "Where are you?"

"At home." He looked around. After the brightness of the afternoon, the dinginess of the shop wore on him.

"Who is laughing?"

"Oh. I have Mia's kids here."

"What are they doing?"

"I'm not sure. They're on the other side of the boat."

"Cody. You left a two-year-old and a four-year-old unsupervised?"

What? "No. They're supervised. I'm right here." He started walking around the boat toward the kids.

"Can you see them?"

"Not exactly." Two more steps.

"They're unsupervised." Her sarcasm came through loud and clear.

He turned the corner and—"Lily, I have to call you back."

It took him a second to understand the picture in front of him. Finn was covered in engine grease. It appeared as though the boy had tried painting his face with the stuff. Maggie had climbed onto the work bench—how?—and sat admiring his row of chisels and saws. In a sprint, he grabbed her hand just as she reached for the business end of his filet knife hung on a magnet on the wall.

"Finn. What were you thinking?"

Finn grinned up to him, mischief dancing in his eyes. "I wanted to be a football player." He held his hands, slick with the grease, up to his hair.

"Don't!" But it was too late. Finn patted the top of his blond head, rubbing the grease in until his curls stood on end.

"Mom does this with her hair," he said.

Cody groaned. Mia was never going to trust him with her kids again. "I'm sure she uses a better product." In fact, he remembered a scent of lilac the last time he'd seen her. It made him think of the tree outside his mother's front door. Hopefully his cheap shampoo from the dollar store would work on the grease in Finn's hair. "Come here." Despite the mess, these two really were adorable. Cody snapped a quick selfie with the kids and sent it to Lily.

———————Cody

See, I've got everything under control.

Lily———————

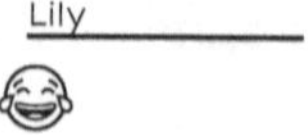

His phone dinged again.

<u>Lily</u>
Should I forward that to Mia?

<u>Cody</u>
Do it and you won't like what I put in your bed
when you come home.

Another laughing emoji and then a GIF of someone pretending to be scared. Then,

<u>Lily</u>
Seriously though, they look happy. That's a good thing. You'd make a good dad, bro.

<u>Cody</u>
Whoa there. I'm just babysitting.

<u>Lily</u>
For now.

He smiled to himself and tucked the phone back into his pocket. His sister's words made him pause. What if he was brave enough to pursue Mia? To tell her that not only did he used to have feelings for her . . . but still did? Had never stopped, really.

Picking up both kids like two sacks of potatoes, he marched back to his bunk room. "Finn, let's see if my shampoo works on engine grease."

Yep. Whiplash. But the best kind.

Nine

OKAY. THIS WAS HER TIME TO SHINE. Mia sat with Dani, Martha, Janine, and other members of the town council around the conference table at the tourism center. They had scheduled video calls for today and planned to put all the fancy tech invested in this room through its paces.

Mia hadn't known what to expect the night before when she picked her kids up from Cody's. But they looked great—all smiles. Finn said something about being a football player, and Maggie babbled nonstop about the big boat. They both smelled faintly of cedar and eucalyptus and engine oil. A scent she usually associated with Cody, actually. They were clean and full and tired and had gone right to bed with just one story.

It was a little like a miracle.

She'd hoped to pick up the conversation with Cody

from earlier, but with the kids being ready for bed, it hadn't been the right time.

Today, she had taken the kids over to Evie's house in Port Joseph where they would spend the night. She'd breathed a sigh of relief on her crossing. Just like every time she'd taken the ferry since Troy's death, she'd been tense the whole time, but the boat made the trip without a hitch.

In preparation for this meeting, Mia had prepared slide shows, one for each candidate. Sure, they were trying to see if these applicants were a good fit for the program, but they were also trying to entice them to choose Jonathon Island. A mutual wooing, as it were. She'd shown the presentation to the council and received mostly approved nods, though Martha's face hadn't given away many of her thoughts.

The computer blooped with the video chat connecting noise, and they all turned their attention to the screen.

Mia gripped her hands together before wiping them on her pants.

Dani led the first part of the discussion with Meredith Olson and her husband. They hoped to open a bakery specializing in treats made with Michigan blueberries.

Each of the other members of the group had a chance to ask a few questions, and then it was Mia's turn. "I've prepared a few slides to show you the store space I think would be perfect for you, it used to be a pizzeria, as well as a house that fits your requests." She'd gone around taking photos of all the homes and businesses.

On-screen, Meredith nodded, a smile cresting her lips. So far so good.

"Let me just share the screen." Mia moved to the computer, past Patrick, and sat next to Dani. She clicked a few buttons, and a photo of Finn and Maggie filled the screen.

"That doesn't look like a house," Meredith said, her voice dry.

Mia heated. "Sorry. Sorry. Just a second." She clicked into the correct program and the old Island Pizzeria popped up. "This is the place I thought you might like to rent." She ran them through the specs ending with, "Of course you are free to bring your own equipment, but the previous owners left a few things behind." She loaded a photo of a huge Hobart mixer.

"I'm prepared to offer a very low rent," her dad's voice rumbled from across the table.

"Yes, we understand that." Meredith looked at her husband. Their faces, projected on the screen, revealed nothing of their thoughts. "Can we see the houses please?"

Mia clicked to the next part of the presentation. "This home on Poppy Lane has been recently refurbished." She noted with pride the changes Cody had made to the space. Everything looked beautiful. She clicked through a few more slides, doing her best to sound like a competent real estate agent.

"I'm sorry," Meredith interrupted. "Did you say there are only two bedrooms?"

"Yes, many of the houses we are offering only have two bedrooms." Mia's pulse rate spiked. "These are all older homes. Some even have historic value."

Meredith sniffed. "We have two children. We will need more than two bedrooms."

"Aren't they both daughters?" Mia realized her mistake as soon as the words left her mouth. Of course, Meredith wouldn't want her daughters to share, otherwise she wouldn't have asked for something bigger.

The room grew heavy with silence as everyone stared at Mia. She thought quickly over the other options. "Okay. I can show you one with three rooms." She maneuvered to another presentation. This meant she'd have to scramble to fit in a new house for the other candidate. "This one has three lovely rooms and a wraparound porch." She concentrated on the photos, pointing out the benefits of the home. Around her the silence grew thicker.

She glanced up at the screen. Oh.

Meredith sat back in her chair, arms crossed, a grim look on her face. "This one won't work either. We need a bigger yard for the dog."

Mia swallowed hard. Her first call and she was already failing. "All of the houses with three bedrooms have the same size yard."

"So, you're saying it's choose a yard or choose more bedrooms?"

Mia's mouth was too dry to speak so she only nodded.

"Well then, I guess we are out." Meredith ended the call and Mia sat back, stunned.

"Well, that could have gone better," Martha said. Her strident voice seemed to wake everyone else from their silence and they all started talking at once.

Dani handed her a water bottle.

"Thanks." Mia cracked the lid. The cool liquid slid down her throat and soothed her nerves.

"This was just the first one," Dani said. "We never thought it would be easy." An alarm beeped on her phone and Dani turned it off. "Everybody, listen up. Next, we have," she checked her clipboard, "Jemma Swanson. She is a glassblower."

Soon, a young blonde about Mia's age appeared on the screen.

"I'm so excited to be part of this project," she said. "I can't wait to move over there and get started."

Her enthusiasm was contagious. Soon, the whole group was firing off questions for Jemma, and she was sending them right back.

Yes, she was from Michigan.

Yes, she'd been on the island before.

Yes, they would give her a low rent, and the houses really were a dollar.

And on and on.

When Mia finally showed the slides she had prepared, Jemma barely even looked at them.

"I'm sure you know which place will be best for me. You're more familiar with everything there. This all looks great." Jemma beamed into the camera. "I will have some equipment that will need to be delivered if my application gets approved."

Dani and Mia exchanged looks before Dani looked around the table. Everyone was nodding.

"Jemma, we're all very excited about having you aboard. We'll let you know a final answer soon. We're having an in-person meet and greet next week. We'd love to have you there," Dani said. On-screen, Jemma jumped up and did a little dance.

"Thank you all so much," she said. "I don't know if I can make it next week, but I'm all in. I won't let you down."

They ended the call. Once again everyone began talking at once, but this time, a happy note rang in the air.

The day progressed with more calls, and each of the council members took a turn leading the discussion. The pile of notes beside Mia grew larger. She had a stack of yeses and a stack of nos. Right now, they were tied. There was also a stack of maybes, people who the council weren't sure about and a few who were themselves unsure.

"Last one on our list," Dani said. "This will be Mrs. Linda DeVoe. She sells specialty clothing. It's Janine's turn to lead the discussion."

Linda DeVoe was an older woman, perhaps in her sixties. Her hair was neatly styled, and she wore dangly earrings and a pastel top. A much younger man sat next to her.

"I hope you don't mind if my nephew's son sits in," she said. "He's helping me with the computer. It can be finicky."

"Don't worry, I'll be quiet," the young man said. "I don't know much about clothes anyway."

The interview ran in fits and starts. There was a strange lag on the audio, and they kept talking over each other.

"Maybe we can hash out these details when I come to town," Linda finally said.

"That would be great," Janine said. "Would you like

to see the business and home we've picked out for you? Subject to your approval, of course."

Mrs. DeVoe nodded and Mia started her presentation, showing her the various details of the places they'd earmarked as possibilities for her.

Mrs. DeVoe pursed her lips. "I don't know. It's not something I can really determine over a screen. I just don't know if I'm ready to make any decisions."

"That's fine." Janine took back the presentation. "We will send you the details of the in-person event soon. Hopefully we can impress you enough for a yes."

They thanked Mrs. DeVoe and ended the call.

The meeting broke up and everyone devolved into a general chaos of hand shaking and back slapping. One by one, the council members filed out.

Cody passed behind Mia's chair, then leaned down and said in her ear, "Good job." Before Mia could respond, he'd walked out the door.

Across the table, her dad cleared his throat. "Yes, good job, Mia."

She nodded at him once, then looked back at the papers in front of her until she heard him get up from the table and leave the room. Dani came back into the room and sat next to Mia.

"How do you think that went?" Dani laced her hands together and laid them on the conference table.

"So-so," Mia said. She flipped through the stacks of notes. "I think we're going to have to go to our second tier of applicants."

"Will there be enough?"

Between them, the computer hummed as it cooled down from the meeting.

"I hope so. I'll take a look tonight." Mia jotted down a few more notes. "I will have plenty of time, the kids are at Evie's."

"Maybe you should take the night off. Do something fun." Dani's eyes lit up. "You could come out with Liam and me."

"And be the third wheel? No thanks." She didn't need pity.

"Oh come on, it would be fun. You could invite Cody." She singsonged his name.

"Stop. You're not being funny." But she couldn't help the giggle that escaped her. "Cody and I actually had a weird conversation yesterday."

Dani propped her chin on her hand, elbow on the table. "Do tell."

"Basically, he told me that he'd liked me when we were younger, but then Troy and I became a thing." She crossed her arms, tucking them tight to her body. "And then, things got intense. He was looking at me and I thought . . ." She swallowed.

"Thought what?"

"I thought he might kiss me."

"What?!" Dani's squeal echoed through the room. "You guys kissed?"

"No." Mia put her hand out to calm Dani. "I said I thought he might. But then Finn came, and the moment was over."

"Uh huh," Dani said. "Okay. So how do you feel about that?"

"I don't know." Mia buried her head in her arms on the table. "I think I might be starting to have feelings for him." Hopefully her muffled voice carried to Dani's ears, because she was *not* repeating that.

Dani rested a hand on her back. "And how do you feel about that?"

She let out a long breath and sat up. "I don't really know. I don't have time to think about it, or feel about it for that matter. I can't let a relationship get in the way of saving my house. Cody and I have always been friends, and we'll just go on that way."

Dani gave her a long, hard look. "Cody wouldn't let you lose your house. You know that right?"

Of course she did, but still. "I'm just not ready, Dani."

"I get that." Dani gave her arm a squeeze. "But don't close yourself off to the possibility. Now, let's pack up and go out and do something together."

"No. I need to get this work done. My kids' home is more important than a night of fun."

Dani sighed. "I suppose you're right. But don't let all this work take over your life. You are allowed to have fun sometimes too."

"I'll remember that." Mia left the building and walked toward her home, trying not to think about the long, lonely night ahead of her.

He should have known better.

Cody's feet pounded along the boardwalk. Unable to sit still this morning, he'd answered the call of the morning sun and went out for a run. In the past few days, he'd tried to put his head down and make some progress on finding the parts for his boat. He planned on making some calls to former clients as well. Fat chance.

Because then Mia called, upset because she wasn't going to make her quota. Then his mother had needed him to help his father move the wood pile from one side of the yard to the other because she wanted to plant blueberry bushes. And was that a pretext to get them together and talking again? Probably. Didn't work. Sorry, Mom. And then Dani had him come tear out some cabinets in one of the storefronts. And suddenly it seemed like everything else was more important than finding the right gasket for a twenty-year-old marine engine.

After an hour of frustration scouring eBay, Boat Parts Unlimited, and Marine Wholesale—usually his go-to websites—he had been unsuccessful in getting the part he needed. Even with the income from fixing up houses and businesses around town, he didn't have the funds to source a new engine, not even a half-working refurbished one. Not if he could convince his dad to sell—he needed every penny he had saved for that.

He'd concluded that the whole world was telling him, "Nope. Not today."

His restless feet had propelled him into his running shoes and out the door.

Stubborn thoughts chased him down the trail. No boat parts meant no boat. No boat meant no fishing business.

And if his dad was going to cling to his decision to give up the commercial license, Cody's dreams were dead in the water anyway. The waiting list for those licenses stretched to the moon. His dad's would be snapped up before Cody even had a chance to add his name to the list.

Overhead, a flock of seagulls whirled and spun in the air. Going nowhere but making a lot of noise doing it.

He put a little more speed into his step.

If he wasn't going to be a fisherman anymore, who was he going to be? Sure, being the island handyman paid the bills, but he didn't want to be fixing toilets and replacing drywall for the rest of his life. He liked being outdoors, even in rough weather.

He stumbled over a high spot in the boardwalk, his momentum carrying him over and down on one knee. He landed hard with a loud crack. Hopefully that was the board and not his kneecap.

"Whoa! Are you okay?"

Wincing, he stood back on his feet. A quick check of his knee showed it was mostly his ego that got bruised. Pastor Arnie sat on a bench near the boardwalk, his shock of red hair lit by the sun. Cody hadn't noticed him before. Pastor Arnie got up and moved over to him. The fifty-something man had pastored on Jonathon Island for almost thirty years. His wife, Tara, was affectionately known as the town mom.

"That looked painful."

Cody grimaced. "Yep." He put his hands on his thighs and bent a little at the waist, breathing hard. Coming to an abrupt stop was not a great way to end a run.

"Sorry. I guess I stated the obvious. Anything I can do? Doesn't look like you're bleeding." Arnie reached out and put a hand on Cody's shoulder.

"I just need to catch my breath a minute." He stumbled a step or two, still bent over.

Arnie reached for his elbow. "You can share my bench, if you'd like."

Cody sat next to Arnie. Closing his eyes, he leaned his head back. The sun warmed his face. Around them, the gulls still called to each other. A fishy smell filled the air. He let a few minutes of silence pass.

Opening his eyes again, he looked at the preacher. Pastor Arnie sat with his elbows propped on the backrest, looking calm and content. Cody got the sense he would sit there all day if he thought that was needed.

"Thanks," Cody said. "I appreciate you sitting with me."

"My pleasure," Pastor Arnie said. "I come out here to think. I was just about to head back to the church when you tumbled by."

"Ha. Funny."

"How is that boat of yours coming?" Pastor Arnie had been among the crowd who'd gathered last fall when his derelict treasure had been towed into the marina and then up to his pole shed shop.

"Slow." He detailed the process and how he'd been stymied at every turn. "Now I can't find the part I need to get the engine running again."

"So, basically everything in the world is distracting you from getting this job done."

He rubbed at the back of his neck. "That about sums it up."

"I don't know." Pastor Arnie paused.

"What?"

"I could be way off base here, but I've known you for years. I don't think you'd let a few setbacks and distractions prevent you from finishing something you set your mind to."

Cody clenched his jaw, then relaxed it again. "What are you saying?"

"Just that maybe there's more to your lack of focus than just some little chores that people ask for help with."

They weren't little chores, but whatever. "I'm still not sure what you're saying."

"Can I be honest here?" Pastor Arnie gave him a searching look. Cody nodded. Bring it on. "It's just that I think there might be other issues you haven't faced yet. You haven't really dealt with what it would be like to be out there again. Without Troy. And possibly in danger again. How often do you go fishing now?"

Oof. Cody sucked in a deep breath. That question had sucker punched him in the gut. But, to be fair, he'd given the man permission. "I guess . . . I haven't really been back out there other than taking the ferry once or twice."

"Maybe you need to figure out what you are afraid of. I'm guessing that's more the issue than the distractions you're allowing to sidetrack you."

A cloud passed over the sun, dappling the light.

Cody sat in stunned silence. Was fear holding him

back? Before he formulated a response, Pastor Arnie spoke again.

"If it really is that you don't have the time to finish the project, well, that's valid too. But if it's fear that's holding you back, let me remind you of a verse from Psalm thirty-four. I'll text it to you." Pastor Arnie pulled out his phone. A few seconds later, Cody's phone pinged with an incoming text. "The Pastor Arnie paraphrase of Psalm thirty-four, verse four says that if we seek the Lord, He will deliver us from all our fears."

Cody tapped into his Bible app and navigated to the verse. "Thanks. I'll think about this."

Pastor Arnie slapped his knees and stood up. "On that note, I'd better get back. My sermon won't write itself."

Cody stood too, then tested his knee before bending to touch his toes. Everything worked. A few stretches later, he began to jog back the way he'd come.

His run and his thoughts carried him past his house and down to the water. In addition to the larger commercial fishing trawler currently berthed in his shop, Cody owned a speed boat. At the shoreline of his lot, a small wooden dock jutted into the water. Bobbing to one side floated his speed boat. He faithfully put it in the water every spring and hauled it out again for the winter. He paid the fee to have it registered and kept the motor full of gas.

But he hadn't actually taken it out on the lake for two years.

Not since the last time he and Troy had taken an early morning fishing trip—the day before the accident.

The brilliant sun now shone overhead, its rays dancing

on the water. The twin lake scents of loam and fish called to him. Pulled him toward the bay and the lake beyond. Except, he couldn't get his feet to follow the tug deep in his belly.

"Are you having a staring contest with that boat?" Liam walked up next to him. "You look like the boat stole your dog and spat on your best pair of boots."

"What?" Cody wasn't sure whether to be annoyed or humored by the comparison.

"Your hands on your hips, feet squared up." Liam shrugged. "Just looked like you were about to ask the boat to meet you outside for a 'conversation.'"

Cody let out a small laugh, devoid of humor. "I guess it kind of is like that." He glanced to the side. Liam wore casual pants and a windbreaker. He'd tucked a ball cap over his designer haircut. Maybe . . . "I don't suppose you'd want to take a boat ride, would you?" If he had to face a few demons, it might be good to have backup.

Liam checked his smart watch. "If we make it a short ride, I'd enjoy getting out on the water. I've got about an hour to spare before I promised to meet Dani. I just came by to show you some pics of the fishing rods I ordered. Will that be enough time?"

Cody nodded. "Works for me." He started walking toward the dock, Liam trailing behind. The ancient structure wobbled as they stepped onto it. "I can show you a few good spots around here for when you're ready to use your gear."

Liam rubbed his hands together. "Let's do it."

A few minutes later and Cody had the boat running.

Liam, sporting the bright blue life vest Cody had tossed him, untied the mooring line under Cody's direction, and they eased away from the dock. A pit opened in Cody's stomach, taking his heart and throat and all of his blood down into itself. He stood in front of the captain's chair at the wheel and Liam perched on the bucket seat next to him.

The dock had slipped twenty feet behind them when bright spots blinked at the edges of Cody's vision. He blinked to clear them. Standing at the helm of his boat was like slipping back into his own skin, despite the memories nipping at the corners of his brain.

He swallowed hard as he swung the boat in a wide arc to come around the bay. "One of my favorite spots is just a little ways off my own dock." As he spoke, a band tightened around his chest. He tugged at the neck of his life vest but didn't get any relief.

The boat rocked in a swell from the left. He turned the wheel to the right, overcorrecting.

"Whoa." Liam clutched at the side of the boat as the inertia threatened to topple him. A spray from their wake hit them.

"Sorry about that, man." Cody focused on watching the swells ahead. *Keep it together.* The bright lights in his vision came back and his head swam.

"Cody? You don't look so good," Liam said. "Are you okay?"

"Fine." He gritted his teeth. Suddenly, his view of the sun-dappled lake in front of him was replaced by an image of a stormy night, a sinking boat. The air filled with a remembered scream.

"Cody, sit down." Liam's commanding voice broke through the memory. His hand was heavy on Cody's shoulder, forcing him back into the captain's chair behind him. Liam turned the key to shut off the boat's engine and silence rushed in. "Want to tell me what that was all about? Pardon the expression, but you're as white as a ghost."

Sitting very still was helping clear Cody's head. The white lights subsided, and his heart rate came back to baseline. Tell Liam? Yeah, he supposed he owed the man an explanation.

"I haven't been out in a boat like this since Troy and Steve died."

"Coulda warned me." Cody cut his gaze to Liam. Liam's eyes twinkled. "I'm just kidding. It wasn't like we were in any danger. We weren't going fast enough. I was just afraid you were going to pass out." Liam rummaged around in an old cooler Cody kept on deck. He came up with a bottle of water. "I don't know how old this is, but the seal is intact. You need to take a few sips." Liam cracked the cap and handed the bottle to Cody.

His hands shook as he took a long pull. Cool water slid down his throat.

"Want to talk about it?"

No. Except his mouth didn't get the memo. "We were out on a late-night run, chasing a school of fish. Like usual, it was Dad, Troy, Troy's dad Steve, and me as a four-man crew. Dad had asked me to check the forecast, and everything looked fine. Or at least . . . Well, I saw a threat of a storm, but it was far off, and I didn't want to call our night."

He could still picture that radar screen, its bright colors seared onto his retinas. Reds and yellows to the south, but those storms were tracking east. Plus, they were far enough away there was no danger to Lake Huron.

Right.

Cody swallowed, but his tongue had run dry. He sipped at the water. "We headed out to the Straits of Mackinac like we always do, but I was distracted. A bunch of chatter came over the radio about the storm north, and suddenly, it hit us. We didn't have time to get off the lake."

Liam nodded. His eyes were intense. Cody looked away.

He remembered the wind blowing sideways, the rain like bullets. "We'd been in rough waters before but nothing like this. Dad was reeling in the fishing lines while I fought to keep the boat under control. I should have asked for help—I was in way over my head. And then the storm pushed us onto the rocks." He shut his eyes, but the scenes still flashed in front of him.

"Steve, Troy's dad, got thrown overboard. He went under instantly. My dad held Troy back from jumping in after him, but then the boat began taking on water and heeled over on its side. Troy was dumped in, along with my dad." Cody swiped a hand over his eyes.

"It's okay," Liam said. "You don't have to say it."

Except, this felt like catharsis. Because he'd never actually told the story in its entirety, out loud—just relived it over and over again in his mind. Torturing himself. But there was something different about processing it verbally, for someone else who hadn't been there.

His voice dropped to a whisper. "I called SOS and then went for the life preservers. By then, the ship was listing so badly, the deck was a playground slide. I pitched in, barely hanging on to the life preservers."

"What? I can't even imagine."

"I don't even know how I reached my dad. Gave him one of the life preservers. Then I spotted Steve and managed to get a life vest under his arms. The waves were crazy, taking us down, slamming us toward the rocks. I finally spotted Troy. He was limp, and I thought he was already dead. I got to him—and no. Alive. But he'd broken his back, was nearly drowned, his lungs full. Barely breathing. I kept telling him to hang on, that he had a family to get back to . . . I couldn't get us up on the rocks, so I held Troy to me, and we floated together until the Coast Guard arrived. The last thing he said to me was to hold on to his wife and kids for him. He died in my arms."

"Sounds like a hero move." Liam laid a hand on his shoulder.

"No. Desperation. I should have read the storm, should have turned for home. And maybe if I'd gotten the life preservers to them sooner—I don't know."

Cody blew out a breath. "We were rescued by the Coast Guard, but it was too late for Steve too. He probably was dead before I gave him the preserver." Cody's voice broke. He cleared his throat.

He could still picture Mia from those days. How she'd met him at the hospital, hope in her eyes, only to be crushed by the truth. He had failed her. Her mother-in-law too. They were both widows now.

"That's horrible, man. I'm so sorry."

"I am finally starting to believe that it wasn't all my fault. Everyone around me keeps reminding me of that fact. It's sinking in." The admission tore out of him. But, like removing a splinter, he felt a little better when it was said. "But bad things happen to me. And I let them happen to my friend too."

"Doesn't sound like it to me. All I hear is that you saved your dad, tried to save your best friend, and were all the victims of a storm no one predicted. Bad things happen to everyone. What matters is how you deal with it."

Cody barked out a sound that could have been a laugh if it weren't so bitter. "My dad blames me. That's why he wants me to get out of the business."

"I don't know your dad, but he should be proud of you, not holding you to something that wasn't your fault."

Cody shrugged. Then his shoulders slumped. "Nevertheless . . ."

Liam stayed silent a while. The choppy lake banged against the hull of the boat. "Drink the rest of that water. Then let's get you back to shore."

Cody complied then helped Liam navigate back to the dock. "Sorry for the worst boat ride ever."

"Thanks for telling me all that. Takes courage to spill your guts." Liam grabbed a line and began tying the boat to the dock.

Cody took the other rope and secured the front of the

boat. "Let's go out again. Maybe once I've gotten this," he gestured to himself and then the boat, "figured out."

"Works for me." Liam took off his life jacket and stowed it.

Cody gripped his shoulder before letting go and removing his own jacket. "Thanks for listening, man."

"Anytime."

When Liam had gone, Cody made his way into his shop and laid down on his bed. His body shuddered as it came down from the adrenaline.

So much for figuring things out. He'd been on the water once and freaked out.

He sat up again. Okay. He was just going to have to go on the water again. And keep going until he didn't freak out.

No one else was going to solve this for him. Which meant it was time to stop sitting on the sidelines of his own life once and for all.

Ten

SEEING LILY AGAIN SOOTHED MIA down to her soul.

Cody's big sister had tagged around with them often and had grown to be a good friend of Mia's, despite Lily being four years older. The curvy blonde in blue leather leggings stood on the ferry dock, shielding her eyes, until she spotted Mia. Lily let go of her baggage and ran, squealing, into Mia's arms. Mia held on for an extra beat, not wanting to let go.

"It's so good to see you, Lil. I love the lavender streaks you've added to your hair. I hope you don't mind that I'm the one to pick you up." Mia reached out and tweaked a strand of Lily's hair. "Cody and your parents all had a minor emergency. Something about the washing machine overflowing? So, Cody called me." Her heart had given a little jump when she saw his name on her caller ID. Maybe he'd called to commiserate with her about the failure of her efforts. Maybe even to return to that discussion they'd had about their relationship. But, no. He'd jumped straight into asking her to pick up Lily, his manner distracted.

"I'm happy for it," Lily said. She walked back to where she'd dropped her luggage. She lifted a bag onto her shoulder and pulled a small suitcase behind, giving it a tug over a rough spot. "It gives us a chance to catch up a little. Have a little girl talk."

"I brought our wagon, so you don't have to try to wheel that thing across the cobblestones." Mia gestured to Lily's suitcase, its small wheels already stuck between two pieces of the road.

"Thanks," Lily said. She stowed the suitcase's handle and then put her shoulder bag into the wagon.

Mia hefted the suitcase into her wagon, and they walked up the inclined Ferry Road. "Want to walk down Main before I drop you off at your folks' place?"

"I'd love that." Lily stopped at the top of the road, eyes wide, head on a swivel as she looked around at Main Street. "Wow. Everything looks so nice. People must really be pitching in to spruce up the place."

Mia's chest swelled. She loved this little town. She blinked against a sudden hot pricking behind her eyelids.

"I love Jonathon Island." Lily echoed Mia's unspoken words. Was that a note of longing?

"You could come back, you know." She pulled the cart to a stop right outside the old fudge shop. "We could use someone like you in town. I know Cody already talked to you about it, but I was hoping to convince you." A line of excitement frizzled through her. Lily could help make her quota. It was perfect. "No one is interested in opening a fudge shop. You could move right into the space your family already occupies—and we could throw in a house for a dollar. Give your two weeks' notice down in Florida and be here and ready to go by mid-July."

Lily's face twisted into a grimace. "I don't think so, Mia. I'm too addicted to the Florida sunshine."

"That's not a good reason."

"I know." Lily twisted a piece of wavy hair. "I just . . . I've got a good thing going there."

"A good thing? I thought your boss was an egomaniac who worked you hard without any recognition." Mia raised a brow. "Or so Cody says."

Lily laughed, something strained in it. "That's the candy business." But despite her words, the way she was looking at the cute pop-out shop windows, and the white siding and the porch, at the green roof on the old two-story building . . . well, she clearly wasn't as indifferent to the pull of the past as she pretended to be.

And Mia wasn't above begging at this point.

Because she needed at least two more people to meet her quota. It would be the icing on the cake if one of those people was Lily. Or maybe the crumbled cookie on top of the fudge. Or something. Mia wasn't good at metaphors.

"Just come inside the fudge shop and look at it." She hurried to the front door then waited for Lily to catch up. Her friend walked like she waded through a vat of cookie-topped fudge.

"Mia, I really don't want to go in." Lily shook her head

slowly. "I don't think running my own business is a smart choice for me right now." She paused. "Maybe ever."

Okay, that sounded like a conversation for another day. She'd let Lily off this time.

Mia released a sigh. "Sorry. I'll stop pressuring you." She led the way back out to the wagon waiting in the morning sunshine. "I confess I have a reason for being so pushy."

"Oh?"

She gripped the handle of the wagon, knuckles white. "I'm afraid I'm not going to meet my quota." Lily knew all about the project, both from Mia herself and from Cody.

"I'm so sorry, Mia. I wish I could help."

"Well, you could move home . . ." Mia held up a hand to ward off Lily's protest. "Sorry, terrible joke. Seriously though, if you hear of anyone who wants to relocate to a beautiful island in the Midwest, send them my way."

She still didn't understand why people weren't flocking to the island. Sure, it was remote, and you had to take the ferry to get to the nearest Target, but the quiet surroundings, the lovely state park, and the community more than made up for it.

She looked around at the little shops surrounding them on Main Street. Some days, her fingers itched to really bring back the full charm of this place she loved. The town had done a great job of cleaning up a bit in preparation for the meeting, but Mia had seen this town before the fire and the pandemic. She knew how amazing it could be.

They walked past the storefront Mia had earmarked for Matt's art studio.

"Why don't you take one?" Lily pointed at the empty

gallery. "You probably have enough art stashed at your parents' house to fill that place."

Something tugged deep in her gut. A gallery of her own . . . Except. "There's no way I can manage a gallery. My kids take too much attention."

"Can't your family help with the kids? Or there's always daycare."

"My mom already is helping Evie a lot. And Troy's mom has moved her mother into her house for the foreseeable future. Not an option. Also, daycare? I don't think this island is big enough for that." A heaviness in her stomach threatened tears. "No, I need something that is more flexible. If we can get more people on island, I'm thinking of focusing on real estate again. I need to be practical."

"Fair enough. But I'd hate to see you give up your art entirely." Lily gave Mia a searching look.

She turned away from the studio. "Cody said something similar to me the other day."

"Speaking of Cody, I saw your video."

Mia groaned. "You and thirty thousand of your friends."

Lily bumped her shoulder into Mia's "He still has that spark in his eye."

"What do you mean?" Mia's hands grew damp around the wagon handle.

"C'mon, Mia, you know Cody has always been interested in you."

"When we were younger." She thought back to their conversation. He'd said teenage crush, right?

"Yes, but also now. I don't think he ever stopped caring for you like that."

Her gaze whipped to Lily. "He told you that?"

"He didn't have to. I know my brother."

Mia looked at herself, reflected in the gallery window. Red top, khaki shorts, hair blowing in the wind. She remembered his words *like a water sprite.* Now she just looked like the overworked mother of two. "You're wrong. Once Troy and I got together, he only saw me as a friend. His little crush died." That's what Cody had said, right?

"First, it was never just a crush. He loved you." The sweet scent of the jasmine in the flower box floated over them. "And I don't think he ever stopped."

Loved her?

Oh, wow.

"Are you sure? He never said anything. Made a move, or anything." Mia wiped her hands on her khakis.

Lily shrugged. "He buried his feelings for you, but I can tell you he very much loved you. Now . . . if you let him . . ." She waved her hand in a circle.

Mia blinked rapidly. Cody loved her? Was it possible?

Lily bumped her shoulder against Mia's again. "What do ya think? Could you ever love him back?"

"No. Yes. Maybe?" Her thoughts tumbled as she tried to sort through them. "Lately . . ." She couldn't complete the thought. Didn't want to acknowledge that her feelings for Cody had been changing over the past weeks. And, yeah. She was scared to fall in love again. Scared to rely on someone else and then lose him.

She wrapped her hand tighter around the handle of the wagon. "I guess I'm just afraid of losing someone again."

Her voice was so low she wasn't sure Lily heard her, but then Lily laid an arm across her shoulders and squeezed.

"I get that. Taking a risk is scary. But look at you. You're already doing hard and scary things. Taking care of two children on your own … You're brave, Mia. And isn't love always worth the risk?" Lily squeezed again and then let her arm drop. "That's all I'll say for now. But promise you'll think about it."

"I will."

Their walk took them out of the downtown loop and into the small west side neighborhood where Cody's parents lived. The houses in the Driftwood Hills neighborhood were larger than hers on Lilac Lane, the owners all more well-to-do.

She pulled to a stop in front of the Hart home and said goodbye to Lily. Walking back downtown, she stopped in front of the old Sampson gallery and stared at it, eyes unfocused.

Could she be falling for Cody? She thought about how Evie had asked if she felt the same way about him as she felt about her brother. Nope. This was totally different then how she felt about Bash. But what was she going to do about it?

Twenty-four hours later and Cody still couldn't get Pastor Arnie's words out of his mind. *If we seek the Lord, He will deliver us from all our fears.*

Except his heart still raced when he thought about his

time on the water with Liam yesterday. Maybe he needed time to let that truth grow in his heart.

He walked down Main Street, hoping to catch Lily on her way from the ferry. And, let's face it, hoping to see Mia too. Talking to Mia this morning before running over to his parents' had ignited a slow burn in his belly. He tried tossing the water of truth on the embers, but no amount of truth like "she's not free" or "she's your best friend's girl" or "she's got too much on her plate to consider a relationship right now" would douse the flames that had been springing up lately.

Was fear holding him back in that area of his life too? He was tired of feeling that way. It was time to take a step forward with Mia.

As though called by his thoughts, a familiar frame, ponytail swinging, came walking toward him. Mia. Could she hear his heart beating from a hundred paces away?

"You missed Lily," Mia called to him as she approached. "I just dropped her off at your parents' place."

"Shoot! I was hoping to catch her before she got out there." He wanted to talk to Lily about this new resolve to pursue Mia. But now that she was in front of him, he wouldn't wait to spend more time with her. "I needed a second pair of hands to hang some shelves. I don't suppose you have time to help me?" Cody hooked his thumbs on his jean pockets. Maybe that would stop his hands from constantly reaching for Mia.

She took a quick look at her cell phone. "No SOS message yet," she said. "I can probably give you an hour or so.

Evie has the kids this morning, and she planned to keep them until lunchtime."

"Thanks. I really appreciate it." He led the way into a nearby building. The small, twenty-foot by twenty-foot interior formerly housed a shop selling anything related to butterflies.

"How about a trade?" Mia's eyes sparkled. "Jemma Swanson, you know, the glassblower? Anyway, her application was accepted, and she's already been assigned a house. She won't be able to make it to the in-person meeting, but everyone liked her so much we fast tracked her approval. She's having some equipment delivered in a few days, and I said I would take the delivery. But today, Jemma emailed me what to expect to receive and it's several very large boxes."

"Okay . . ." He led her through the storefront to where the shelves needed to be hung. He'd already refinished the wood floor, and a smell of linseed hung in the air. He didn't know which business had been assigned here, but Dani had requested he hang shelves along the far wall. "And?"

Mia spun in a circle. "I cannot get over how you've made these businesses come to life again. You have a real talent. Anyway . . ." She turned to face him again. "Would you come and help me move the boxes? I don't think I can do it alone."

Moving without thought, he stuck his hand out. "It's a deal." When she took his hand to shake it, the zing racing up his arm landed solidly in his heart. Yep. He should've kept it to himself. "Uh, the stuff is over here."

They walked to the wall, and he made sure to be a step away from her, avoiding contact.

"I've already marked where the boards will need to go." He picked one up and held it in place. "If you hold it, I can put the hardware in."

"Got it." She placed her hands near his. "What did you do yesterday?" She moved closer to mirror his grasp on the board.

His hands shook, and he gripped the board more tightly to keep them from slipping. "I actually took my speedboat out."

"Sounds like fun."

"You got this?" She nodded and he let go of the board. "Fun is not the word I would use." He kept his tone neutral.

"Oh? What then?"

"It was just something I needed to do. It's been a long time coming." Hefting the screw gun in his hands, he lined up the hardware and drove it in.

"Wait, you haven't been out there at all in two years?"

He bit back a sigh. "Nope. Just the ferry once or twice." She didn't need to know that those times he'd had to ride inside the cabin of the ship, not able to have the wind whip against his face.

"Then I'm proud of you for getting out there. A real hero." Mia's eyes shone. Were those tears?

He hadn't felt like a hero. "You wouldn't have been proud if you saw me."

"I'm proud of you for reclaiming something you always

loved." Mia's gaze moved back to the shelf she still held. "I look forward to hearing about the next time you go out."

"Maybe you should come with me sometime." Where did that come from? Nothing like inviting the girl you maybe kinda couldn't get over to witness your breakdown.

"Maybe." She lifted one shoulder, let it drop.

He drove in another screw, gave that side of the shelf a wiggle. It held steady.

"It felt weird being out there without Troy." He moved to the other side of the shelf and put his hand next to Mia's. "You can let go now." She ducked under his arm as he finished securing that side.

"Being out on the water was his happy place. Fishing with you made him happy. You two were better together." Mia crossed her arms. "Troy would be proud that you got back out there. Honestly, I haven't been out on the water either. I used to love fishing, but now I come down with the shakes when I think about being in a boat."

"Look, I'm not one to talk, but I think you also need to get back out there. You can't let his death steal this from you too." He turned to her, searching her eyes. Shoot. The tears were back.

"You're right. I miss the water. And I don't want to teach my children to be afraid of it. I don't want them to be afraid of anything." She dashed a hand over her cheeks.

"Mia, listen to me. You are the bravest person I know. You could never teach them to be afraid." He chuckled. "Though, a little healthy fear might be good for Finn. He can take things too far sometimes. Seriously though, you're a great mom."

"Thank you." She looked up at him, cheeks flushed. "Thank you for always encouraging me. For being there for me these last two years—almost our whole lives, really, and for seeing me when others didn't. You're so good to me."

His mouth went dry at her gratitude. "Mia . . ." This was an opportunity—to affirm their friendship.

Or take the plunge.

Cody swallowed. "I don't do those things because I'm kind. I do them because . . ."

"Because what?" Her right hand rose and rested on his bicep. Fire shot through his arm and into his heart.

His eyes flicked to her lips then back to her eyes. Her gaze was steady on him.

Here went nothing. He'd either sink . . . or swim. "Because I care about you."

She inhaled sharply, tipping her head up and coming an inch closer. "I know. You're a good friend."

"No, Mia." He closed the gap between them, hooking an arm around her waist. "Because I care about you. Not just as a friend. As a woman." Cody lifted his hand and brushed his fingertips against the soft skin of Mia's cheek. She shivered beneath his touch—and it was heady, the way she melted into him. "A beautiful woman."

"Cody." The ragged bent to her voice sent a flash of yearning through him.

His gaze took in the high color in her cheeks before dropping to her mouth. He looked back up to meet her eyes and she gave a slight nod.

He lowered his head and claimed her lips, soft and

pressing. Her grip on his bicep tightened and she deepened their kiss. Fifteen years of longing poured out of his soul and into her embrace. He pulled her tighter, wrapping the other arm around her.

Being with Mia was coming home. He never wanted to let her go.

Cody rocked on his feet and knocked over the drill. The clatter shocked him, and he pulled away.

He breathed hard, a grin splitting his face. But Mia's wide eyes and the way she put a hand to her mouth . . .

"Mia, I am so sorry. I mean, not sorry for kissing you, but for coming on too strong. Was that too much?" His heart thundered. The last thing he wanted was for her to think he was anything like Matt.

"No. I wanted it too." Mia touched her lips. "But maybe we should slow down. I'm sorry. I just need more time."

"I'm okay with that. I don't want to push you. I'm not going anywhere." He started putting away his tools.

She stretched out a hand to him. "I thought we had more shelves to hang up."

"I'll finish it later." He had to get away. Had to put some space between them before he did something crazy like taking her back into his arms and kissing her until they both forgot Troy ever existed.

"Oh. Um. Okay. I should probably pick up the kids anyway." Mia brushed a hair away from her face. She turned to go through the door. The next few minutes flashed in front of his eyes. She would leave, and he would have screwed up their whole relationship.

"Wait." He reached for her but dropped his hand before

it connected with her shoulder. Too much temptation if he made contact. Her gaze pierced him. "Are we okay?"

"Yeah, we're okay." She left without another word.

He meant what he said. He wasn't going anywhere. He just needed to give her time to see that he was the right guy for her.

Eleven

AT LEAST IT LOOKED LIKE THE WEATHER was going to cooperate. The past few days had gone by in a blur of preparations and last-minute arrangements for the in-person meeting with the possible new business owners today.

She didn't have the luxury to think about the kiss with Cody or what it meant. He'd reached out a few times, but she hadn't had much time to do more than send a quick text response. He stood near her on the dock. His navy Jonathon Island T-shirt highlighting his eyes. Her gaze drifted to him again. That shirt was working for his muscles too.

Stop it! Focus!

Mia tucked her hands into her jacket pockets. No reason to let anyone see them trembling.

Lord, help me today!

The ferry pulled up to the dock a few feet from where

she stood with her dad, Dani, Cody, and Tara Chamberlain, a "welcome to Jonathon Island committee" of sorts. Mia had dropped off Finn and Maggie with her mom earlier, grateful that she didn't have to keep track of them while also doing this part of her job. The stakes of impressing everyone were high enough without Maggie wandering off or Finn falling into the water.

Earlier, her dad had greeted her with an awkward hug. All these years later and she still didn't know how to behave around him. Maybe Evie was right, and she needed to sit down and talk things through.

Too bad there wouldn't be time for that anytime soon. But once her mortgage was paid off . . . maybe then she could figure out the rest of her life.

Cody included.

Focus, girl.

She and Dani had haggled about how many to invite to this meet and greet. They'd only wanted finalists from the interviews. She'd argued that inviting more guests than they needed to fill the spaces made the most sense. After some pushback, Dani had agreed. Already two had canceled, citing arrangements to bring their businesses elsewhere. The remaining thirteen meant they had an extra, which felt tight to Mia, but doable.

The ferry boat captain laid on his horn as the boat pulled into its slip. A few moments later, passengers began filing down the gangway. She recognized a few of them from the video chats they'd held over the past week. There was Mr. and Mrs. Olson, dressed in a fedora and a cloche hat respectively. Mr. Olson even sported a bow tie, and were those spats? With Mrs. Olson's red wool jacket, they looked more like a couple who wanted to start an antique shop than a pizzeria. But she knew the next couple off the boat, the Millers, were the antiques dealers. She'd pegged them at around mid-fifties, both dressed casually in jeans and sweatshirts. A man in a kilt walked down next.

Huh. She'd seen this guy's social media profile. He was another artist, and he'd been in a kilt in some of his photos. Who knew that it would be an everyday type of outfit?

Matt came next. The sight of someone she could rely on unknotted one of the ropes currently restricting her breathing.

One woman shoved her way forward before leaning over the guard rail and retching into the bay. Mia ran to her side to assist her. She recognized her as Ms. DeVoe, a woman who sold specialty clothing.

"I'm sorry." The woman wiped her mouth with the tissue Mia tucked into her hand. "I've never traveled by boat before. Is it always that choppy? I thought I was on a roller coaster."

"Ms. De Voe, right?" Ms. De Voe nodded, lips tight. Mia looked out over the water. Today it lay smooth and calm. The sun beamed down on them from its place in the noon sky. "I'm sorry it didn't agree with you. Can I get you something to calm your stomach? We will be walking to the Tourist Bureau in a moment, and there will be refreshments there."

Ms. De Voe waved her off. "I'll just get some water when we arrive. Standing on solid ground is helping." She moved a few paces off and bent at the waist, putting her hands on her knees.

Mia shrugged. Not much else she could do right now. One situation at a time. She greeted the rest of the guests as best she could before stepping onto a bench and clapping her hands three times like a tour guide.

"Welcome to Jonathon Island, everyone. I'm so glad you could make it." She glanced around the group as they all quieted down. Cody caught her eye and gave her a thumbs up. A flush stole across her back. Biting her cheek to hold back her smile, she continued. "We'll be starting our day off by taking a short walk to the Tourism Bureau, where we can get some refreshments and get to know one another better. We'll also have a question and answer session. Then we'll move on to a tour of town. Anyone interested in taking a look at some of the houses will have an opportunity to do that as well. Any questions?"

When there were none, Mia climbed off the bench and began walking toward the Tourism Bureau, the group falling in behind and around her.

She found herself walking next to an older, bald man dressed in jeans, cowboy boots, and a leather jacket. "Too bad we have to walk," he said. "My Harley would love to eat up this road."

"Mr. Somerton, right?" He nodded and she shook his hand. "Nice to meet you. You have a motorcycle?"

"Yes, ma'am. She's my baby. I had her custom made then picked her up in Milwaukee myself." He pulled out his phone. Was he seriously going to show her photos of his motorcycle? Yep. That's exactly what he was doing.

His lock screen was a picture of him astride a very large machine—Mia had no idea what to call the behemoth. Then he swiped open his photo app, and for the next four hundred and thirty-seven seconds, he showed her approximately four hundred and thirty-six pictures of a red, white, and blue Harley-Davidson motorcycle. Mia mmm'd and ahh'd through the lot. Hopefully, Mr. Somerton didn't notice she was less than enthusiastic about them by the second hundred.

"You do remember the rule about motor vehicles, right?" She finally broke in.

He waved a hand as though swatting a gnat. "Merely a formality."

"It's not—" But he didn't let her finish as he turned away to show Ms. DeVoe his photos.

"Isn't she a beaut?" Mia heard him ask before they were lost in the group.

Finally, they reached the building housing Dani's office, the Tourism Bureau, and a small museum highlighting local history. Mia led them into the museum, the biggest space in the building.

"Everyone, please help yourself to the snacks and drinks. We'll start with the question and answer time in just a few minutes." The room filled with noisy chatter as Mia pulled Dani toward the front of the room. "Everything going okay on your end?"

"I'm nervous, is that weird?" Dani clutched her hands together.

"Not weird at all." Mia put her arm around Dani. "This whole thing was your idea. Of course you want it to succeed. Don't worry, you'll do great, cuz." She squeezed Dani's shoulder and gave her a smile. After a beat, Dani smiled back.

"Okay. We got this," Dani said. "Let's get this show on the road."

Once again, Mia clapped her hands, calling for attention. "Huddle up, everyone. Feel free to bring your drinks and snacks to the chairs."

The Jonathon Island Welcoming Committee moved behind a small podium amid the general squeaking of chair legs against the tile floor as the group got situated.

Her dad stepped to the mic mounted on the podium. Despite their differences, Mia couldn't help being impressed with the way her father commanded the room. "It has been a privilege to welcome each of you to our island. Thank you for taking the time to apply for our newly minted program and for your interest in becoming year-round citizens. I know each of you will love living here as much as I do. I've loved raising a family here." He cut his eyes to Mia, an unreadable expression in his gaze. "And I'm loving watching my grandkids grow up here too." He moved back as Dani stepped to the mic.

"We've been in touch with each of you and answered many questions, but I'm sure there are many more out there. Especially now that you've gotten a chance to get a taste of the town. All of us are available to answer, so fire away."

Mr. Somerton lumbered to his feet. "Is it true that I can't bring my Harley to the island?"

"Yes, that's true." Dani gripped the sides of the podium, her knuckles whitening.

"What am I supposed to do with her, then?"

"Most people rent a space on the mainland for any vehicles they own. Except boats, of course."

"Is there some sort of appeal process?"

"No. This has been a law for a hundred years." Dani bit off her words like she was snipping a piece of string.

"I didn't buy a fancy machine just to be separated from her for most of the year." Mr. Somerton crossed his beefy arms. "The town council will be hearing from me. I bet I can sweet-talk them into letting me bring my girl."

Her dad stepped back to the mic. "Mr. Somerton, I'm the mayor here. I can tell you right now that there will be no exception made for your Harley-Davidson. I'm sorry."

"I mentioned it in all that paperwork. That gal there," he nodded toward Mia, "she knew I had a Harley."

A pain stabbed Mia's gut. Had she told Mr. Somerton he could bring his motorcycle? She thought fast about their conversation. Nothing sprang to mind.

Her dad gave her a side-long look, and she returned it with a wide-eyed shake of her head. She hadn't made any promises.

Besides, there had been other members of the council there. They would all have remembered something like that.

Her dad leaned an arm on the podium. "I don't know what you think you were promised, Mr. Somerton, and I'm sorry you were under the wrong impression, but we won't be able to make any exceptions."

Mr. Somerton's chair clanked in protest as he dropped back into it. "I'm out." His voice rang clear over the gathering.

Mia winced. Hopefully his stormy look wasn't contagious.

After a few more benign questions, the Q&A ended on a more positive note. Mia found herself by the drinks table. A few empty water bottles rested there, and the cans of pop had been decimated. She straightened a few up and tossed out the empty bottles.

"What a meeting that was," Mr. Miller said. The antiques dealers were the only ones who hadn't spoken up in the meeting. Instead, they had spent the whole of it alternating between jotting down notes and smiling encouragingly at each speaker.

Hopefully her wry smile came off as genuine and not sarcastic. "It certainly could have gone better."

"Don't let that man get to you." Mrs. Miller put her hand on Mia's arm. The warmth comforted a few of her jumpy nerves. "I think this plan is lovely. And it's helping us to fulfill our dreams."

Mr. and Mrs. Miller shared a long look. "We came to the Grand Hotel on our honeymoon thirty years ago," Mr. Miller said. "We fell in love with the island and promised each other we'd move here someday."

"Our life took a lot of twists and turns," Mrs. Miller said. "But now the last of our five children is away at college, and we wanted to explore moving our empty nest to the place we'd always dreamed about living."

Mia felt an unexpected pricking at the backs of her eyes. "What a beautiful way to live your life."

"Is there such a thing as a holy coincidence?" Mr. Miller asked. "Because coming across your plea for new residents felt like the nudge we'd needed all these years. Thank you for helping us realize our dreams."

They both beamed at her expectantly. Mia's throat tightened, and she coughed in an attempt to clear it. "Uh, you're welcome," she said. "I'm glad you're so enthusiastic. It's going to take a boatload of that to pull this whole thing off."

"I'm sure everything will get figured out," Mr. Miller said. "All it takes is a shared goal where everyone pulls their weight. At least, that's how it's worked for us."

"That's right. Trust, mutual respect, and helping each other." Mrs. Miller looped her arm through her husband's. "That was our family motto. And when things got hard, we just held on to each other harder."

The image of a couple clinging to each other through a storm whispered a promise to Mia's heart. If they could make it, maybe she could take a chance too. Could she be courageous enough to pursue a relationship with Cody? Maybe try for a fairy-tale ending.

Near the door, Matt stood with the other artist who had arrived on the ferry. The two appeared to be in an intense conversation, the other man's face red and blotchy. Matt had his hands near his hips, clenching and unclenching them in a gesture Mia recognized from college. He was trying to keep himself from saying something rude.

Suddenly the other artist raised a hand and shook

his finger in Matt's face. "Fine, then." His roar echoed through the hall. "If you're not going to bow out, then I will. There is not room on this island for both of us!" The man stormed out the door, slamming it behind him. Was that guy for real?

Matt gave a helpless shrug to the roomful of people who stared at him. "Guess he can't handle competition." He raised his eyebrows in a "can you believe it?" expression. A few people chuckled before returning to their conversations.

Mia made her way over to where Dani stood. Her cousin held a clipboard and was jotting notes down.

"How many?" She leaned over Dani's shoulder and looked at the list.

"If these numbers are right, we're two short." Dani tapped the ones she'd crossed out.

Mia's whole body suddenly weighed a hundred pounds heavier. "Oh no. If I can't fill those last two spots in two weeks..."

Dani looked at her, eyes wide. "Can you call some of the people who were near the top of the list? There have to be more people interested."

She thought back over the stacks of applications, most of which were eliminated for one reason or another. "I hope so. Maybe I can even issue another call for applications. I'll figure it out."

She had to.

Cody stood next to his dock, hand on his hips. He

wouldn't let fear beat him. He shoved all thoughts of Mia and the kiss, and the brilliant way she'd handled herself at the meeting yesterday, into the far corner of his mind. Going back out on the water would take his full concentration.

"Ahoy there, Captain." Pastor Arnie walked up next to him on the shore. Cody recognized his polo shirt and boat shoes as his casual uniform. He put his hand on Cody's shoulder. "Are we ready to do this thing?"

No.

"Yes." Cody's stomach folded in on itself. "We can only go out for a short time; I promised Mia I would help her move something."

"I think that's probably a good idea anyway, just until you get a feel for things."

Cody had spent an hour in Pastor Arnie's study a few days ago talking over what had happened on the water last time with Liam. Arnie had agreed to go out in Cody's speedboat with him as soon as he was ready. The day after his kiss with Mia, he called and said he was ready.

Ready for a lot of things, actually. If Mia needed time, he'd give it to her. But eventually, they would be discussing that kiss.

Discussing what it meant—sooner or later.

Taking a few deep breaths, he made his way to the boat, Pastor Arnie close behind.

The day had dawned bright and clear, but he knew rain was in the forecast for later. Early summer in Michigan meant lots of rain. Shielding his eyes, he looked to the horizon. Dark clouds were building but were still a long way off. The air was still and the lake calm.

He stepped into the boat and it rocked slightly. Pastor Arnie stepped in and Cody handed him a life vest.

"These are mandatory on my boats now," he said.

"Understandable." The other man slipped it on over his green polo shirt.

Cody turned the key in the ignition. The loud rumble of the engine succeeded in drowning out his thoughts for a moment.

I can do this. This is fine.

"Pull in the rope, please." He pointed to the line tying them to the dock. Pastor Arnie did as he was asked, and Cody eased the boat into the open water.

"What's that verse again?" His fingers tingled.

"Psalm 34:4," Pastor Arnie said. "'I sought the Lord and he answered me and delivered me from all my fears.'"

As they made their way around the island, Cody's pulse spiked and his hands grew slick on the wheel.

"Okay, stop the boat and breathe with me." Arnie put a hand on Cody's shoulder. They floated for a few minutes, the boat rocking gently. "Nice and steady."

Cody concentrated on the man's soothing voice. Soon, his heart rate was back to normal and his sight had cleared.

"Thanks, Pastor."

"My pleasure." Arnie gestured to the bay. "Should we keep going?"

Cody started the boat again. After a few more moments of panic, Cody began to settle into the boat. When they'd been out an hour, he started having fun. He felt more like himself than he had in years.

"Let's turn back," he said. As they rounded the outcropping just before home, the engine sputtered and died. Cody bit back a curse. Why did bad things keep happening to him?

He opened the top of the outboard motor and poked around.

It was no use.

"What's the diagnosis?" Pastor Arnie stood over his shoulder.

"I'll have to take it back to the lab for an autopsy." Cody shot the pastor a smile.

"I'm glad you're able to joke about this. It shows real progress." Arnie smiled back.

Cody checked the time. He was going to be late for meeting Mia if they didn't hurry.

"Do you want the good news or the bad news?" He asked Arnie.

"What's the good news?" Arnie moved back to his seat in the bow.

"I have paddles on board." Cody went to the storage chest along the side of the boat and unsnapped its lid.

Arnie stood. "Okay, What's the bad news?"

Cody handed him a paddle. "We have to use them."

The two men stationed themselves on either side of the boat. They paddled hard. They made it about halfway back to their goal when a cold breeze whipped over them. The distant clouds weren't quite so distant anymore. Now, they covered the sun cooling the air.

Soon, the water began to churn, waves tossing the speedboat as they paddled.

"Harder," Cody said and both men doubled down on their efforts. Cody could see his dock achingly close.

He didn't have time for fear as they maneuvered the boat to the shore. He needed to get it in, tied off, and covered before the rain hit. They'd just bumped the side of the dock when the skies opened overhead.

"Tie her off," Cody called. "I'll hold us." He kept a grip on one of the dock cleats while Pastor Arnie tied off the line on the back of the boat. Then he tied the one on the front.

"Do you have a cover?" Rain streamed down Arnie's face.

"In the shop." Cody shed his life vest and stepped out of the boat. Both men hurried across the lawn to the shed. Inside, they dripped on the floor as Cody collected the boat cover. The pulsing of the pouring rain beat on the steel roof. He tossed Pastor Arnie his dad's rain slicker and put his own on.

"Thanks for coming with me today." He rested his hand on the doorknob, steeling himself for the onslaught of rain.

"My pleasure. I'll help you with the cover and then dash home," Pastor Arnie replied.

The two of them wrestled the canvas over the boat, securing it with the snaps made for that purpose.

Cody waved as Pastor Arnie took off toward home. A rumble of thunder ground through the sky.

Shoot. He was really late now.

Without stopping to change his clothes, Cody made his way downtown. Surely Mia would forgive him for being late when he told her about his progress.

Twelve

MIA DIDN'T KNOW WHAT TO DO WITH the emotions swirling through her. Cody's kiss had awakened something in her, something she had been denying for the past several weeks. She was falling for him.

If it was true what Lily said about Cody being in love with her, maybe it was time to jump in with both feet. She could trust Cody. He'd never let her down.

Dani was meeting with some of the prospective businesspeople who had stayed over after last night's meeting, leaving her free to follow through on that favor for Jemma, the glassblower. She bundled the kids against the cool wind and walked to Jemma's store. She paused at the door. The teal building boasted a mural along the side, featuring a lighthouse and the island shore. Inset along the bottom of the walls ran a double row of seashells. The fun and eclectic location would be perfect for Jemma and her glassblowing business. Mia imagined wind chimes hanging out front and colorful vases and other blown art in the window. Shaking her head at the whimsy, she unlocked the door. Finn and Maggie pushed past her and into the echoing space.

Outside, the sky hung gunmetal gray. She could smell rain in the air. Hopefully the delivery would come before the skies opened up.

This space was everything Jemma said she'd needed. The full wall of windowpanes let in plenty of light. Or they would when it wasn't overcast. The floors were poured concrete, speckled with a glittery epoxy. About two-thirds of the way back, a low wall partitioned off the back of the room. It would make a perfect workspace; customers could watch her at work while staying out of her way.

Mia decided to put the delivery boxes back there.

"Finn, Maggie, some boxes are being delivered. I need you to stay out of the way." She rummaged around in the backpack she'd brought, then handed Finn an iPad. "Here, I've loaded a couple of *Bluey* episodes on there."

She led them to a spot that would be out of the way. Soon, the cartoon sounds of the Australian dog family filled the room. She checked her phone. No messages. Not that she expected Cody to text her or anything. She looked around for a doorstop and spotted a small, wooden triangle near the entrance. That would come in handy for the delivery.

The low moan of the ferry's horn groaned through the building. The delivery would be here soon. Where was Cody? He was late. That wasn't the Cody she knew. Moving to the front window, she looked down the street. No familiar set of strong arms and quick smile. A few drops of rain hit the pavement.

She walked back and forth in front of the window.

A rumble preceded the arrival of an ATV pulling a trailer, boxes stacked high.

Two men jumped down. She recognized them as the freight delivery guys from the ferry service. The dark haired, tall one was Luke, and the shorter blond was Martin, maybe? They moved to the back of the cart and began unloading boxes. One of the boxes towered almost as tall and wide as an apartment-sized refrigerator, about her height and twice as wide. Perhaps that was the furnace Jemma had talked about.

"Hi, guys." She held the door open for them, then kicked the stop into place. "You can bring them straight in."

"Sorry, Mia. We can't do that," Luke said.

"What do you mean, can't?" Mia propped a fist on her hip.

"It's company policy to drop them off. We need to make all our deliveries before the ferry leaves again." The man gestured at the full cart behind him. All those boxes would take hours to deliver, even on this small island.

Where was Cody?

"Leave it here then, I guess. I'll drag it in."

The boxes hit the sidewalk with a thump. In less time than she'd thought possible, Luke and Martin moved off, leaving Mia alone on the sidewalk, surrounded by a dozen boxes of various sizes. Overhead, a crack of thunder warned of the coming storm.

She craned her neck into the building, checking on Finn and Maggie. They sat hunched over the iPad, its blue light reflecting on their faces, shading them in tones of cartoon. Her heart pinched, but she supposed another few minutes of children's programming wouldn't rot their brains too much. She just needed to get these boxes under shelter before the storm. A drop of rain hit her cheek.

Right. Double time.

Lifting a stack of the smallest boxes, she shouldered her way through the door and set them inside, out of the way.

She paused a moment to palm her cell phone, typed out a message to Cody. *Where are you? I could use some muscles.*

She blushed, backspaced the sentence and wrote:

Mia

I thought we said 10 a.m?

She would call him, but texting was faster. And speed was definitely needed. As she stepped outside for a second load, raindrops began pattering on the boxes. A smell of petrichor filled the air—that particular scent of ozone, and dust, and water, and wet cement in the first moments of rain. She closed her eyes briefly and inhaled deeply. Then opened them to see the boxes getting wetter by the second.

No time for whimsy. If she didn't focus on this work, some very expensive equipment might be ruined.

Another load of boxes later, there was still no text from Cody. Had something happened to him?

Her stomach clenched. She was alone. Always alone. Maybe she should call Dani to come and help.

Nah. If Dani wasn't at work, it would take longer for her to get here than for her to do it herself.

Above her, the skies opened up. Cold rain sliced into her, soaking through her jacket.

She stared at the last three boxes, hands on her hips. She would have to drag them into the store. She didn't have a two-wheeled dolly cart, and she sure couldn't lift them. Putting her arms around the shortest one, she grasped the handles cut into the cardboard. She pulled back and felt it move an inch.

Now the wet dog scent of damp cardboard was all she could smell. The box scraped against the sidewalk as she scooted it toward the store.

She looked to the side. The top of the other box darkened with rainwater.

Her progress was halted by the lip of the doorjamb. Bending at the knees, she tried to lift the box the two inches to clear the jamb. No joy.

"Looks like you could use a hand."

Her heart leaped, but the low rumbling voice did not belong to Cody. She peered around the box and found Matt standing on the other side. A sharp pain bit into her somewhere near her heart. Matt's square jaw, covered with the slightest amount of stubble, his piercing blue eyes and dark wavy hair should have made her heart pitter-patter. But all the rugged appeal in the world still didn't make him Cody.

Which wasn't quite fair to Matt, who'd never done anything wrong but be the wrong man. First, not Troy, and now, not Cody.

"Thanks. Cody said he'd be here, but . . ." She shrugged and gestured at the sidewalk, empty of anything except ginormous boxes and the growing puddles. "If you grab that handle, I'll take this one."

Moving slowly so the compromised cardboard wouldn't tear and drop the expensive cargo on the unrelenting concrete, they moved the box into the shop and to the left of the front door.

"We can leave that here for now," Mia said.

Another crack of lightning strobed the store, and the lights blinked out. In the corner, Maggie whimpered.

I know how you feel, little one.

But she couldn't show her fear to the kids. "One more box, kiddos, and then we can go home."

Moving faster now, she and Matt pulled the second and third boxes into the building.

"Should we take them to the back?" Matt reached out to the first box they'd dragged in.

"This is fine." Mia pushed at a stray hair. "These boxes are so wet, I'm afraid to move them any farther." A draft from the door whispered over her, and she shivered. She hugged her arms to herself.

"Let me." Matt came over and reached for her. A moment later, his strong hands moved over her upper arms, heating them.

She should tell him how she felt about him. She looked up into his warm eyes. There had been a time when they held such promise for her. But now? Nothing. He leaned toward her, angling his head.

Um, was he coming in for a kiss? No, this was all wrong.

His face inches from hers, she put a hand on his chest to push him away. He tightened his hold on her arms. She started to speak. "Matt—"

The door closed with a bang. Cody stood in front of it. His face stormy and his hair damp from the rain.

"Oh. Hi. Um, sorry to interrupt." His words scraped out like they'd been run over a piece of sandpaper.

"Cody. Hi." She sprang away from Matt but stumbled. His hand shot out to steady her. Cody's gaze bore into where he grasped her elbow.

"Thank you," she said to Matt then pulled her arm from his grasp. "Thanks for the help too. I couldn't have done it without you."

"I was happy to help. More than happy."

She still needed to let him down gently, but with Cody staring daggers into the man, now was hardly the time. Still, Mia didn't want to be rude. She smiled. "It's good to have a reliable friend like you around."

Cody coughed, but Mia stayed focused on Matt. She'd deal with Cody—and ask why he was late—once they were alone.

Matt's smile widened. "I'm here anytime, Mia. Anytime."

Looking between the two men, one thing became clear. Of the two of them, she'd rather have Cody.

But by the look on his face, he might not have her.

It's good to have a reliable friend around.

Cody was too late. To help with the boxes—and maybe to win Mia's heart too.

Again.

He turned away from Mia and Matt—the memory of the man's arms around her burned into his brain—and put his hand on the doorknob.

He wouldn't do anything to jeopardize Mia's happiness. And if that meant she wanted Matt, well, he'd stepped aside once before, he could do it again.

Except. *Fight for the girl.* Lily's words slipped into his mind, stilling his hand on the doorknob. What if . . .

He shifted back around again. Mia wasn't looking at Matt. She was looking at him. She'd stepped a generous step away from Matt too.

Maybe he'd stay.

Fight.

He and Mia had a conversation to finish.

He took in the surroundings, clocked the huge boxes scattered across the floor. No wonder she'd asked him to come. He checked the window. Yep, it was still raining harder than earlier.

Okay. He was convinced. He'd stick around a while longer. If he found out that Mia cared for Matt, he'd back off. Even if it killed him. Which, judging by the stabbing sensation going on in his ribcage, it just might.

"Cody!" Two small bundles bumped into his legs. The smile that crossed his face was immediate and involuntary. One of the worst parts of losing Mia, again, would be losing these two too. Swooping down, he scooped Finn into his right arm and Maggie into his left. No matter what happened with him and Mia, he vowed right then to be the best "uncle" these two could ever have. He owed that much to Troy.

"Hiya, guys," he said. He spun them in a circle, their giggles dulling the pain near his heart.

"You all wet." Maggie's giggles almost masked her words, but he had gotten good at toddler speak in the past few weeks.

"I was out in the rain." He set the kids down, his words for them, but he kept his eyes on Mia, an apology in them. "Out on my boat."

"Cool!" Finn propped his hands on his hips in a gesture Cody recognized as pure Mia. "My dad used to go on a boat."

"Then he died." Maggie punctuated her matter-of-fact tone with a nod.

Mia flinched and his gut tightened. "Kids—"

"No," she said. "It's okay. It's true. Troy used to go out on a boat, and he died." She hugged her arms to her chest. He saw Matt reach a hand to her, but she went to the kids and knelt between them. "But that doesn't mean we are scared of boats, right?"

"We are brave," Finn said. "Like Dad."

Mia hugged both kids.

Outside, thunder ripped through the air. Mia flinched and pulled the kids closer.

"Hey guys, you know what my dad used to tell me about thunder?" Three pale faces turned up to him. He reached for Maggie again, tucking her onto his hip. Then rested his hand on Finn's head. "He told me that the thunder was a mother sheep running around in the sky, protecting her lambs. Just like your mom always does for you." He met Mia's eyes. "So, the next time the thunder booms really loudly, you can just remember how much your mom loves you, even if sometimes she's really noisy about it." He winked at Mia. Maggie giggled.

Matt cleared his throat. "Okay. Well, I'll be taking off now. Unless you still need me, Mia?"

"No, I think I'm good. Thanks. I've got everything I need right here." Her gaze found Cody's, and his throat went dry. Mia stood and faced Matt again. "Are you sure you don't want to wait out the storm?"

"Nah." Matt checked his watch. "I have a call in a few minutes. I'll just make a dash for it. Cody." Matt stuck his hand out and Cody shook it. The other man tightened his grip, but Cody wasn't going to be intimidated. Matt let go first then turned to Mia. He gave her a brief hug and an air kiss. "See you later, Mia."

She waved him off with an indifference that almost had Cody doing a fist pump. "See ya, Matt."

A cold breeze washed over them as he walked out of the building, but the heat inside soon wiped it away. Finn and Maggie went back to playing on an iPad near the wall.

"I'm sorry I wasn't here to help." Cody motioned at the boxes. "This couldn't have been easy."

"I was grateful Matt showed up when he did." Mia put her hands on her hips before stretching out her back. "But I understand. Sounds like you had an eventful morning. And you showed up right on time. Matt was . . . being pushy."

Heat flared through him. If Matt had hurt Mia . . .

"I see that look in your eye." Mia reached out a hand and grabbed his wrist. A heat of a different sort ran up his arm. "It wasn't like that. He just wants more than I can give him. I was feeling a little cornered, and then you came and made me feel safe. You always make me feel safe, Cody." She started to say something more, but then her eyes hooded. She pulled her hand away and turned from him. "Tell me about your morning."

What? No. He wasn't going to let her off that easy. There had been something more, he was sure of it. If he was going to fight for her, it started now. "What aren't you saying?"

"Nothing."

"Stop. I know you. I've known you almost your whole life. I know when you're not telling me something."

"It's just that, I'm worried about how you make me feel." She kept her gaze on the ground.

"Um. Okay?"

"Being with you feels good, safe." A blush crept up her cheeks. "I like being with you. But I think I'm afraid to depend on anyone else because I've found out the hard way that life can be short. I relied too much on Troy, and now I'm struggling to provide for my kids. But with you . . . I want to depend on you. I just don't know how." She swept her hand toward the kids. "I need to be able to take care of us on my own. I realized that while I waited for you to show today." She glanced his way quickly then back to the ground.

"Look, Mia. I know you're not sure if you want more

than friendship with me—and I'll accept whatever you decide—but I need you to know something." He plowed right through her quick intake of breath. "First, I'm not going anywhere. And second, it's not good for you to try to do everything on your own. God made us to be dependent on each other."

"It just makes me feel so weak."

"Stop. It's not a weakness. In fact, it can be our greatest strength." Cody put a hand on her shoulder and waited until she met his eyes. "I know I didn't do a good job of showing up for you today, but I will always be here for you. You can trust me."

"My heart knows I can trust you. I'm just having a hard time convincing my head." She looked away for a second then back again. "I guess it's not just about trust. It's also about needing to prove that I can make good choices for myself. To prove to this island that I'm not just that pregnant teen. I'm not just a widow. I'm a survivor."

"You have nothing to prove." He ached to hold her closer, but that right wasn't his. Not yet. "You have two great kids, you're making a life for them. You're doing a great job. No one judges you for your past except you."

She sighed. "I guess. Maybe it's just that when I visit my parents, I feel the weight of Dad's judgment and project that onto the whole place."

"Hey, I may be way out of line here, and I shouldn't tell you what to believe, but I don't think your parents are judging you. Every time I talk to them, they are super proud of you and how you've handled yourself."

A spark lit her eyes. Anger? No, he didn't think so. But it wasn't joy either.

"You've been talking to my parents about me?" She raised one eyebrow.

"No. I mean, yes. I mean, when I'm talking to them and the subject of you comes up." Was she really going to make him flop around like a fish on the end of a line? At least she looked less ashamed.

"Relax, Code. I'm only teasing." Her face softened. "I guess I still don't know how to act when it comes to my parents. Especially my dad." She gave a little shrug. "Problem for another day."

From the front door, a beam of light crept across the floor. The clouds must have moved on, allowing the sun to shine through the pane of glass.

"You were wrong before," Mia said.

He put a hand to his chest in mock horror. "Who, me? What could I possibly have been wrong about?"

"I am sure about our friendship . . . and I don't want to be friends anymore."

The stabbing in his heart resumed as though it had never left. He took a step back. "Okay. I understand."

"No. Wait. You misunderstood me." Mia closed the gap. "I think I want to try being . . . more than friends." She tipped her face up to him. "But I'll need to take it slow. For myself, and for the kids."

He couldn't stop the grin creeping across his face, but he pulled himself back from swooping her into his arms and swinging her around and around.

Slow. He could do slow. He'd show her she could rely

on him, even if it took a hundred years. "We can take all the time you want. Will you go out with me tomorrow?"

She laughed. "I don't know if that is slow, but, yes, Cody. I will go out with you."

And right then, right there, were the words he'd been waiting his entire life to hear.

Thirteen

WHAT HAD SHE BEEN THINKING? Going out with Cody would be a huge mistake. They lived in a small town. People would see them, and they would talk. Mia reached for her cell phone sitting on top of her dresser. She'd just text him that the date was off.

"Knock, knock!" Dani called from the front of the house. When Mia had asked her cousin to babysit, she'd sworn her to secrecy. Dani had promised but couldn't quite eradicate the twinkle in her eye.

Mia heard Dani greet the kids, who were watching an episode of *Sesame Street* on YouTube, before coming down the short hallway. Dani rapped a knuckle on the open doorway. "Can I come in?" Without waiting for an answer, Dani moved into the room. "What are you wearing?"

Mia glanced down at her cutoff shorts and graphic tee. "What's wrong with what I'm wearing?"

"Everything."

"It doesn't matter. I'm not going anyway." She looked down at her phone, trying to summon the right words for her Dear John text message.

Dani put a hand to her hip. "You most certainly are going." She dropped her hand and strode to Mia's closet. After riffling through it for a minute, she tugged out a yellow and blue floral sundress and shoved it at Mia. "You can never go wrong with a sundress."

Mia splayed a hand over her churning stomach. "But what if people talk?"

"Let them!" Dani tossed the dress on the bed then began rummaging through Mia's shoes. Grabbing a pair of white sandals, she pointed them at Mia. "Look. No one is going to judge you for going out on a date. Your husband has been gone for two years. And, even if they do, let them! You aren't doing anything wrong or sinful. Just enjoying an evening with a man. You need to let go of what other people think of you and cling to what God says about you." Dani placed the shoes on the floor next to the bed. "You are forgiven. You are loved." She speared Mia with a look. "But we both know that's not the real problem here."

Maybe Dani knew her a little too well. "Fine. You're right. I'm also a little scared of falling in love again." Just the thought made her queasy.

"And I get that. But life without love is no life at all." Dani gave her a hug. "Now get this dress on and wow the socks off your man."

"He's not—" But Dani had already left the room.

Constance, Lily, and now Dani had basically all said the same thing. Love is worth a risk. Mia took a few deep breaths and then slipped into the sundress. She had just finished tying a ribbon around her hair when she heard Cody at the door.

"Cody!" Finn's voice echoed down the short hallway.

"Hey, buddy." The thrill of Cody's voice went straight through her and down to her toes.

She walked out to the group in front of the door. Cody straightened and gave her a long look.

A smile worked its way across her lips. The sound of the kids' chatter faded away as she took in his red button-down shirt, gray slacks, and boat shoes. His strong jaw and intense eyes made a devastating combo. Why did she want to cancel again?

A few minutes later they were on their way.

Cody led her straight to the front of the old Hansons' house.

"Did you need to check on something here?" She motioned to the house.

Cody reached for the doorknob but paused before opening the door. "I hope this is okay. I know you wanted to move slow, and I figured that meant not alerting the whole island to us being out on a date, so I set up a spot for us here."

The tension in Mia's gut uncoiled. "Thank you, Cody. This means a lot."

On the floor of what used to be the Hansons' living room, in front of the new fireplace, he had laid out a blanket. A lamp stood nearby, alongside a cooler and an insulated bag. A small portable speaker was playing soft music.

"I stopped by Kelley's right before coming over and picked up some burgers. I don't think they should be soggy." Cody led the way to the blanket. Mia sat as he began doling out the food. He flipped on the fireplace before settling next to her.

Mia searched for a topic to talk about. *Come on. This is Cody.* Where did this shy streak come from? "What's the update on overhauling your boat engine? Did you get it running?"

"I finally found the part I needed, but I'm still negotiating the price." He fiddled with his fork.

She took a deep breath, blew it out. "You look nice tonight." Cody's russet red shirt accentuated his strong shoulders, and he must have gotten a haircut. It looked good on him.

"Thanks, you do too. Look nice, I mean. Beautiful, actually." His eyes traveled over her in a slow appraisal. "How was your day?"

"What did you do today?"

Their voices jumbled over each other as they spoke at the same time.

Mia laughed. "I don't know why I'm so nervous. We see each other all the time. We talk all the time."

Cody leaned forward. "Look. We don't have to feel pressured here. Our relationship isn't dependent on tonight's date. We can just enjoy the food. We don't even have to talk." He took a big bite of his burger. A dollop of ketchup oozed out the back of the bun and plopped onto his shirt.

Mia couldn't tamp down the giggles. "Good thing you're wearing that color." She reached over and dabbed the spot away with her napkin.

He caught her eye. "Uh, Mia, you don't have to do that. I can get my own spills."

She felt her face flame and dropped back onto her side of the blanket. "Sorry. Hazard of being a mom."

He winked at her. "Not that I mind having your hand on my chest."

Her cheeks heated again, and she bit into a fry, the salty treat exploding with flavor. "What's something you've never told anyone?"

He choked on his drink. "What?"

"It's just that we know each other so well, I'm not even sure how this is supposed to work. I thought maybe we could take turns asking questions."

"Okay by me."

"Sooo . . . what's something you've never told anyone?" She ate another fry.

A strange look passed over Cody's face. But then it cleared, and he said, "I don't like fudge that much."

"Cody! Your family owned the fudge store!"

He shrugged before shoveling a handful of fries into his mouth.

She pointed at him. "Don't think you're getting away with making that statement and not following up. I'll wait for you to swallow." She crossed her arms and sat back. He took a long drink of water, and she raised her eyebrow at him.

"Fine." He grinned at her and set the cup down. "I never told anyone in my family, and you are totally sworn to secrecy, but I would pick fruity candy over chocolate any day. Maybe it was a byproduct of always having fudge around. Give me Skittles." He pointed at her with a french fry. "You cannot tell my mom. Or Lily. Or anyone."

She mimed zipping her lips and then threw the key over her shoulder. "Your secret is safe with me. Hey, remember Gushers?"

"I haven't thought about those candies for a long time."

"I used to love those things. Like an explosion in your mouth when you bit down. I don't think Doug's sells them anymore." Huh, when had that happened? It was like a bit of her childhood had disappeared without her noticing.

"Too bad. I bet Finn would love them too." He crossed his arms and gave her a long look. "Tell me about a time you felt unsafe."

That was a loaded question. She looked around the plain white walls of the living room as she thought back. "Do you remember our trip to Washington DC in eighth grade?"

"The one we had to sell chocolate bars door to door to raise enough money to go? Of course." He fake shuddered.

She kept her gaze on her plate. "And we had to pair up with two other kids—our trip buddies?"

"I wish they'd let us choose our partners. You, me, and Troy would have had a blast together. Instead, I had to hang out with Lily and one of her friends." He rolled his eyes.

"I got stuck with two ninth graders. We got separated and I got lost. I ran around trying to find them, but I finally had to figure it out by myself." She paused. "Anyway, I took care of myself and found an adult. They had a cell phone, but as they were calling our group leader, I spotted your neon green backpack."

He popped a fry into his mouth. "I don't remember this at all."

"That's probably because you only had eyes for Lisa Miller." She took a big bite of her burger.

"I never—"

She held up a hand. "Don't deny it. You picked her as your lab partner every time." The music changed to a rock ballad.

"Only because you and Troy always picked each other." He pointed a fry at her.

"Only because the teachers would never let us have three in a group." She countered.

"What happened to the ninth graders?"

"They denied that they had ditched me. Said it was my fault." She shrugged.

"I'm sorry that happened."

"It was a long time ago. Anyway, I'm glad you had such a bright backpack." Huh. She hadn't remembered that before. Cody had always been there for her even when he hadn't meant to be. It was just how their relationship had always been.

And she'd taken it for granted. Taken *him* for granted.

Cody stood. "Wanna take a walk? I have a surprise for you."

"Oh! I love surprises." He held out a hand and helped her up, his palm warming her fingers.

Cody led her out through a door in the kitchen to the backyard. Outside, Mia threaded her arm through Cody's. The sun was sinking in the sky, painting the scattered clouds pink and golden.

Mia gasped. Set up in the backyard were two makeshift easels with a posterboard on each. She looked up to see Cody smiling at her.

"I thought we could do some painting," he said. "I know these aren't high quality supplies, but they were the best I could do on short notice—they didn't have much selection at Doug's Market."

"This is amazing, Cody. Thank you." A warmth spread through Mia. "Look at how the sunset is making that birch tree look like it's lit from inside."

"Lead the way, Madame Monet. Let's get that tree on paper."

Maybe her friends were right. Being with Cody was worth the risk.

Cody put his hand over Mia's tucked into his elbow. He never wanted this night to end.

He let go of Mia when they reached the easels.

"So, did you ever kiss her?" Mia picked up a yellow paint pot and uncapped it.

"Kiss who?" He opened the blue pot.

"Lisa Miller."

"Are you still on that? No, I never kissed Lisa Miller. Didn't her family move away after that trip?"

A frown line had developed between her eyebrows as she concentrated on making a few strokes with her paintbrush. "Who was your first kiss, then? I can't believe I don't know this already."

"I don't think I like this game anymore," he growled.

She laughed. "Too bad. You agreed to play. And it was my turn to ask a question."

Did she really not know? "You."

She stood up straight. "What?" She searched his face.

"I know you want to move slow, and I respect that, but Mia, you should know that I've never kissed anyone but you." He met her gaze. Her mouth opened into an O. He wanted to kiss it shut but held back.

"Well. That's unexpected. I know you dated a few girls." She held her paintbrush aloft and a yellow drip fell onto the grass.

"I didn't want to kiss anyone until I was sure of the relationship. Our school and this island are so small, it would have gotten awkward fast if I dated around." May as well jump in with both feet. "Plus, none of them were you." Sure, he'd tried to date other girls, but gave up after high school. It wasn't fair to keep comparing them to Mia.

He looked at her painting. Somehow, even while using the goopy grocery store paint, she'd managed to create something amazing.

Overhead, the sky darkened to a velvety navy and the stars began to twinkle.

"Code. I don't know what to say."

"You don't have to say anything at all." He looked deep into her eyes for a heartbeat then shifted to look at her painting again. "How did you get your painting to look like that? Mine looks like a four-year-old did it."

Mia leaned over to inspect his work. "I have bad news for you. I think Finn can do it better than that. Let's call it impressionism."

"Want to sit out here for a minute? I can run in and grab the blanket." At her nod, he headed inside and picked up the blanket. When he got back outside, she'd cleaned up the paints, but she must have taken a minute to add a little to his painting, because instead of a blob of yellow, green, and purple paint, it looked incredible. "You made that mess look like a masterpiece. Mia Franklin, you are a marvel. You keep making things better in my life."

She smiled up at him. "You had the right idea. I just tweaked it a little." She shivered.

"Let's sit." He laid a portion of the blanket on the ground, and after they sat, he wrapped the top part around their shoulders. "Is that better?"

"Yes. Thanks." She nudged him with her shoulder. "I think it's your turn for a question."

In the low grass around the edge of the yard, lightning bugs winked at them.

"What's something from your childhood you wish you could have back?"

She went silent. Then, "My relationship with my dad. I used to be his shadow. He was the first person to let me use a paintbrush." She laughed. "Granted, it was to help him paint the porch, but still. Then Nora came, and things changed. I love Nora, of course, but being the middle child is nothing like being the baby. Then of course, everything with Troy and Finn . . ." She raised one shoulder then let it drop. "That sounds really self-centered. Wanting all of my dad's attention."

"No. I know it's not about that. I get it. Losing things you love is hard. I know that too well." May as well admit the rest. "I always lose what I love."

"What makes you say that?"

"Because it's true." He braced an arm behind her. "Do you remember my puppy, Cheezit?"

"A little. You only had him for a short time, right?" Crossing her slim legs in front of her, she leaned against him, settling in.

He picked up her hand and laced his fingers with hers. "I had begged Dad for a dog for years. Finally, he brought home Cheezit." He could still recall the joy of that day. The squirming puppy in his arms.

"I don't think I like the direction this story is going." Mia shuddered.

"Yeah, it's not a happy one." He gathered his thoughts. "I had promised to walk Cheezit every day, and I kept my word."

"I remember how smart he was. You taught him tricks, right?" She snuggled in tighter.

A shooting star raced over the sky, he pointed to it.

"Make a wish," Mia said.

Why would he? He had everything he needed right here.

"Better finish your story." Mia poked him in the side. "It will be good. Catharsis."

"You already know sort of where this is going. One day I walked Cheezit, and I put him in the backyard, but I didn't latch the gate." Cody swallowed hard. "I ran inside to watch some show I didn't want to miss, and Cheezit got out. It wasn't until bedtime that I realized he was even missing. We looked for him for several hours but didn't find him."

Mia was stroking his knuckles now. "I remember how frantic you were. You even came to our house way out on the tip of the island."

"A few months later I saw a dog that looked like Cheezit walking with someone else. I tried calling to him, but he wouldn't come." A lump grew in his throat, but he swallowed it away. "I ran up to the man he was with and tried to explain that Cheezit was my dog. The man said he'd found *his* dog badly injured and had cared for him since then."

"Oh, Cody." Mia rested her head on his shoulder.

"My dad said that losing Cheezit was typical of me. And that I always lost important things. My mom tried to tell him that I was only a child, but he said I couldn't be trusted with anything important."

"What a terrible thing to say to a child."

He squeezed her shoulder. "I suppose. And he probably was speaking in the heat of the moment. But he wasn't wrong. I do lose everything that is important to me. Cheezit was a little thing compared to the loss of Troy and now, maybe, the fishing business."

"Okay, but loss is a part of life. You've got your focus

wrong. Instead of always looking at the things you've lost, fight for the good things you've gained."

Seemed like everyone in his life was telling him something similar lately. "I can do that."

"Besides," she tipped her face up to him, "you haven't lost me."

Her skin looked like porcelain in the moonlight, and he noticed a few freckles sprinkled across her nose.

Darn that promise to go slow.

He dropped a kiss onto her forehead. "I'll take that good thing any day."

And Mia was right. He'd done far too much focusing on the bad things in his life. It was time to focus on the good.

Fourteen

MIA SHOULD HAVE BEEN THRILLED. She counted the applications on her lap. Never mind that she'd already counted them seven times already. They always added up to thirteen. Thirteen applications stamped with approval from the town council. Thirteen new businesses coming to Jonathon Island, new owners moving into abandoned houses, thirteen new reasons to woo tourists back.

A part of her was excited to see the town she loved come alive again. Except thirteen meant she was still short of her goal.

That morning, she'd gotten an oh-so-delightful text from Martha reminding her of the deadline and her commitment to filling all of the businesses they'd agreed on.

I'm not doubting you can do it. Just wanted to remind you.

Way to keep the pressure on.

The subdued noises of a library on a weekday morning surrounded her. Mia had met Evie here earlier and promised to watch Evie's kids during story time.

A roll of laughter rang out from the nook where several island kids gathered around Allean Meyer, the librarian. As usual, the short, slim woman wore a funny hat—one shaped like a giant teacup today—and sat in a chair the kids had dubbed "the reading throne." Once again, Mia shot a word of thanks heavenward that the public library stayed open year-round. Keeping two small children entertained without resorting to YouTube all the time proved to be a full-time task. Story time at the library became the highlight of their week.

She ran a thumb along the edge of the papers again. All her hard work from the past few weeks in a neat stack. She ought to be thrilled.

Except it wasn't good enough.

She needed one more business filled to keep her own from foreclosure. Her deadline, highlighted in red on her phone calendar app, was only a few days away. She'd gone through all of the eligible applicants, posted several new videos, and sent the information about the opportunity to any contact she could think of. But no one was interested in the last slot.

Another wave of laughter drifted her way, Finn's loudest in the crowd of under-fives. She wanted to put her fingers in her ears. Her chest grew tight at the thought of taking Finn and Maggie away from here. Tighter still at the thought of moving away herself.

She glanced at the Cat in the Hat clock on the wall. Story time would run another ten minutes. She could use the computer until then.

A few minutes later, she spotted Evie coming across the room. She quickly minimized the search she had up and spun in her chair to greet her sister.

"Thank you for keeping the kids today. I know you have a lot going on." Her sister twirled her hand in the air as though to say *with all this*.

"Somehow, adding a few to the mix can sometimes be easier. They entertain each other," Mia said. She put her elbows on the desk in front of her, knocking the mouse to the side. All of the searches she had minimized sprang to life again on the screen.

"What is this?" Evie stepped closer to the computer, peering at the photos of apartments as though they were hieroglyphics.

Mia slapped at the mouse, but too late.

"Are you going to move?"

"Keep your voice down," Mia said. "I haven't talked about it with the kids yet."

"Why in the world are you thinking about moving away?" Evie's voice pitched higher.

The tightness in her chest squeezed harder. She blinked rapidly against a pricking in her eyes. "I failed on this job for Dani. I couldn't meet the quota."

Evie put her arm around Mia's shoulder. "You're not a failure. Everyone knows how hard you've worked on this project." Evie paused. "I know you don't want to ask Mom and Dad for help, but—"

"That is so not going to happen. I told you that already." She crossed her arms. The library air conditioning kicked on, and a cold breeze fluttered the edges of her shirt sleeves.

Evie swiveled Mia's chair and looked her in the eyes. "It was worth a try. But if you're not going to ask Mom and Dad for help, at least you can ask God."

Mia's heart thumped.

No one judges you for your past except you. Cody's words echoed in her heart for the thousandth time since he'd said them to her. *I don't think your parents are judging you . . . They're super proud of you.*

"Cody said something similar to me. He's on your side about Mom and Dad too." Mia began packing her work away.

"I can see you're done with this conversation, but at least promise me you will talk to me before you make any decisions about moving. And talk to God about it too." Evie handed her a stack of papers from the edge of the desk.

Mia nabbed them from her and added them to the stack. "Fine. I promise."

"So. Cody?"

"We've been spending time together." Her face warmed as she recalled exactly how they'd spent their time a few nights ago.

Evie's face softened.

"It's natural for us to spend time together, you know." Mia put her hands on her hips. Except, why was she denying her feelings for him to Evie, one of her best friends and confidant ever since they were kids? She put her hands down. "The truth is, I don't know what is up with us. I . . . kissed him. And then he took me on a super romantic date."

"What?" Evie's squeal drew some attention from the library patrons in the magazine section.

"Shh. It's the library." Mia resisted rolling her eyes. Barely.

"I promise to be quiet." Evie held up her hand Scout's honor-style. "But you need to tell me all the deets. Right. Now."

Mia told her about the kiss and the date. "I'm finally ready to let him in, but recently he totally flaked on me."

A crease appeared between Evie's eyes. "That doesn't sound like Cody."

Okay, she had to admit that was stretching things a bit. "Yeah, I guess you're right. He had a good reason. He'd taken the boat—"

"He went out on a boat!" Evie clapped her hand over her mouth at Mia's pointed stare. Then, quieter, "Sorry, I just know what a big step that would be for him. For you too, while we're at it."

Mia's stomach roiled at the thought. She put her hand on it. "Anyway, his motor died, and I had to do it all on my own. Well, not totally alone. Matt showed up and helped me."

"I see that look in your eye. Is this going to be some rom-com love triangle?"

"Stop. It's not like that."

"Good, because wasn't he the guy in college that called

you a fishwife when he heard you were marrying Troy?" Evie's eyes flashed. "And said something about settling for mediocrity?"

"Yeah. But that was because he didn't want my talent to wither away." Looked like he was right.

"Still, doesn't sound like the kind of thing you'd want a potential boyfriend saying."

"You don't have to worry about it. In fact, Matt kind of made me feel uncomfortable. He was pushier than I remember him being in college." She waved away Evie's look of concern. "He's harmless. Just more invested in pursuing a romantic relationship than I am. Cody walked in while he was hugging me." And, yeah, her life did sound a little like a soap opera all of a sudden.

"I'm sure you can clear all of that up with a simple conversation."

Mia rolled her shoulders. Over by the reading throne, the kids were starting to stand for a round of "Shake My Sillies Out," their traditional closing song.

"The thing is, we did clear that up with a simple conversation. But . . . I don't know. I'm afraid to rely on him too completely. And afraid that I will lose him too."

"Give it time. You can trust Cody. Allow him to show you that. And am I beating a dead horse if I remind you that you can pray about this too?"

She gave her sister a smile. "You're right. As always."

The kids interrupted any further conversation, but Mia was still thinking about Evie's words when she arrived home after the library and dropping some paperwork off at Dani's office.

Lunchtime led to quiet time, and then Mia found herself all alone. She sat in her chair across from Troy's empty one. Speaking of moving on . . . Maybe Constance would like to have that. She'd mentioned needing a better place for Grandma Harmon to sit, and Mia needed to start letting go of more of Troy's things. She'd never liked the chair, as it didn't fit with her other furniture, but he'd insisted on keeping it. She sent her mother-in-law a quick text, offering to bring it over.

That task completed, thoughts of eviction and Cody warred for top spot in her mind.

Fine, Evie, you're right. I should talk to God about all of this. "Lord, you know my needs. Help me figure out how to stay on the island." Her parents' faces swam into her mind, but she pushed them away. "And give me wisdom with Cody too." A short prayer, but long overdue. Her heart calmed as she sat in silence a moment more. Her phone pinged.

Constance

Sure, we'd love to have the chair.

Mia

I'll carry it over after the kids get up from their quiet time.

Before making promises, she should have tried to move the thing. Mia stood and crossed the room. Putting a hand on each armrest, she shifted the chair a foot. Okay. This would be doable. Something rustled near the wall.

What the?

She shifted the chair out another foot.

Peering around the back of the chair, she spotted several pieces of paper. She tugged them free.

Plum-colored crayon covered the front and back of an application she had printed weeks ago. Maggie. The little girl must have hidden one of the papers back here so she wouldn't get into more trouble.

Mia gave a little laugh. God didn't always answer this clearly, but today she couldn't deny He was showing His love for her. She remembered reading this proposal but had forgotten it existed in the hassle of the rest of the job. A woman had proposed a curio shop that specialized in maritime-themed treasures. The attached photos of the product she intended on carrying, as well as some design ideas, looked perfect for their hopes for downtown Jonathon Island.

Her heart moved quicker than a school of minnows when someone tried to catch them as she dialed the number written on the paper. Hopefully, this Grace Marconi would still be interested in moving.

"Hi, is this Grace?" She twirled a pen through her fingers.

"This is she."

"Hi, this is Mia Franklin from Jonathon Island? I'm calling you about your application." Mia explained to Grace that the council was still looking for candidates for the revitalization program. "Are you still interested?"

Several minutes later, she hung up the phone and pumped her fist in the air. She dialed another number. "Dani? I have some really good news."

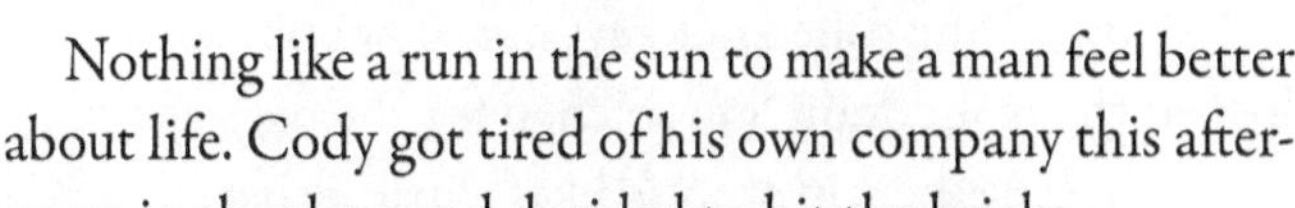

Nothing like a run in the sun to make a man feel better about life. Cody got tired of his own company this afternoon in the shop and decided to hit the bricks.

His route took him along the road, past businesses, and then through the older, residential area of town. Most of the houses he'd worked on were through here. A run past them couldn't hurt. Couldn't hurt to run past Mia's either. Maybe catch a glimpse of her dark curls pulled back by that bandanna that brought out the green of her eyes.

I think choosing you might be a good choice. Her words sank into his heart and found a nice spot to live.

He hadn't stopped thinking about their date the past few days. The way Mia had looked in the moonlight . . . Yep. They needed another one. Soon. How often could he take her out while still honoring her wishes to go slow?

So, yeah, that part of his life was going well. The "what to do about the fishing business" part . . . not so much. He hung a left down Lilac Lane. At the dead end, he would turn back around and head home. His smartwatch buzzed, alerting him that he'd run four miles already.

Shoot. Mia's house looked as dark as a night out on Lake Huron. Lights off, curtains pulled. Must have a meeting in town. His feet pounded past her place, but he pulled up short at the Franklins' house. Mrs. Franklin held a grocery bag in each arm with a plastic bag dangling from her right hand. As she reached into the purse slung on her left elbow, her bags tipped.

He jogged up the short sidewalk. "Mrs. Franklin. Let

me help you with those." Careful not to drop her groceries, he took the paper bags.

"Thanks." She fished her keys out of her purse and unlocked the front door. She reached for the bags again.

"I can bring them in, if you'd like." A pause that stretched long and thin fell between them. Constance Franklin had not had much to say to him or his father in the years since her husband and son passed away.

He understood that. He had a hard time talking to her too. He was alive, and her son wasn't. The guilt of that tore a hole in his gut every day.

Walking into the Franklin house hit just as hard. How many times had he been here with Troy over the years? He knew this place almost as well as he knew his parents' home.

He breathed in the cinnamon scent of the candles Mrs. Franklin loved, walked past the "wall of fame" featuring Troy in his high school uniform, in his cap and gown, and various ones with friends and family. He paused at the one with Troy in a tux and Mia in her wedding gown, before entering the kitchen to set the bags on the table, scarred from many years of use.

Mrs. Franklin put down her things too then went to the sink and filled an electric teakettle.

He braced a hand on the back of one of the wooden chairs ringing the table. "I guess I'll—"

"Stay for a cup of tea." Mrs. Franklin didn't look at him as she reached for a pair of coffee cups still in the second cupboard from the left.

Hokay. "I'm a little sweaty from my run."

She looked at him then. "I was married to a fisherman for almost thirty years. Sweat at my kitchen table is not going to be a problem."

He pulled out his usual chair and sat down, his arms naturally finding their places on the armrest.

"I'm going back to check on Mom, before the kettle whistles." Mrs. Franklin slipped out of her jacket as she left the room.

He looked around the warm room. Light-colored cabinets lined the walls. A flowery curtain hung over the window above the sink. The once familiar place held so many memories. He'd been here almost as much as at his own house in high school, then less often after Troy and Mia got married. Then not at all these last two years.

The kettle whistled, and he stood and poured water over the teabags in the mugs.

She'd given him Troy's cup from pottery class. He remembered their pottery unit in school. He and Mia and Troy had all decided to make matching cups. His and Troy's had turned out a little lopsided, but Mia's had been perfect. Looked like Mrs. Franklin had held on to Troy's, despite its flaws. The blue rim had a chip in it.

Cody moved back to the table and sat. A few moments later, Mrs. Franklin joined him again.

Mrs. Franklin cupped her hands around her tea and stared down into it. "Thank you."

He barked out a laugh. "For what?"

"For being willing to brave this awkward situation with me."

He remembered her self-deprecating humor. "My pleasure."

"I'm glad you offered to help today. It forced me to act. The truth is, I've been a coward. There are things I need to say to you, things long overdue." She rolled her shoulders.

He waited. Gave her space. It was the least he could do.

She took a long swallow of her tea then looked him straight in the eye. Her face hard, lips in a tight line. "I want you to know that I don't blame you or your father for what happened to Steve and Troy."

The floor shifted as if it might give way under him. It was a good thing he was seated. "Okay . . ."

She put a hand up to stop him from saying anything else. "I know it would be easy for you to think that I do blame you, that that's the reason I don't talk to you. But I know that accidents happen, and that's what that whole incident was. An accident."

Cody took a full, deep breath, his first since coming in the house. "It means a lot to me to hear you say that—" But Mrs. Franklin hadn't finished.

"I can't talk to you, I can barely look at you, because I am reminded of him. Of my boy. What would he look like two years older? How would he be as a dad to his growing kids?" She fisted a hand and raised it to her mouth. A long, sharp, icy shard pierced his heart. "Steve I can mourn, I can let go. I'm still dealing with that grief, but it's manageable. But no mother should outlive her son." The last words came in a whisper. The clock above the sink ticked a few seconds past.

She folded her hands in her lap and looked at him again.

"But I'm a coward for not telling you over and over these past few years that nothing that happened was your fault. You are not guilty. And I'm a coward for pushing you away and not holding you close. I lost two sons that day."

"You didn't lose me." His voice roughened by unshed tears. *You are not guilty.* Yeah. He'd be reliving those words often. "I'm right here. If you want me to be."

"I don't know if I'm ready for that. I'm sorry, but that's the truth. And when I saw you jogging up my walk, I vowed to tell you the truth."

"That's okay too. Take the time you need." He started to stand.

"Wait," she said. "There's more I want to say." He settled back down. "Gossip around town says you are trying to reopen your dad's business."

"Yes. That's right. I wanted to honor Troy's memory. We'd always planned to take over the business together, as you know. But that's a dream that I'm thinking about letting die. Everything seems to be against me."

A frown line crossed her forehead. "But why let it die?"

He outlined the trouble he'd had sourcing parts, the interruptions every time he started making progress on repairs, and finally, he told her about his dad refusing to transfer the fishing license.

She nodded slowly. "Those are a lot of problems. Maybe it's not my place to say, but I think you should still try. Troy would tell you to never give up. To keep running, like he used to cheer when you were in track. He loved being out on the water with you."

"That sounds like Troy."

"It would honor Troy's memory. But ultimately, you need to do what is right."

"Being a fisherman is all I know. I love it." His heart lightened.

"Speaking of love . . ." Her face softened for the first time that afternoon. "Don't you think it's about time you ask Mia out?"

"What?" The word exploded from his chest.

"Come on. You've been pining for that girl since ninth grade. Maybe even longer. Don't get me wrong, I saw how you supported her and Troy, and I've always admired you for that. But you don't have to step aside anymore. Troy would want his family taken care of, and I can't think of anyone who would do a better job . . . if that's what you and Mia both want, of course."

"I appreciate that." More than she would ever know. He opened his mouth to tell her that he'd taken Mia out a few nights ago, then hesitated. He should check with Mia before spreading that news. Even if Mrs. Franklin did just bless their potential relationship.

Mrs. Franklin set her cup down and pushed her chair back. "While I'm feeling brave, I suppose you should come through to the backyard."

"Okay . . ." He felt like a broken record, but all of this was giving him conversational whiplash.

She led him out the back door and toward a shed. Next to the shed was a large shape covered with a tarp. He knew that shape. It was the speedboat Troy had been tinkering with throughout high school and beyond. Many Friday nights found the two of them fiddling with the outboard motor or slapping some duct tape over a new crack in the seat cushions. Mia would sit in a lawn chair nearby, her long legs crossed, Pharrell Williams on the radio, the three of them laughing at something stupid.

Mrs. Franklin walked fast toward the boat. She peeled back a corner of the tarp. "Troy would want you to have this."

He hauled up short. "No. Absolutely not. I already have a boat. Besides, that should belong to Mia."

"Nope. Not this. It means more to you than it would to Mia. Plus, I know you spent a lot of your money on it too. Almost as much as Troy. That boy never could keep a dime in his pocket."

He ran a hand over the hull. The blue paint sparkled in the June sunshine. He remembered long debates with Troy over the color choice. Cody would have gone with a racing red, but Troy picked blue. Once finished, Cody had to admit the blue really worked.

"The boat is yours. I already put the title and registration in your name. When we go back through the house, I will give them to you. Keep the boat or sell it, I don't care, but that boat is yours."

"I don't know what to say."

She waved away his words. "Like I said, it might be a while before we can go back to the way things were, but I needed to get this stuff off my chest."

They walked back through the house. When they got to the front door, he noticed movement out the small window. He saw what looked like a walking couch cushion, topped with a purple bobble. Behind that, marched another cushion, this time topped with a pair of bright eyes under a mop of curly blonde hair. Trailing behind was Mia, carrying the chair that the cushions must belong to.

He hurried out the door and down the walk, just in time to catch Maggie as she tripped on the cushion, falling forward onto it, bobble flopping.

"Whoa there, little lady." He swooped her up, laughing. Mia set down the chair and brushed a hair out of her eyes. Could Maggie hear the beating of his heart? "Let me help you guys." He set Maggie down and picked up the cushion.

Maggie put her little hands on her hips. "I do it mine self."

"I see." He bit his lip against a smile. "Stubborn, like your mama." He shot Mia a wink. "Fierce too. Maybe she will let me help her."

As he took the chair from Mia their fingers brushed. A zing ran up his arm and landed somewhere in his heart. "Let me help you with that."

"Thanks." Mia held his gaze. "It's not heavy, just awkward."

"I can see that. Where are we going with it?"

"Grandma Harmon's room," Mia said. "Were you just at Constance's?"

He smiled at her over the top of the chair. "This has been a banner week for me. Mrs. Franklin and I had tea. I'll have to tell you about it later."

He walked up the yard to the Franklin house, Mia at his side and Maggie and Finn tottering along with their cushions—and finally, some peace in his heart.

He still didn't know what the future held—with his

dad's fishing business or with Mia—but a guy sure could get used to this kind of life.

Fifteen

HOW COULD SHE HAVE FORGOTTEN Troy's boat?

Mia stood on Cody's wooden dock, slightly swaying with the waves. The water looked beautiful today. Troy's boat floated in front of her, blue paint sparkling. The thirteen foot Boston Whaler looked even better in the water than it ever had in Constance's backyard. A small pleasure cruiser that doubled as a fishing boat, the whaler had four swivel seats, a modest diving platform off the back, and an outboard motor. Troy had replaced all the torn upholstery with a white faux leather. It surprised her to note that it still looked bright even after being in storage for so long.

Cody had called in a few favors, and he and Liam and a few others had pulled the boat on its trailer from Constance's all the way down to the water. Then he'd called and convinced her to bring the kids down for a ride.

"Let's test it out." He'd pleaded.

"Not today, Cody. Grace is supposed to call back with a good time for her video interview with the council. If she decides to move forward with her application, that is." Now was not the time for slacking off. After all, she was still short on applicants. It was not the time to go for a pleasure cruise.

"So, you're just going to sit around waiting for a phone call? There's cell service on the boat. I give you my word we won't go far from shore. Besides, Finn and Maggie will love it," he'd said.

Those words had finally convinced her. He was right. The kids would be over the moon with this ride. They loved going on the ferry the few times she'd taken them to the mainland. Right now, they practically vibrated with excitement as they waited to board the boat.

She and Cody and Troy had spent so much time with it in high school. Troy was constantly trying to improve the vessel. He'd tinker with the outboard motor, then they'd take it for a tour around the island. He'd painted it this sparkly, blue color just before high school graduation. They hadn't had time to put it in the water that summer. As far as she knew, he'd never put it in the water. Not during their marriage anyway. Too many other priorities, Finn being the most important.

She was glad Constance had given the boat to Cody. Glad that he'd thought to share it with her children.

Now, those two were attempting to board, Finn with his legs spread in wide splits—one foot on the dock and one in the boat. She reached to steady him as Cody leaned out of the boat to swing Maggie in. He settled Maggie into one of the captain's chairs before strapping her into a life vest. Then he held Finn by the elbow as the little boy navigated his other foot into the boat. Finn pulled a jacket over his head and snapped the clips shut. Cody tested the straps to make sure they were snug. When the kids were safe, he put his hand out to Mia.

She placed her hand in his. His rough calluses rubbed her palm, sending a zing up her arm.

"What's in the bag?" Cody held her gaze as tightly as he held her hand. His thumb caressed the knuckle of her pointer finger.

"Um." Yeah, real intelligent. She slipped her hand out of his and unslung the heavy tote from her shoulder. "I thought it might be cold out here on the water, so I brought hot chocolate and a blanket. Plus a few snacks."

He rubbed his hands together in exaggerated glee. "Snacks!" The kids laughed.

"Snacks!" Finn echoed. "I'm hungry now."

"Finn, you are a bottomless pit. Do you think we can make it five minutes on the boat before you eat all the snacks?" She put her hand on her hip. "You need to learn a little patience. No snacks until we can see the lighthouse."

"Imagine what he'll be like as a teenager." Cody shot her a wink, and suddenly she didn't think she would need the hot chocolate. Her insides already felt warm and gooey.

"But, Mom." Finn's whine managed to make the word into three syllables.

"Finn, you gotta respect your mom's rules," Cody said. "No snacks until we can see the lighthouse. Which means we better get going. I want hot chocolate." He revved the engine as Mia untied the mooring line from the cleat on the dock. Soon, they eased their way out into the open water.

The late afternoon sun glinted off the water, making rainbows out of the spray coming off the boat's wake. Cody stuck close to the island shoreline. Her chest expanded and lifted. Braving the Straits of Mackinac would have been too much. Finn and Maggie spun around and around in the two seats at the back of the boat. Their giggles carried over the sound of the motor.

"Thanks for your support back there." Mia laid a hand on Cody's shoulder.

"Eh. It was nothing." Cody glanced her way before turning back to the water. "Finn just needed to be encouraged to obey."

The gooey feeling got warmer. "Not nothing. I'm used to enforcing the rules on my own. Having backup felt . . . nice."

He pretended to tip an imaginary cap to her. "By the way, I'll be signing the title of this boat over to you."

"What? Why? No way."

"It's the right thing to do. It belonged to Troy. Now it should belong to you and the kids."

"I don't want it." She crossed her arms. "Troy would want you to have it. You worked on it almost as much as he did."

He pulled a face. "What am I going to do with another boat? I can barely keep the one that I already have."

She faced forward. The wind from their speed brushed

her face and tossed her hair. The clean scent of water and sky filled her. "I don't know. Sell it maybe. Use the money to buy yourself an engine that actually works."

He grunted in response.

"It's good to see you captaining a boat again," she said.

"As you know, I almost had a breakdown out here."

She glanced at him, saw the whitening of his knuckles as he gripped the wheel. "It's not surprising, given what you went through." Mia tugged a stray hair out of her eye. "You're out here now though."

"Yeah, Pastor Arnie and I went out again." He shot a look her way. "It was the morning I was late to help you."

Oh.

"With his help, and a lot of prayer, I was able to wrestle down a few demons." He rubbed at the back of his neck.

"I'm proud of you. Will you tell me the story some-time?"

"Definitely." He slowed the boat. "How about you? Are you doing okay? Being out here, I mean."

She breathed in, the air going deep into her lungs. Her heart rate was steady. When Cody wasn't grinning at her, anyway. "It's funny. I thought this would be so hard, but it turns out that being out here with you is the most natural thing in the world." She reached out and put her hand on top of his.

Cody swung the boat to the left around an out cropping of rocks.

"Lighthouse!" Finn's cry made her jump, pulling away from Cody. "I see the lighthouse."

Sure enough, the tall, white building rose up in front of

them. As they came closer, Mia saw the long pier beside it and the old whaler nearby.

"A deal's a deal." Cody slowed the boat to a stop. "Time for snacks. We can drift here a while."

She handed each kid a thermos and two graham crackers. "Sit in the chairs with these. No spinning while you have hot chocolate. Anyone cold?" They both shook their heads and then spun their chairs to face the back of the boat. Finn began explaining how lighthouses work to Maggie. Mia reached into the bag again and got out the other thermos and two cups.

She rejoined Cody at the wheel and handed him a cup.

"Where's my graham cracker?" Mischief danced in his brown eyes. "I waited patiently until I could see the lighthouse."

"Oh, you." She started to swat his arm, but he caught her hand in his. His gaze became intense and her belly tightened.

A hundred yards away, another boat sped past. The deck rocked beneath her, and she stumbled. Cody caught her elbows. She looked up at him from under her lashes.

"Cody," she said, then licked her lips.

"Yes?" His voice was hoarse, eyes boring into hers.

She leaned into his warmth. Looking toward Finn and Maggie, she saw they still faced away and were intent on something across the water. She could risk a small distraction. Putting her hand on his chest, she could feel his heart beating faster than the sputter of a speedboat motor. She tipped her head up, meeting his eyes. They were dark and intense. "I know we said we'd go slow, but I'm going to kiss you again. Is that okay?"

In answer, he dipped his head to hers. A light touch of their lips fell into something deeper as the boat rocked again. She grabbed his bicep, and it flexed under her hand. A bigger wave hit them, and the deck rocked them apart. Cody steadied the wheel just as Maggie started screaming.

Mia whirled around and saw her daughter on the floor of the boat. A gash at her hairline streamed with blood. The near edge of the boat bright with a red smear. In one leap, she grabbed Maggie and one of the blankets. She wrapped her sobbing, screaming daughter in the warm wool.

"Maggie fell," Finn said. "When the wave whooshed us. Maggie fell down and hit her head. I told her not to stand up, but she didn't listen to me and then the wave whooshed and she fell down."

"Let me look at it, baby." Mia kept her voice even. Inside she was screaming along with Maggie.

Cody tossed the anchor over the side and came back to them. "What do you need?"

Mia used the edge of the blanket to dab at the wound. With her other hand she held Maggie's hands down and away from blood. "Can you see if there is a first aid kit anywhere onboard?"

She heard Cody rummaging around as she focused on trying to staunch the blood flow. Head wounds bleed a lot, but this seemed like it was serious. Mia pulled the blanket away from the cut. The deep gash rippled her skin, and the blood mixed with the chocolate all over Maggie's face. She must have spilled her drink as she fell.

"I can't find one." Cody crouched down where they sat. "Do you need to use my T-shirt?"

"This blanket seems to be working." Mia glanced at him. "Can you get us to the clinic? I think Maggie is going to need stitches."

"You betcha." Cody stood then tousled Finn's hair. "C'mon, bud. I'll show you how to steer." He lifted Finn into his arms.

Soon, the motor was running and they sped back the way they had come.

The low rumble of the boat seemed to soothe Maggie, and she calmed as they pulled into the public marina. Cody must have called ahead without Mia noticing, because the island's only ambulance waited for them on shore. Cody tossed up a line, and one of the EMTs tied up the boat to the dock.

"Looks like you folks ran into a bit of trouble." Emily Watson, a girl from Mia's graduating class, reached out for Maggie.

"Maggie fell down," Finn said from his place in Cody's arms.

"We'll take good care of her," Emily said, her short, sturdy legs braced wide on the dock.

Mia handed Maggie to Emily and then climbed off the boat. Maggie began wailing. "I'm right here, baby. Let this lady take a look."

Emily carried Maggie to the ambulance, Mia trailing

in her wake. Behind them, she heard Cody talking to the other EMT.

Mia tried to concentrate on what Emily was asking while beating down the nausea rising in her. No, Maggie hadn't had a tetanus shot. Yes, she had medical insurance—thank goodness for Healthy Michigan's low-cost plans for low-income families. No, she didn't have any other medical concerns.

"I think we'll need to take her in for stitches," Emily said. "Do you want Finn and Cody to ride along too?"

She looked at her son's pale face. His skinny arms clung to Cody's neck. "Yes, they need to come along."

She wasn't going anywhere without her guys.

Bringing them on the boat had been a big mistake.

Cody sat on the edge of Maggie's bed in her room. Next to him, the little girl slept under her pink unicorn quilt, clutching her purple bobble hat and her stuffed bunny. The bandage at her hairline made her look so vulnerable. Her gentle snore lifted the corner of his mouth. Mia sat next to him, eyes closed, a hand on Maggie's chest. After the trauma of the clinic, he welcomed this peace. Well, outward peace anyway. Inside, his gut churned. Across the room, Finn's bed lay empty. They'd called Constance to pick him up at the clinic, and she'd volunteered to keep him overnight.

The sharp tang of the antiseptic the nurse used on Maggie's wound hung in the air. She should never have been in a position to have the stitches in the first place.

"Mia, I'm sorry, this is all my fault." He swiped at his eyes then crossed his arms. They ached to gather Maggie up, or Mia, or both of them. But that was a bad idea. Having Mia in his arms was part of the reason they were here in the first place. They should have never taken their eyes off the kids. "I never should have taken you out there."

Mia's eyes flew open. "Code. Stop. Accidents happen with little kids. There is no way this is your fault." Keeping one hand on Maggie, she rested the other on Cody's knee. The heat from her touch soaked into a frozen place inside him.

"One of your kids got hurt." Cody couldn't look at her. Didn't want to see the truth reflected in her eyes. "Loss follows me, and I should have remembered that."

"What in the world are you talking about?"

"I thought I'd gotten to a good place, started to believe that maybe . . ." He inhaled sharply. "But the truth is, I got your husband killed, and now I almost killed your daughter. And it doesn't matter how much I plan or try to be careful . . . loss just seems inevitable."

Mia laughed, a short, humorless bark. She patted Maggie and then gave his knee a squeeze. "Come on. Let's go into the kitchen where we don't have to whisper. Plus, this kind of conversation needs more hot chocolate."

While Mia heated water for the instant hot chocolate, Cody took two mugs out of the cupboard. Soon, cups filled, they sat at the table. The steam curled up between them.

Mia reached for his hand. She held it in both of her own. Her thumbs tightened her grip. "Listen to me carefully. I need you to hear me." She paused, took a deep breath and squared her shoulders. "I don't blame you for Troy's death. I never have."

He kept his eyes on the table. Her words dinged against the armor he had built for himself.

"Please look at me," she said.

He raised his gaze to meet hers. Expecting pity, he saw something closer to grace instead, maybe even love.

She waited a beat, keeping eye contact. "What happened that terrible night was not your fault. It has never been your fault."

"And I'm starting to believe it. But"—the words tore from him, leaving a raw wound in their wake—"my dad blames me for all of it."

"Has he told you that?"

"Not in so many words. But he doesn't have to say it. He's told me in a thousand other ways."

"I can't believe an old fisherman like your dad would blame you for the weather."

"Why do you think he won't sell me the business? He doesn't trust me anymore. And I don't think he ever will."

"Again, has he ever said that to you?"

"Yes." Or did he? What did he say? Cody thought back over their conversations. Huh, he couldn't remember a time his dad had actually said those words. "I guess he's more or less just said things like 'you know why I won't sell to you.' I know he means that I can't be trusted with a boat."

Mia was silent for a moment. "I still can't see it. That doesn't sound like your dad at all."

"People change. These things can affect you . . ." He stopped himself. Obviously, Mia didn't need his platitudes. She knew even better than he did just how much these things could change a person.

"I think you should talk to your dad about it. Don't let him off the hook. Yourself either. You can't keep being so passive." Mia's eyes flashed. "Ask him straight up if he blames you for the accident. At least that way you will know for sure. You will have a way to move forward."

"And risk losing a relationship with him for good? I don't think I can take more losses in my life."

"Cody." Mia squeezed his hand. "Loss is inevitable here on earth. It's how we deal with it that matters."

He covered her hands with his other one. "When did you get so wise?"

"Eh, I've always been an old soul." Mia flipped her hand, palm up on the table. He fitted his fingers between hers before meeting her eyes again. Unshed tears pooled in them.

"What's wrong?"

She swiped at a tear that escaped. "It's not your fault Troy was there that night," she said. "But it was mine." She let go of him and covered her face.

What?

He scooted his chair closer to her and gently tugged her hands away from her face. Her eyes were red and full of tears. "What are you talking about?" He cupped her cheeks with his hands and wiped away a tear with his thumb.

"Troy didn't want to go that night, but I told him we needed the money to help pay for Finn's birthday gift. Your dad said he didn't have to pick up the shift, but I talked him into it." She covered her mouth with her hand as her eyes welled again. "So, you can stop blaming yourself now and blame me instead."

"What happened to Troy is not your fault. Hey, look at me." He tipped her chin up until she met his gaze. "It's not on you."

She blinked. A wetness formed in the corners of her eyes. Moving his hand up, he rubbed a thumb across the tear before it fell.

"I've felt so guilty these past two years. Like I stole Finn and Maggie's father from them."

"The lake stole Troy. Not you." They had both carried so much guilt. He was finally letting it go. Perhaps he could help her do the same.

Her voice had dropped to a whisper now. "I've never told anyone about that. I just wish I could have apologized to him. I wish he knew how much I appreciated him."

"Here's what I know, Mia. Troy was crazy about you. He would have never held this against you."

"I just wish I could hear him say it."

"Let me say it for him. Mia, you are forgiven. But I really don't think there was ever anything to forgive. Troy always did what was best for his family. If he was on the water that day, it was because he believed it was best."

She gave him a watery smile. "What a pair we are, eh?"

"So eager to take the blame for an act of nature." He tried for a grin, but it probably fell short.

"I've been trying to keep in mind that God is in control. I can't do anything that isn't seen by Him. Like the sparrow, you know?"

Her words dropped into his heart, and peace spread in its wake. "I like that," he said. A lump in his throat made it hard to swallow. "I think the worst part about all of this is that it makes me worry that I will harm someone again. I think that's why I keep delaying my boat project. Somewhere inside, I don't think I should take the boat out again in case I kill someone else."

"Oh, Cody." Mia stood and moved around to where he sat. She put her arms around his shoulders and pulled him to her. He rested his cheek on her stomach and wrapped his arms around her waist as she held him tight. One of her hands stroked his hair. "Not only did you lose a friend that night, but you lost the thing you loved, your dreams of owning your own fishing company."

"I thought I was making progress—going out with Liam and Pastor Arnie, and then again with you guys. But now Maggie is hurt, and it happened on my watch. It's hard to imagine ever going near the water again."

"That's a real bummer, because we live on an island. Gonna be hard to avoid it."

Her wry remark brought a smile to his face. He pulled back. His gaze roamed across her face. "Are you saying to get over myself?"

A slow smile lit her eyes. "I'm saying to cut yourself some slack. We all suffer losses, and we all will continue to, but that doesn't mean we should stop living. I believe they call that the human condition."

"Okay, but you need to take your advice too. What

happened wasn't your fault. We both know that Troy made up his own mind about things. He didn't need you to convince him to go out on the water. He loved being out there. You don't have to be stuck on the loss of him either." Cody let go of Mia. The clock on the wall ticked past a few seconds.

Mia sat back in her own chair. His arms ached to reach for her again, but he held back.

"So, we both have things to work on," Mia said. "No more feeling guilty. You need to talk to your dad. And we both need to focus on God being in control. He's got the whole world in His hands and all that."

The last thing he wanted to do was try to talk to his dad again. But Mia had a good point. Being passive had lost him so much over the years. It was time to fight for the things he loved.

After all, so far, it had worked with Mia. Maybe it would work for the fishing business too.

Sixteen

THAT ELUSIVE THING CALLED "CALM-ness" had finally arrived.

Which was good, because Mia could use some peace in her life right about now. She'd finally gotten the kids to settle down for a quiet time, careful not to call it a nap, or Finn would have protested. She counted on at least an hour with both kids in bed. Maggie still slept for a longer nap sometimes, but Finn was long past that phase. When Constance had dropped him off that morning though, she'd mentioned that he hadn't slept well the night before; he'd been too worried about Maggie. Hopefully, now that he saw his sister was fine, he'd be able to settle down for some rest.

Sitting on the couch, cocooned in an afghan her grandma had knitted her, she gazed at the devotional in her hands. Had she comprehended a single word? Nope.

Yesterday's boating adventure, out on Lake Huron,

Cody at the wheel, had been fun. Until it wasn't. Mia wrapped the blanket tighter around herself. She closed her eyes tight against the memory of Maggie's face covered in blood. Nope. More vivid that way. She pushed the thought aside, opting instead to remember the tender moments afterward with the kids and Cody.

In fact, she should probably take some of her own words to heart. *Are you saying to get over myself?* Cody's words drifted through her mind. Huh. Maybe she needed to cut herself some slack too. We all make mistakes. She certainly didn't have the time or energy to dwell on the past right now. Because by the end of the week, the storm would hit.

Tomorrow would be the day the town council made their final decisions about the last of the businesses moving to Jonathon Island. After the meet and greet, they'd extended several contracts, but still had spots to fill. She'd set up interviews for a few more people, working with Dani every step of the way. She had no doubt they would all be approved, and her quota would be fully met, but after tomorrow, her life would be busy with getting the final preparations finished for the new people, then helping everyone move in and settle down.

Not to mention receiving her paid-in-full notice from the bank. The minute she had that paperwork in hand she planned to have a bonfire and burn that mortgage statement.

Her heart lifted at the thought.

Not having a mortgage would mean that she wasn't dependent on someone else for her children's home. It would make all the difference in their lives, and hers. She could even start thinking about the future. She still needed to make money somehow. Real estate? The last few weeks had been so intense she hadn't been able to spend a whole lot of time thinking about how exactly she would provide for her kids.

Speaking of children, she really should get moving on something for supper. She needed to check Maggie's stitches too.

While unwrapping herself from her blanket, she noticed a missed call notification light up her phone. Weird. The phone lay next to her the whole time she fought to concentrate on her daily devotional. Why hadn't the phone made a noise? Probably time to add buying a new one to her list. She might be able to afford one after her mortgage was paid off. She swiped open the voicemail.

"Hey, Mia," Matt said, voice tinny on the recording. *"Listen, I have some bad news for you. Good news for me though . . . I've received an offer to share a studio space in Boston. The other artist works with sculpture, so her style and mine complement each other well without being direct competition."*

Mia's fingers and toes grew numb while her head heated as Matt's words began to sink in. He described how sorry he was and ended with *"I wish things had worked out there on Jonathon Island, but in the end, I have to do what is best for my career, and Boston is it."*

The voicemail ended, and Mia stood in her living room and stared at the silent phone.

Matt was backing out. That meant that even if everyone was approved tomorrow, she was still short of her quota.

Fumbling, she dialed his number.

"Matt, please don't do this."

"Hello to you too, Mia." She could hear water and an engine on Matt's end of the line.

"Tell me you're joking about leaving Jonathon Island." Okay, so she was a little desperate, but come on, it was her kids' home and future on the line. An image of the apartments she could afford flashed into her mind. Not good.

Matt sighed. "Look, Mia, the truth is, I saw your video and remembered the good times we had in college. I did a little digging and saw that your husband wasn't in the picture anymore. I was checking out some new spots to relocate to and thought, two birds with one stone, you know?" He paused and the silence grew long and taut. "When it was obvious you weren't into me—sorry, I know that sounds like I'm full of myself, but it's the truth—I decided it would be better to move on."

"You won't move here because I won't date you?" Mia pulled the phone from her ear and looked at it. She put the phone back to her ear. "That doesn't make any sense. Are you serious right now? We can still work together in a platonic relationship."

Matt was silent for a long moment. He cleared his throat. "You maybe can, but I can't. You were the only reason I would have chosen Jonathon Island. I took my shot and lost." She pictured him on the other end of the line, running a frustrated hand through his hair. "Now I need to move on. Look me up sometime in Boston. I wish you well, Mia. I truly do."

He hung up and Mia stared at the phone again. Great. Just great.

Her legs gave way, and she dropped into the chair behind her. A spring gave out with a twang. The sharp end poked through the fabric and scratched the back of her leg. The pain was minimal, but tears sprang into her eyes.

From their bedroom, Maggie began crying.

"Mom!" Finn's voice quavered. "Maggie still has an owie."

Mia ran a hand over her wet eyes. She straightened her shoulders and heaved herself out of the chair. No time to check if her scratch was bleeding as Maggie's cries became more insistent. "I'm coming, guys."

In the bedroom, she was greeted with the pungent odor of ammonia. She looked at Finn. He sat on his bed, eyes on his lap. Oh, buddy. Finn hadn't wet the bed in two years. These past few days must have overwhelmed him.

Maggie stood on her bed, her wailing getting louder and louder. Mia picked her up and spoke to Finn. "It's no big deal, honey. Let's get you cleaned up and your bedding changed." She shushed Maggie, brushing her hair back from her hot, red face. "Okay, Mags. You're okay. We'll get you a new Band-Aid when we get Finn's bed taken care of." She set her daughter down, but Maggie cried louder.

"Hold Mama," she sobbed.

Mia scooped her back into her arms and looked to Finn. "Can you get yourself some clean clothes? I'll strip your bed, then we can all go into the bathroom."

Arms full of a sweaty, still-crying Maggie and a load of damp sheets and blankets, Mia stepped into the hallway and collided with something. Cody stood there, a sheepish look on his face.

"Sorry. I did knock, but it sounded like you had your hands full in here, so I let myself in. How can I help?"

Mia's eyes pricked again. That silly scratch must be bothering her more than she thought. "Can you help Finn get some clean clothes?"

Working together, they cleaned up the mess, changed Maggie's bandage, and got both kids settled down in front of PB&Js for some supper.

"Thank you," Mia said. She moved to the sink and began washing the dishes.

Cody picked up a towel and dried the cup she set into the sink. "No problem."

"Why are you even here?" She glanced over at the kids. They were dancing their sandwiches across the plate before taking a bite. "Sorry, that came out wrong."

"I wanted to tell you that you were right. I've been doing a lot of thinking about what you said last night. I'm going to talk to my dad soon. I'll ask him straight up what he thinks of me." Cody flashed her a smile as he reached for the next cup. "I feel better even having made that decision. You're always right."

Ha. That was a laugh. "Not always. Turns out you were right about Matt. He called and told me he was pulling out of the agreement."

"What? When?"

"Right before both kids had a meltdown. I was getting ready to call you when . . ." She waved her hand in the direction of the kids' bedroom as if that explained everything.

"I'm sorry, Mia. I know how much having Matt here meant to you."

"It wasn't Matt, or at least it wasn't only him. It was the idea that someone would be in that art space. It would feel like maybe everything from my past was redeemed." Like she had a piece of her old self left. "And now I don't have that. And I won't meet my quota." Her heartbeat ramped up.

Cody opened his mouth then shut it again. Then he took a deep breath and said, "How about we get on the phone right now with Mrs. Harper? She was the last name on the short list, right? We could see if she's still interested."

"No. It's too late. We don't have enough time to get her on board."

"Mia, this is worth a try."

His soft pleading went straight to her heart. "Fine. Let's call her." Frankly, at this point she'd even beg.

After checking on Maggie and Finn, who had moved on to eating mandarin orange slices, Mia dialed Jocelyn Harper. She put the phone on speaker and held it between them.

"Hello, Mrs. Harper? This is Mia Franklin. I'm wondering if you are still interested in the offer to relocate to Jonathon Island?"

"Oh!" There was a rustle on the other end of the phone, then they heard Mrs. Harper say quietly, "It's the JI council. They want to know if we're still interested." A rumble came over the phone as someone answered her. Another rustle and then her voice came clearly again. "I'm definitely interested. But my husband needs to talk over some things with someone before we sign anything."

She widened her eyes at Cody. "I'd be happy to answer any questions he has. Feel free to put him on the phone."

"Oh, no. He wants to meet in person. He says he has to look someone in the eye to see if they are a good person to do business with. He has a sixth sense about these things."

"The town council meets tomorrow, Mrs. Harper. They can arrange a video call for you. In fact, they will probably insist on it." She glanced at the kids. Still eating peacefully. Thank God for minor miracles. "I don't think anyone can meet you in person before that. We have the forms all set up online for you to sign."

"My husband doesn't trust online forms. Isn't there any way we can do this in person?"

"You could come on the ferry in the morning?" Mia's shoulders tensed.

Another rumble, then, "I'm sorry, we can't come tomorrow. Can someone come here tonight?"

Maybe? Mia glanced at the clock. Her heart fell to the pit of her stomach. The last ferry had already left for the day. "I'm sorry. That's just not possible." She put a hand to her forehead. "The soonest anyone can meet with you is the day after tomorrow." It might not save her house, but she'd committed to doing a good job for Dani. And that meant filling all of the businesses even after they'd foreclosed on her house. Mia made arrangements with the Harpers to meet them at their home and then hung up.

Fatigue rumbled through her body. All of her muscles gave way, and she slumped into a chair. "I guess that's that."

"Mia." Cody sat next to her and took her hand. "I'm sure the council will give you an extension. Especially if they know the Harpers are still interested."

"I guess they might, but I doubt it. And what then? I'm just fooling myself to think I can make a go of it on island. I need to get practical and move somewhere I can have a real, paying job. Something that keeps the roof over my kids' heads." It was time to face facts. She would need to say goodbye to her little house on Lilac Lane.

"What if I go over to the Harpers tonight?"

A roll of thunder cascaded over the house.

Mia raised an eyebrow at Cody. "You are not going out in the rain."

He raised one back at her, and her heart did a flip. "I'm a fisherman. I'm used to getting a little wet."

She went gooey that he would even offer. Not too long ago he wouldn't have gone out on the water at all. "No. Absolutely not. It's not worth the risk."

"You are worth it—"

"Mama!" Maggie's shriek cut off whatever Cody had been about to say and brought Mia back to the present. "I done."

Later, after helping get the kids cleaned up, she walked Cody to the door. "Stay dry out there."

He leaned in and kissed her cheek. "See you later, Mia." Another roll of thunder chased him down the walk.

Mia shut the door and then leaned her forehead against the wood. She might not have her house for much longer, but she had Cody, and she had her kids. That would have to be enough.

Mia shouldn't lose her house when there was something he could do about it. Cody might be fast friends with loss, but that didn't mean Mia and the kids had to be as well.

As he walked home, the rain slackened to a light drizzle. He pulled out his phone and keyed in the number he'd spotted on the Harpers' application. They agreed to meet him at the dock in Port Joseph and grab a piece of pie together at a nearby shop that evening.

The storms must have moved all the way off, because an hour later as he docked his boat in the public slip, his rain slicker held only a few drops on it, which could easily have been from the spray off the boat. Spotting the neon sign for the café, he hustled toward it.

Inside the combination convenience store and café, the wooden booths and smell of cinnamon were a welcoming embrace. Near the door sat an older couple, late sixties at least. Must be them.

"Mr. and Mrs. Harper?" Cody held his hand out and Mr. Harper shook it, his grip tight.

"Thanks for coming over," Mr. Harper said, giving an additional squeeze before letting go. "We were just about to order some pie."

Cody slid into the booth across from the couple. They looked like they fit together in that way people do after having been married for a long time. Maybe he and Mia would look like that someday.

"I'll get right into it." Cody laid his hands on the table. "Your shop would be a great fit for our community. I'd be happy to answer any concerns you have, and then we can get those papers signed tonight for the meeting in the morning." Guilt twinged at having snagged the paperwork behind Mia's back. But she would forgive him when he returned with them signed, and her house secure.

Mr. and Mrs. Harper shared a long look.

For the first time, Cody's gut clenched. They were going to sign, weren't they?

Before they could say anything, the waitress arrived with three slices of apple pie. Cody dug into his first bite. Sweet apple and the spicy cinnamon notes burst on his tongue. No wonder the place smelled so good.

"Jonathon Island is a great place to live and work." Sure, he was quoting verbatim from Mia's website, but they were good sales points, couldn't hurt to use them on the Harpers. "We're a tight-knit community, but very open to bringing new people into the fold." He took another bite of the pie.

"Let me stop you right there," Mrs. Harper said. "We've been doing a lot of thinking about this opportunity, especially since getting that call this afternoon. And I'm sorry to tell you . . ." She paused and looked down at her plate. The apple pie turned to ash in his mouth.

Mr. Harper cleared his throat. "We won't be signing the papers. We thought we were ready for a new adventure, but once it became a reality, we realized we like it right here."

"But you seemed so excited." Even as he spoke the

words, Cody knew they were futile. "Is there anything I can say to change your mind?"

Mrs. Harper looked him in the eye again. "We do love Jonathon Island. We've visited many times. And we appreciate the gesture of you coming over here to talk to us. But we're too old to be making that change. In fact, all of this discussion made us think about selling our shop and starting our retirement."

The last of his hope died a swift death.

A few minutes later, Mr. Harper laid some bills on the table then stood and clapped Cody on the shoulder. "Have a safe trip home."

Cody stood from the table and wandered through the convenience store. He'd failed. The words kept ringing through his mind. He'd lost the Harpers, and now Mia would lose her house.

He stopped in front of a candy display without really seeing it until a bright yellow package caught his eye. Gushers. *I used to love those things.* Mia's words from their date jolted through him. Thinking about her that night, in her yellow sundress, lit a fire in him. He would go home, talk to Mia, and they would come up with a plan together.

Nothing was lost yet.

He paid for a few packages of the candy and raced to his boat. As he pushed away from the dock, a crash of thunder rolled over him.

The sun raced for the horizon as though it were being chased there by the dark clouds forming to the east. Its orangey-purple light did little to illuminate the lake. He motored out into the straights and flipped on the boat's running lights before checking his smartwatch. With any luck, he'd be back before Finn and Maggie were in bed. Hopefully Maggie was feeling better. He could help Mia get them into their jammies and tucked in. He'd love to read them the story about the pigeon and the bus he'd spotted on their bookshelf.

And then, once the kids were settled, he and Mia could have some quality alone time.

A bolt of lightning sizzled overhead followed by another ominous boom of thunder. He pulled up the weather app on his phone. Sure enough, a new storm had kicked up on the lake. His pulse kicked up in response.

Because of course there was a storm.

Wind whipped at him right before the rain began coming down in sheets. He tugged on a baseball cap to try to keep the worst of it out of his eyes. He glanced behind him. The far shore he'd left ten minutes ago had disappeared in the waves. Better to keep moving forward. Toward home. And Mia.

He turned the boat to a forty-five-degree angle into the waves, knuckles gripping the wheel until they streaked white. Acid pooled in his stomach. *This is nothing like before, just a little wind, a little rain.*

The spray from a wave hit him in the face. Not that there was much difference than the rain pelting him. The boat rose over a wave and nosed down the back of it. He forced the images of what could happen out of his mind.

Pitchpoling.
Capsizing.
Broaching.

Dangerous words rang in his ears. Or maybe it was the grumble of thunder overhead. Cody fought to hang on as another monster wave hit almost broadside. He wrenched the wheel back the other direction, attempting to tack on the slight calm between waves.

The sky hung fully dark now. The distance between Port Joseph and Jonathon Island only stretched about eight miles, but he may as well be at sea. He couldn't see either shore. He squinted at the compass mounted on his boat. The arrow swung northeast. He'd gotten turned around. Biting back a curse, or was it a shout? He swung the wheel into the next wave. The boat tilted starboard.

A prayer ripped from his lips. *Please, God, save me.* And he didn't have time for any more words because another wave caught him. Tipped him portside. He swiped at the rain on his face. It tasted salty. Maybe not rain, then.

Just then he saw another boat, another captain fighting this storm. *Bad things happen to everyone. What matters is how you deal with it.*

Okay, Liam had a point. *Focus on the good things.* Mia's words chased in.

In that moment, he made a decision. He didn't want to focus on losses anymore. No more waiting around for bad things to happen, for more loss to crash in. He was going to cherish the good things in his life for as long as he had them. He loved Mia and he couldn't wait to tell her.

Another wave crashed and there was no time to analyze that truth. He fought the lake rising in front of him.

Wait. Was that . . . ? A moment later, another flash. Land ho! Keeping his eyes on the light, Cody tacked up and down the waves, making slow progress. A grueling fifteen minutes later, he motored into Jonathon Island Marina, soaking wet, but alive.

Overhead, the thunder lost its power and the rain fell to a trickle.

He'd survived. The lights of downtown beckoned him home. He couldn't wait to get the boat docked and secured.

After tying up the boat, he hurried toward Lilac Lane.

In moments, he was turning up Mia's front walk. He tapped lightly at the door in case the kids were already in bed.

The door opened wide, framing Mia, hair in a tumble, with a red-cheeked Maggie on her hip.

"Cody! I'm so glad to see you." She reached for him and pulled him tight to her, Maggie sandwiched between them. "I know it's only been a few hours, but I missed you."

"I missed you too." His heart sank as he thought about the bad news he was about to deliver.

"The kids have been asking about your mama sheep story and the thunder. I think you've made an impression on them." She pulled back and smiled at him. "What brought you back? And why are you all wet?"

In answer, he pulled the Gushers from his pocket. Her face lit up, and she reached for the candy. "Gushers! Where did you find these?"

She looked beautiful. A band tightened around his chest.

"Can I read the kids a story?" He really wanted to

know what happened with that pigeon in their book. And spending time with the kids would help warm him up.

"They're both exhausted from the day and the storm." From the sound of her voice, the kids weren't the only ones who were exhausted. "I'll just lay them down and then we can talk."

All right then. He'd have to think of another way to warm up. Looked like he and Mia would have some alone time after all.

He sat on the couch and waited for her. The room was different without Troy's chair in the corner. Lighter somehow. Or maybe he was projecting, because despite the bad news he'd come to deliver, right now he felt lighter, and the specter of Troy didn't seem to matter as much between him and Mia.

Mia came in. She'd tied her hair back, but a tendril of it framed her face. His fingers itched to stroke that lock. She sat in the easy chair next to the couch.

"Cody, why are you wet?" A furrow creased her brow.

He pulled his hat off and ran a hand through his wet tangles. "I, uh, was out on the lake."

She shot to her feet. "In the storm?"

"Yes."

Her eyes flashed. "I hope you had a good reason."

"I did have a good reason, but before we talk about that, there's something I have to say." Her face turned stony, which wasn't super encouraging. But he'd promised himself he'd tell her. He stood too. "Mia, I've waited too long to tell you this. I love you. I think I've loved you since the day you came to the island. You are talented and kind and funny. You bring out the best in me." She opened her mouth then shut it again. Were those tears in her eyes? "I want to be with you. I want to stay in the lives of those amazing kids of yours. I want it all, Mia."

"Cody." Mia's voice tightened, and he reached for her. So, they were tears. She shook him off. "The last few hours have been traumatic for me. When the storm came up, I had flashbacks of the night Troy died. And now I find out you were in that storm? And all you can say is that you love me? It's too much." She pressed a fist to her mouth then tapped it on the arm of the chair. "Why were you even out there?"

"A good reason, I promise. I went over to Port Joseph. I met with the Harpers."

A look of horror crossed her face. "You went over there after you said you wouldn't? It wasn't enough that I sent one man to die, you thought you'd make it two?"

"I'm sorry, I—" She gave him a sharp look, and he bit off the rest of the sentence. Except, wait. "You didn't send me. I wanted to go. I offered, remember? And I never said I wouldn't go." Was it cold in here?

"But you wouldn't have gone if it weren't for me. I told you I'd figure it out. You didn't need to endanger your life for this. You didn't think I could do it?" She tightened her lips and breathed deeply.

That wasn't what he'd thought at all. "I wanted to help save your house." Yeah, it hadn't worked, but they could figure that out together. "I don't get why this is such a big deal."

"What's a house compared to you dying?" The words

should have been loving, but the hiss she delivered them in stung. "You didn't trust me to do it on my own, so you took an unnecessary risk. And for what? A contract I could get signed in a few days?"

His gut clenched. "Mia, they didn't sign. They don't want to move here."

All of the color drained from her face. She opened her mouth. Shut it.

"We can figure it out together." He reached for her again, but again she shrugged him off.

"I don't think I can be with you."

"What? You're overreacting."

"Don't tell me I'm overreacting. My husband died out there. Do you get that? Died." Every word she said punched him in the gut. "My children have no father." She pointed toward the hall. "Maggie never even met him. It doesn't matter how I feel about you. I can't open myself and them up to that again. If this is how it's going to be, I can't do it."

"I can't promise I won't go back out on the water." He squared his feet. "And I won't apologize for doing it this time either. I was trying to help you."

"Some kind of help. It didn't even work." She crossed her arms. "Sorry. That was uncalled for."

He scrubbed a hand over his face. "Look, Mia, going out on the lake is part of my job, part of the life I've chosen. But I'd give it up to be with you."

"I can't ask you to give up your dreams."

"But that's just it. You're my dream. Mia, I love you and I want to be with you."

"Have you not been listening? I can't be with you."

"But you love me, right? I know you. I can see that you feel the same way about me." He leaned forward. "We can figure this out together. I will fight for you."

"Love doesn't have anything to do with it. The kids and I can't handle losing another person. I know you want to reopen your dad's business, and Cody, you should do that." He longed to meet her eyes, but she gazed somewhere in the middle distance. "You should follow your dream. Do it for yourself, or do it for Troy even. But I can't be with you." Tears streaked their way down her face.

He ran a hand through his damp hair and gave it a tug. Who cared if it stuck up now. "So, it's choose the business or you?"

"No. I'm taking myself out of the equation." She swiped a hand across her face and turned away from him. "Have a good life. Catch lots of fish. But I can't be waiting onshore wondering if you will be coming home."

A heat flared in him, and he reached for her again. If she would just listen to him . . . "Mia, anything could happen to anyone at any time. Don't close yourself off from love just because you're scared."

Maggie called from down the hall. "Mama?"

"See you around, Cody." Her voice broke. "Will you lock the door on your way out?" Then she walked away from him.

He was too late.

Maybe if he had told her how he felt earlier, before going out on the water, it would have made a difference.

No. He knew better. He always lost everything he loved.

The revelation on the lake evaporated in the face of this. The worst bad thing to happen to him.

Seventeen

EVERYTHING FELT SORE. MIA STRETCHED out her limbs, but they still protested. This feeling was familiar. After Troy died, Mia learned that grief could show up in physical ways. Sure, her heart ached from turning Cody down last night. And, yeah, she did love him. He was right about that—she could admit it now. But she couldn't watch him die.

After Cody had left, she'd fallen into bed and dampened her pillow with a thousand tears.

She'd made the right choice to let Cody go, but that didn't make the choice any easier. Cody's words kept beating on the door of her heart. "Don't close yourself off from love just because you're scared." Well, too bad, Cody. She wasn't that brave. And she couldn't open her kids up to that potential loss. Cody had a special place in their lives, but she needed to keep it distant.

She checked the clock ticking on the wall. Any minute now, Dani would be calling with the news about her meeting with the council. She'd called Dani last night and told her she couldn't make it to the meeting, and that she was out of ideas for filling the quota.

Mia cleared the last of the breakfast dishes off the table and set them in the sink. Maybe she'd have the energy to wash them later.

When the phone rang, Mia jumped. Dani.

"I'm sorry, Mia. I have very bad news."

The oatmeal Mia had eaten for breakfast turned into a rock in her stomach. "They voted to foreclose on the house." Tears sprang to her eyes. She'd failed.

"Yes." Her cousin sniffed. "I argued for you for as long as I could, but they stood firm."

Mia sank into one of the kitchen chairs. "I would have hoped Dad would also be on my side. Didn't he stand up for me at all?"

"He wasn't able to be at the meeting. I'm not sure why. I'm coming over," Dani said. "I'm packing up right now."

"No. You don't have to do that. I'm fine." Or she would be, somehow. She just needed to figure out a way to land on her feet again. "I'll talk to you later." She hung up with Dani and then watched the clock as it ticked off the seconds. Each click sounded like a death knoll.

Enough.

In the dining room, her laptop rested under stacks of paperwork. She shoved those aside and opened the lid.

She called up the tab on her laptop where she'd saved the housing searches. Two of the apartments were now unavailable, and the other two, both one bedroom, appeared smaller than when she'd first hunted around.

Finn and Maggie wandered in, Finn clutching a car from Cody in his hand. A frown crossed his mouth. "Mom, are you crying?"

Was she? She put a hand to her cheek, and it came away wet. "It's nothing, honey. I'm okay." She cleared her throat. "I'm looking at some new places where we might live."

Finn peered at the laptop screen. "Like that yucky brown one?"

"It's not yucky." But she couldn't deny that it was brown. Very brown.

"It is gross." Finn put his little hand on his hip. "It looks like p—" She quickly put her hand over his mouth before he could finish the sentence.

Okay. That eliminated one more choice. She did some quick calculations. If she worked part-time, and maybe even got back into the realty business with its flexible hours, she might be able to afford something larger. But how was she going to find childcare?

She looked down at Finn and Maggie. They smiled up at her. Even if she could find a job, childcare, and a place to live, and those were some mighty big ifs, how could she take them away from their family and the island that they all loved? If she lived on the mainland, there was no way she'd be able to afford to take the ferry crossing as often as she wanted.

She thought of the empty bedrooms in her parents' house. Evie's words about having a conversation with her dad came to mind, and she tightened a fist. Scrawling some numbers out on a paper, she estimated how long it would take to save for a down payment on a better place.

She dialed her mom's cell phone. "Hi, Mom. Can I come over?" For her children's sake, she would put aside her pride and become the proverbial prodigal.

Putting the kids in the bike trailer made for them, Mia rehearsed what she would say to her dad. Finn and Maggie jabbered the whole way there. Their happy voices turned her resolution into steel.

A mile of hard biking and her parents' house with its sweeping porch and turrets came into view. She knew when the weather warmed, her mom would hang baskets of flowers along the porch, and her dad would drag the Adirondack chairs out of storage. She shook off the memories of this place she hadn't called home in years. She was here for her children. Not because she belonged.

Sure, she'd been back many times, but always with a buffer of other people. Today she was on her own.

Mom opened the door. She gave Mia a quick embrace. "Dad's in his study. I'll take care of these two." Mia rested a hand on each child's head briefly before they ran off to the kitchen where they knew Grandma would have a treat.

Mia walked down the hall toward her dad. Along the wall hung pictures of the whole Jonathon family. It felt like walking through time. She started with their baby pictures and then she and her siblings grew up over the course of school photos, a few family portraits thrown in here and there. Evie's wedding photo marked the change into a new generation. Mia paused at the last family photo with all of them in it.

Taken right before she'd left for college, the family appeared perfect in every way. Too bad she'd spoiled all of that less than a year later.

She moved on. No photo of her courthouse wedding graced the wall. But here were Finn and then Maggie as scrunched-up babies. Then more of all the cousins.

Too soon, Mia reached her destination. She hadn't been in her dad's study since the night almost five years ago when she'd broken the news that Finn was on the way. It hadn't changed since then. A faint smell of leather and sandalwood hung in the air. She rubbed her damp hands along her pant leg.

Her dad sat at his desk. She hesitated in the doorway until he turned to her. A smile lit his face. His thick, salt and pepper hair framed a face with more wrinkles than she remembered. Was he getting old? How had she not noticed that? They hadn't spent much time together lately, but still. You should know if your dad is getting old.

"Hey kiddo!" He still had the same booming voice. "Mom said you were coming by."

"Hi, Dad." She crossed to him. He rose and gave her a hug. Her arms stayed stiffly by her side.

"Let's sit over here." He led her to the two leather chairs framing the wall of bookshelves. "I heard Cody was out on the lake last night. I'm glad he made it home safely. That's a relief. I like that kid."

"Yes. He weathered the worst of the storm." The thought of Cody poked her heart again, so she shoved it away. That was over now.

Her dad must have noticed the look on her face. His

grin dropped away. "This doesn't seem like a pleasure visit. What can I do for you?"

Mia twisted her fingers together. "Dad, I know things haven't been great between us, but I was wondering if you would allow me to move home for a while."

"You want to move home? I thought you liked your house? Lilac Lane is a pretty part of town."

"I—I can't afford to live there anymore." She gripped her cold hands together as she outlined how Troy's insurance had been eaten away and then their meager savings. "As you obviously know, I had that deal with the city and the development committee to pay off my mortgage with a dollar." She breathed deep. She could do this. "But I didn't meet my quota."

"I heard that the council voted against paying off your mortgage but . . ." His face creased. "That means you're losing your house? Why didn't you say anything?"

"I thought you would have found out by now." She shrugged. Maybe her money problems weren't as much of a source of gossip as she thought.

"I knew about the deal, but I never suspected it was out of necessity. I thought you used Troy's insurance policy to keep paying for the mortgage."

"I did for a while, but his policy was so small . . . The kids and I have been living off the rest." Did she have to repeat herself?

Her dad reached out a hand to her but let it drop to his knee. "I'm sorry. I didn't realize how hard it has been for you. Why didn't you come to us before?"

"You've never approved of anything I've done, from

marrying Troy to any of the decisions I've made since then. I guess I just didn't want to disappoint you again." She laughed without joy. "Look how that turned out."

"Honey, it was never about disapproving of your choices. Was I surprised when you got pregnant? Sure. I didn't handle that very well, and I'm sorry for that." He reached out to her again, but she didn't reciprocate. "I should have told you that you are loved unconditionally and the choices you made and the baby, Finn, who was a result of those choices, didn't change the fact that I love you, and I always will."

Tears pricked at her eyes. "You turned away from me."

"What do you mean?"

How could he not remember? "That day. When I told you about Troy and the baby . . . I was crying, and you just sighed then called for Mom and walked away."

"I—" His eyes reddened. "I wasn't turning my back on you. I was starting to cry. I wanted to be strong for you, to pull myself together so we could make a plan. I knew your mom could give you some comfort, so I left the room. By the time I got back, you were gone. I'm so sorry I made you feel unwanted. I should have responded better."

"It just seemed like you were so angry with me. I wish I had known that was what was happening. We could have cried together." All fight left her, and she slumped in her chair. "You looked so disappointed."

"Your mom and I wanted the best life for you. We didn't know how that would happen if you were a mother at nineteen, but then we saw how happy you were with Troy and how much he loved you and took care of you. We wanted to make amends."

Mia remembered then that they had tried to reach out to her, but she had continually kept them at arm's length. She didn't want her poor decisions to affect Troy and Finn, so she'd avoided situations where her parents could pass judgment on them.

"I'm sorry, Dad. I misjudged you." Ironic, since that was what she thought he'd done to her. She leaned forward and took his hand. His eyes were red and shiny with unshed tears. Hers probably were the same. "I should have given you a chance to explain. By the time Troy and I were married, it seemed to matter less. And then Maggie was on the way, and then Troy . . . I should have listened to you. I thought I needed to do it on my own."

Her dad stood and pulled her to her feet. A moment later, she was engulfed in his arms. She breathed in the safety of being held by him.

Just like that, he was her dad again, broad shoulders that could help carry her burdens. "We all need each other." She heard his voice deep in his chest where her ear rested. He pulled back a little, not letting her out of his embrace, just enough to look her in the eyes. "More than that, we all need God. People will always fail us, but God never will. You don't have to do this all alone."

"Thanks. I think I'm finally figuring that out."

"Of course you can move home, but maybe a better option would be for us to help you with the mortgage?"

She let go of him, and he released her as they both sat back down. "No. As much as I would like that solution,

I can't manage any part of the mortgage without a job. I don't want to be in debt to you and Mom. I need to find a cheaper solution. Living in the house on Lilac Lane is a dream that needs to die." Tears pricked her eyes again as she thought of leaving her little home. But the thought didn't hurt as much as she'd expected. The knowledge that her mom and dad were on her side helped.

Her dad nodded. "Okay, I'll respect your decision on this. It sounds like you've thought it through."

She reached into her bag and pulled out a sheet of paper. "I still have my real estate license." She handed him the paper where she'd outlined her expenses and a possible timeline. "I think if I start a real estate business, I wouldn't have to live here very long before I can afford to rent something nicer in Port Joseph or another town over there than what I can currently afford." She pointed at the bottom line. "Once people start moving back to Jonathon Island, business will pick up. And, when the hotel is finished, we'll probably see a housing boom too. If I can sell that many houses a year, I might be able to save for a down payment on another house."

He rubbed his chin as he looked at her numbers. "This all looks good."

Her heart swelled. "Thanks, Dad."

He handed back the paper and leaned back in his chair, steepling his fingers. "Where does Cody fit into this plan of yours?"

She rubbed at her chest. "Cody?"

"What does he think of all these plans?"

"I don't know. He doesn't know about the meeting and the vote." She swallowed hard.

A line appeared between her dad's eyebrows. "Don't you think he would like to discuss this with you?"

"Why would I discuss this with him?"

"I know I haven't been a stellar father to you lately, but the whole island is aware that you and Cody are in a relationship. I just think it would be a good idea to discuss everything with him."

She dropped her gaze to her hands. "I told Cody I couldn't be in a relationship with him. It's too hard."

"Sweetie, love is hard. But it doesn't always end in tragedy. You can't let what happened with Troy cut you off from love. Where would it stop? Would you stop loving your kids because they will leave someday?" He covered her clasped hands with one of his own. His heat seeped into her fingers. "Don't harden your heart. Sure, being vulnerable is hard, but the rewards are so very worth it."

"When I learned that Cody was out in the storm, I was so scared. What if I lost another man that I love? Plus, I don't think he trusted me to make it on my own."

"Sounds to me you are already losing him, but this time by a choice you are making. Does it hurt less?"

Her gaze flew to her dad. A softness lingered around his eyes. "No. It hurts pretty much the same." In fact, it felt like tearing out her heart with a filet knife.

He smiled. "I think this is more about your desire to control the loss in your life. You think if you can control it, it will hurt less. But it doesn't work that way. All loss hurts. And there will be plenty of pain in life, but you don't have to choose this one. It's worth the risk." Her dad leaned toward her. "I hate to break it to you, but none of us can make it on our own. We all need each other."

Her dad's words jangled through her brain, chasing her home and all through the bedtime routine with her kids. After she'd tucked Finn and Maggie in for the night, she laid on the couch and stared at the ceiling. *Being vulnerable is hard, but the rewards are so very worth it.*

She pictured Cody, his goofy smile, his kindness with the kids, his wisdom, his poetic nature. And he'd never said she couldn't do it on her own, just that he wanted to help her, to support her and her decisions.

Yeah. *You're right, Dad.*

Loving Cody was worth the risk.

Cody woke up feeling like he'd wrestled a six foot, one-hundred-pound lake sturgeon single-handedly into his boat.

He'd walked like a robot through the day yesterday after Mia had broken things off with him. Then, last night, he'd tossed and turned in his bed, hashing through the arguments for and against all of his dreams. He'd cried out to God throughout the night, asking for wisdom.

Then, this morning he'd called Liam and told him what had happened on the water and how Liam's words had helped.

"That's great," Liam said. "You sound tired."

He told Liam what he'd been wrestling with all night. "I don't know if I should give everything up or keep fighting."

"You don't have to let one bad thing define you. Or even a series of bad things." Liam cleared his throat. "God loves you, man, and that's what defines you. Do what He created you to do."

He hung up with Liam with a renewed determination. He respected Mia's decision to not have a romantic relationship, even if the thought felt like having fishhooks stuck through his heart. But he could still chase after the dream of reopening the fishing company.

Even after the storm the night before last, he couldn't deny that the passion for being on the water burned bright in his chest. While he would have given up all of that for Mia, he couldn't imagine a better life.

He briefly toyed with the idea that he should give it up just to show her he was serious about her, but he knew she wouldn't be happy if he did that. Part of respecting her decision was making some of his own.

He pulled on a pair of joggers and a lightweight jacket and then his running shoes. He'd take his morning run and end up at his parents' house.

Time to confront his dad once and for all. Time to fight for what he wanted and not to just wait for loss to find him.

The sun shone bright in the blue sky as he pounded the trail. After running a mile out and back, he turned up the road that led to his parents'. When he got close, he saw that the shed door stood ajar. He slowed his pace, evened out his breathing, and went in.

"Hey there, Cody." His dad stood near the tool bench, a fishing rod in his hand. "Lily caught her first fish with this rod. For a while I thought she might be the fisherman between you two. She could catch a fish just by looking in the water."

Cody laughed. "Our good luck charm." Was his dad really starting to talk to him again? Incredible.

His dad hung the fishing rod back on a hook then took down a different one. "This is the rod you caught your first fish on, do you remember that?"

Cody remembered the bright summer morning, the feel of the tug on the line, then the overwhelming pleasure of landing the fish. It had flopped around in the bottom of the boat until his dad picked it up and showed him how to pull out the hook. "I think I cried."

"No shame in having some emotions. That was a big day for you."

Did he accidentally turn down Memory Lane? "Dad, I didn't come over here to reminisce." He leaned a hip against the tool bench. "But I guess that's a good place to start. You know how much I love fishing. Both tossing in a line for breakfast on the beach and doing the commercial fishing with you. You taught me to love it."

His father nodded but wouldn't meet his eye. "You used to be the most passionate fisherman I've ever met."

"And I want to rekindle that fire. You can't ask me to give that up. I don't want to give it up." He noticed his hands flailing and tucked them into his pockets. "Why, Dad? Why don't you want me to buy your business? And the fishing license?"

The hand holding the fishing rod trembled. "I lost my best friend out there. Not to mention Troy. Two fine men."

"Do you still blame me for the accident? Is that why? Because you don't trust me out there?"

"Blame you? I don't blame you. If anything, I blame myself. I should have let that one go. We'd already put in a full week." His dad passed a hand over his eyes. "I heard about that school of fish, and all I could think about was how it could be an extra mortgage payment for your mom and me. We didn't really need the money, but I thought if I could pay off the house, I could save up to take your mother somewhere nice for our thirtieth anniversary." His dad looked at him, eyes pleading for understanding. "I don't blame you, Cody. You did everything right."

"Then what? You still haven't answered my question. Why can't I buy you out?" His belly still churned. The admission from his father salved some of his wounded heart, but if it wasn't that his dad blamed him for the accident, what could it be?

"I'm scared!" The words exploded out of his father. He turned and braced both of his hands on the bench. His shoulders hunched, knuckles white. "I don't want to lose my only son the way I lost my friend—the way you lost yours. Every time you talk about going back out on the water, a kind of panic comes over me."

"Dad—"

"No, let me finish. It's been a long time coming. You were right to make me talk about this." His dad heaved himself up and away from the bench. He faced Cody square on. "When I thought about you going back out on the water, I thought I would lose my mind. Your mother reminded me that all my worrying wouldn't keep you safe, only God can do that. She said you are written on His hand." He rubbed the top of his head, a gesture Cody recognized as resignation. "I've got a ways to go, but your mother was right. I need to leave your safety up to God. People die all the time from all sorts of things: cancer, car crashes, heart attacks. It's out of our control."

Something loosened inside him. "I'm not likely to be struck by a car on this island."

His dad met his eyes. Then started chuckling. Pretty soon the both of them were laughing together.

"My sides hurt." Cody wiped at his eyes. "I needed that."

"Me too. Things were getting a little too touchy feely there for a minute." His dad smiled, all his teeth showing. He breathed deeply, his shoulders rising and lowering. "Listen. The truth is I've lost the taste for fishing. Some part of me wishes you had as well."

"Oh." Cody started to say more, but his dad held up a hand to stop him.

"But I've been giving it a lot of thought, and your mother keeps after me about it." His dad raised an eyebrow. They both knew how stubborn Cody's mom could be when she set her mind to something. "Just because I've given up that life doesn't mean you have to."

Cody lost a breath for a moment. "What are you saying?"

"I will give you the license and sell you the rest of the equipment. No timeline. You can start using it whenever that boat of yours is seaworthy, and you can pay me some with every catch." His dad handed him the fishing rod from his first catch. "The business is yours if you still want it."

Cody whooped and hugged his dad. "Thank you!" A thousand fireworks were going off in his stomach. He grinned so wide he thought his face would split in two. His dad grinned right back at him.

A few minutes later, he stood in the yard blinking at the bright sunshine. Were his feet touching the ground? Everything in him ached to run to Mia. He clenched his hand.

A bittersweet day.

Time to get back to work on that boat engine. He'd need it soon now.

He started walking back to his shop. At the junction of Partridge Lane and Main Street, he spotted Dani walking down Jonathon Lane.

"Hey, Dani." He waved at the blonde.

She startled. "Hey, Cody."

"Sorry. Didn't mean to interrupt your thoughts."

"I was just imagining all the new people who will be moving on island over the next couple of weeks. It's an exciting time." Dani blew a hair off her face.

"You don't look excited."

"I just can't keep myself from worrying about Mia."

His heart stopped. "Mia? Why? Is there something wrong?"

"Didn't she tell you? She didn't meet her quota, so the council can't honor her one-dollar mortgage."

"Can't or won't?" Something like a growl worked its way up in his throat. They wouldn't seriously turn a widowed woman and two small children out of their home, would they?

Dani shrugged, palms up. A grimace passed over her face. "I tried to talk to them, but they stood firm. The Kelleys said that I shouldn't get a vote because I'm biased. And Uncle Seb wasn't at the meeting. She signed the contract, so they feel justified. She told me yesterday that she's moving home." Dani frowned at him. "I thought Mia would have told you all this."

Right. So sometimes news didn't travel fast on Jonathon Island. "Mia and I broke up. Or whatever you call it when two people went out on one date and are developing feelings for each other and one of them calls it off."

Dani swatted him in the chest. "Why did you break up with her?"

"Me? No, she broke it off with me."

"And you just let her?"

"I—"

"Is there something wrong with my cousin? Is she not good enough for you?" Dani put her hands on her hips.

"No, she's the best thing that ever happened to me. I don't want to lose her." The realization wrapped around him. He straightened his spine. The promise he'd made to her about waiting a hundred years still held. He loved Mia, and he wasn't going to let that good thing go.

"Well, get her back, you idiot!" Dani propped her hands on her hips. "Why are you still talking to me? Go, fight for the girl. But go slow with her, she is scared to love again."

"How? I want to respect her wishes. She's afraid to lose

me like she lost Troy. So how can I show her that love is worth the risk?"

"She's not just worried about that. She's worried to need you. But she does need you—so show her that. Do something for her that she can't do for herself."

"Like what?"

Dani tapped her chin. "I think I have an idea."

Eighteen

MIA WOKE JUST AS THE SUN BEGAN cresting the skyline. She threw off her covers and went to the window. Outside, the sun's rays held the Midas touch. Her fingers itched to paint the way the sun streamed through the barren branches of the oak on the side of the yard, casting each twig in gold. She grabbed her cell phone and snapped a few photos. The phone's camera didn't do the vibrant colors justice, but it would remind her when she set up her easel later.

Her easel. Huh. Funny how that thought had slipped into her mind.

Now that she didn't have to worry about where she and the kids were going to be living, her creative thoughts knocked on the door of her brain and demanded entry. Yeah, moving back in with her parents felt a bit like taking a step backward, but it was worth it just to have the thousand-pound elephant off her shoulders.

Today, she would paint again. A pulse of gratitude flooded her. Cody had reawakened her desire to paint with his romantic date.

She couldn't stop grinning as she pulled on an old pair of pants and a grubby T-shirt. She'd called Cody a few times to tell him she wanted to meet up so she could tell him she was ready for a relationship, but it went to voicemail. Something this big shouldn't be said in a message. She would go over there later to talk it over with him.

Knowing that she would be creating again made her feel more like herself than she'd felt in a very long time.

So. Painting. But first, pancakes.

Finn and Maggie came out to the kitchen while she mixed up a batch of blueberry pancakes. She dragged a chair to the countertop so Maggie could help drop the batter onto the electric griddle, then she hoisted Finn into her arms so he could flip them.

A dozen imperfect pancakes later, they sat down to eat. "Finn, can you say a prayer for us?" Beside her, Maggie scrunched her eyes closed and knit her hands together under her chin.

Finn sat up straighter in his chair and began. "For this food that breaks our fast, for this morning come at last, for this love that we share, thank you God for all Your care."

"Thank you, Finn," Mia said. "After we eat, do you guys want to do something fun? I want to show you how I used to use paints."

Both kids finished their pancakes in record time.

She buttoned Maggie and Finn each into one of Troy's old shirts and rolled up the sleeves before donning one herself. She decided to set up in the kitchen. The light was good in there, and the sink was handy for cleanups. She covered the table with a few plastic garbage bags.

The kids trailed behind her as she moved around the house taking out her supplies from the places she'd stashed them. She made them stay down in the hall, though, as she went up into the attic crawl space for a large canvas she'd put up there.

Mia's hands shook as she uncovered the supplies. Was she really going to do this?

She took a deep breath. Yes. This was the right choice.

Back in the kitchen again, she showed them how to squirt a little paint onto their paper plate pallet and mix the colors.

"It's fun to see what kinds of contrasts you can make," she said. Finn splatted blobs all over his canvas while Maggie, tongue between her teeth, made long streaks across hers from edge to edge. Mia pulled up her sunrise photo on her phone. She mixed a few colors together, trying to get the golden shade of the morning. Take it slow. It'd been a long time.

Today's painting wasn't about getting it right or being perfect. It was about having fun with her kids and letting her hair down.

Cody had been right. She should share this part of herself with her children. And she shouldn't deny that she needed to create. Cody had also showed her how to be more relaxed with the kids. That they could have fun together sometimes.

The doorbell rang.

"I'll get it!" The mainland probably heard Finn's jubilant shout, but Mia let it go this time. She felt a little like shouting herself.

She heard the door open and then footsteps back to them in the kitchen. She looked up.

Cody.

He leaned in the kitchen doorway, one arm propped on the jamb. He wore dark pants and a fitted blazer instead of his usual jeans and flannel jacket. His hair was tamed, and she caught a whiff of his styling product, something spicy and heady. A smile ghosted his lips and her breath caught.

How could she ever have thought she could go on without him?

"I hope you don't mind me barging in," Cody said. "Finn said you're painting?" A note of surprise crept into his voice and lit his eyes.

"You were right. I need to do this once in a while." She motioned to the canvas in front of her, its streaks of gold already taking the shape of an oak.

"I need to talk to you."

"I'm glad you're here." Mia and Cody spoke together.

"Sorry, you go first," Cody said.

Mia shot him a weak smile. "We should probably clean this up first. I don't want the kids getting paint on your nice clothes."

"I don't mind a little paint."

"All the same . . ."

Mia showed the kids how to rinse out their paintbrushes, and Cody capped the paints and stacked the supplies into their boxes. She left the canvases on the table to dry. She patted the one she'd been working on, the lines still fresh in her mind. *I'll be back for you.*

A few minutes later, the kids were in the backyard playing on the ancient swing set Troy had dragged home one day shortly after Finn was born. Mia tugged two plastic chairs together, and she and Cody sat and watched the kids.

"Dani told me you're moving home." Cody leaned back in his chair, the plastic squeaking in the chilly air.

"Yep. After all our hard work, I didn't meet my quota for the mortgage." Mia hugged her arms to herself.

"How do you feel about that?"

"It's funny, I thought I'd be more upset, but I'm learning to trust God. I'm very sad to be leaving this house, but I'm proud of the work I did trying to keep it. The island will have some great new businesses."

"You did a really good job. It's not worth much, but I'm proud of you."

"That means a lot, thank you." Mia's heart warmed at his words. Being admired by Cody was amazing. "Was this what you came over here to talk about?"

"No, actually." Cody leaned forward and put his arms on his knees. His eyes grew intense. "I've done a lot of thinking the past few days. I even went over to my dad's and hashed things out with him."

"Code, that's great."

"Yeah, story for another time." Cody waved it off. "Mia, I gave up too easily the other night when you said we couldn't be together. It's been a pattern of mine throughout my life, a pattern I'd like to change. Starting today.

I'm learning that God wants good things for me, and I shouldn't be afraid to follow my dreams, even fight for them when necessary. So, here I am, fighting for the dream of being with you."

Mia stared at him. This determination was a good look for Cody. Her mind scrambled to find a reply. *You are my dream too . . . I'll fight with you . . .* But she must have been silent a beat too long because Cody stood.

"I understand. I can even understand your fears. I'm reopening my dad's business, and I know what that might mean for us. But I couldn't let you go without telling you everything and making sure you knew that I love you. And that I will wait for you as long as you need." He took a step away. "You're not alone, Mia. You can depend on other people, on me."

"I love you." The words burst from her in a rush. Cody's gaze flew to hers. She stood and moved across the space between them. "You were right the other night. I do love you, Cody. I think my heart knew it all along, just took my mind a little time to catch up. I've realized something the past few days. I tried to call you to tell you this morning, but you didn't answer." She reached out and touched his forearm. It warmed under her caress. His eyes searched her face. "My life is better with you in it. You were right that we can't protect ourselves from every pain or fear. I want to fight for us with you and walk through these things together. I've realized that raising my kids, and doing my job, and anything really, I can't do it alone. And more importantly, I don't have to."

Cody put his hand over hers on his arm. "Go back to what you said before."

"I don't have to do it alone?"

"No, the other thing." His eyes crinkled at the corners.

Her lips turned up in response. "You were right?"

"No, the other other thing."

A zing zipped along her spine. "I love you?"

"That's the one." His smile bloomed.

She put her hand on top of his. A hand sandwich. "I do love you. I love your spontaneity. I love your gentle spirit. I love your love of doorknobs." She gave him a wink. "And it doesn't hurt that you're also very cute."

"I was going for debonair." He gestured at the clothes.

"That too." She leaned toward him. "Cody?"

"Hmm?"

"You can kiss me now."

He pulled his hands free and cupped them around her face. Slowly, he rubbed his thumbs over her cheekbones, sending a delicious shiver through her. He leaned toward her and met her lips. She saw his eyes crinkle in a smile for a second, but then hers slid closed. She pressed closer to him, and he moved his arms around to her back. He tightened his grip before moving one hand to cup the back of her head.

Cody's embrace was like being wrapped in her favorite blanket, safe in her own living room, but it was also like lighting a thousand fireworks. Surely the people in Port Joseph could see the sparks all the way across Lake Huron.

"Mommy, are you kissing Cody?" Finn's voice of absolute disgust broke the spell around them.

Mia kept her arms around Cody but pulled back to speak to Finn. "Yes. I am. Is that okay?"

"I guess." He wrinkled his nose. "Can I have a hot chocolate?"

Cody released her. A terrible loss. "I actually wondered if you guys would like to take a walk with me," he said. "I have something I want to show you."

Finn stared at him out of the corner of his eye. "Can we take the wagon?"

"Sure, bud. Maybe we can get hot chocolate after." He held a hand out to Mia. "How about it? Want to take a walk with me?"

Looking into his eyes, she knew that she would go anywhere as long as they were together.

Life didn't get much better than this.

Once again, Cody and Mia and Mia's kids walked the familiar path into town. This time though, Cody couldn't stop grinning.

"What are you so happy about?" Mia bumped him with her shoulder. He looked down at her. Pale yellow sweater, slim jeans, a matching yellow bandanna in her hair, she was sunshine embodied. Behind them, in the wagon, Maggie's purple bobble hat bounced to the rhythm of their steps. Finn pretended to be driving a race car, or maybe it was a boat with the growling and splashing noises he made.

"Can't I just be happy to be walking with a beautiful woman and two great kids?" He tucked her hand into his.

"I suppose." Her smile dimmed.

"I know that look. What's up?"

"It's just that I'm a little sad to be leaving this neighborhood." She waved her arm in an "all this" gesture. "Don't get me wrong, it was wonderful of my parents to allow me to move there, but their house is a little isolated up there on the northern tip of the island . . . and Lilac Lane feels more like home, you know?"

He nodded. With all the time he'd spent there the past few weeks, it had come to feel like home for him too.

"I just wish I knew when the bank was going to repossess it. They haven't given me an exact date, so it's hard for me to plan. I don't want to move Finn and Maggie out until the very last minute. Maybe that's selfish of me."

"I don't know. It doesn't sound selfish to me. You want the best for your kids. That's admirable. And you're probably the least selfish person I've ever met."

The pensive look faded from her face and was replaced by a toothy smile. He gave her hand a squeeze. "Okay, that was a switch. Now what are you so happy about?"

"I was just remembering a few weeks ago when I was walking this route alone. My life has changed so much since then."

"For the better I hope." Cody waggled his eyebrows at her.

"Definitely for the better." She looped her arm into his and smiled up at him. Behind them, the kids were singing a song about the wheels on a bus.

Yeah. His had changed for the better also. Now that the burden of guilt about Troy's death had rolled off his back, he felt a hundred pounds lighter. Of course, the ability to move forward with his fishing business helped too. Add in the newfound footing he and Mia had found, well it was almost enough to make a grown man break out into song.

The only cloud on his horizon was the one that wondered if he'd overstepped with his surprise.

Guess they'd find out in a minute.

He pulled the wagon to a stop at the old Sampson gallery. The sun seemed prepared to help him out, perfectly lighting the scene. Even from outside the doors, he could see that the warm, yellow paint inside the gallery was making the interior glow. He unlocked the door and ushered them all in, leaving the wagon on the sidewalk.

"I still can't believe how wonderful this place looks," Mia said. The kids made a beeline for the hidden door.

"Don't worry. I made sure the door won't lock us in again. And I latched the hidden door open, so it won't close on the kids."

"Thanks." Mia sighed and turned in a slow circle. "It's too bad Matt doesn't want this place. It would have been fun to have an art gallery in town again."

"What is that?" She pointed at an item he'd covered with a light tarp.

He uncovered it with a flourish. "This is the first piece for the Mia Franklin Art Gallery. Or whatever you want to call your business."

Her hand flew to cover her mouth and her eyes widened. "Where did you get that?"

On the wall, Cody had hung one of the paintings Mia had brought home from college. An oil painting depicting two people walking hand in hand in the rain under a bright red umbrella. "Your mom had it in storage. She said you told her to throw it away, but she knew you'd want it again someday. She also said she had a bunch more just waiting for you."

"What do you mean 'first piece'?" Mia had dropped her hand and walked closer to him.

"You are now standing in your very own art studio slash realtor business." He opened his arms wide. "You can pick up the rest of your art and start selling it until you get some realty clients."

A line grew between her eyebrows. "I'm confused. What are you talking about?"

"I sold Troy's boat to Patrick Kelley. He wanted it for his daughter, Olive. Then I used a little of that money to put the down payment on this place. The rest can be used to supplement the rent and everything else for the next twelve months. That way you can focus on building a business and finding more time to paint. And another way to help pay the rent is to split it with another company."

Her brow wrinkled. "Do you think we can find someone?"

"You're looking at someone." He thumbed his chest.

"What?"

"My dad agreed to sell me the fishing business and his license. I figure I'll need somewhere to meet with clients once in a while and somewhere to do some bookkeeping and whatnot. I don't want to live in my shed all the time, so why not split the rent? If you'll have me, that is."

"Cody, this is amazing." She reached up and put her

hand on his chest. He covered it with one of his own. "Of course I'd love to."

He slipped an arm around her shoulder and drew her closer. "I have even better news. Dani and I convinced your dad to call an emergency meeting of the town council. They agreed that having three new businesses in town definitely qualified as meeting your quota. You will not have to move out of your house."

Her mouth fell open, and he had to resist the urge to kiss it back into place. She clapped her hands and danced in place. "I can't believe you did all of this for me. Especially since you didn't know I'd changed my mind about you."

"Did I overstep?"

"Maybe a little. But I love that you did. I needed the reminder that I need other people. You make me a better person, Code." She reached up and pulled his head down for a kiss.

"Mom, come look!" Finn interrupted them before Cody totally lost his head and forgot that they were in a public place.

They walked to the back of the store. Finn pointed with both of his hands at the hidden door, now bolted open. He watched Mia as she took it all in. Inside the little room, he'd added a narrow bookshelf, a toy cupboard, two bean bag chairs, and some old Christmas lights from his mom.

Mia looked up at him, eyes wide.

He smiled down at her. "I figured the kids would be spending a lot of time here. They should have a space to call their own. I hope you like it."

"Like it?" Mia threaded her fingers through his. "I love it. Looks like the kids do too."

They stood hand in hand and watched as Finn and Maggie pulled books off the shelves and settled into a bean bag chair.

How had he ever thought God didn't want good things for his life? God had proven Himself faithful over and over.

Cody glanced down at Mia, then over at the kids again.

Yep. He'd given Cody good things in abundance.

READ ON FOR MORE FROM

Jonathon
Island

Return to Jonathon Island in book 3,
Meet Me at the Fudge Shop
by Lindsay Harrel and Rachel D. Russell.

Two rival families. One historic fudge shop.
And a second chance at love
neither saw coming.

All Lily Hart wants is to prove she's not the failure everyone thinks she is. After a series of setbacks—including failing out of business school and losing her dream apprenticeship—Lily returns to Jonathon Island with one goal in mind: save her family's 74-year-old fudge shop and finally show the world she's a capable businesswoman. The island is starting to bounce back, and Lily's determined to be part of its revival. But when she arrives, she finds a major problem: her former high school sweetheart, Declan Kelley, is back too—and he's claiming the shop for his family.

The Harts and Kelleys have been bitter rivals for nearly fifty years, ever since Declan's grandfather started his own competing fudge shop. Declan's return isn't just about family pride, though. He's here to save his grandmother's house from foreclosure, and reopening the Kelley fudge shop is the only way to do it.

With the lease in dispute, Lily and Declan strike a deal: whoever sells the most fudge in one month gets the shop. Forced to share the space, sparks—and old feelings—begin to fly. Lily's creative flair and Declan's business acumen might just be the perfect recipe for success...if they can stop fighting long enough to realize it.

But with Declan's future in Chicago and Lily's heart set on staying, can they truly find a way back to each other? Or will their families' long-standing feud—and their own desires—pull them apart for good?

Sweet, swoony, and full of heart, this is the story of two people discovering that sometimes, love is the sweetest thing of all.

One

GENIUS DIDN'T ALWAYS STRIKE AT three a.m. on a Friday in June, but when it did, it involved caramel, a decadent truffle center, and roasted cashews—all wrapped in a hand-dipped, dark chocolate shell with a zigzag of white chocolate garnish to make it pop.

Lily Hart's secret ingredient? Bergamot oil, just the right number of drops to create a citrusy, herby deliciousness.

Elusive. Mesmerizing. Sublime.

So what if she hadn't slept last night? Hadn't even gone home after working a grueling twelve-hour shift. But that's what was demanded if you wanted to be an apprentice to Master Chocolatier Oscar Granger at Palm Coast's Florida Sullivan Resort.

Who needed sleep, anyway?

This was brilliance. And yes, it had taken her all night,

but these candies were her ticket to having Oscar's ear at long last. To being more than a grunt worker.

To finally proving to herself—to everyone back home—that she *was* successful. Or at least was on her way.

She glanced past the gleaming commercial-grade, stainless steel prep station, where The Sullivan's kitchen staff would soon be cooking up one of the best breakfast spreads this side of Orlando, toward the gleaming glass clock set over the swinging double doors that led to an opulent dining room. Soon, Oscar and her fellow apprentices would walk into the kitchen and make their way toward the pastry section in the back corner, roll up their sleeves, and begin another day of creating the award-winning desserts worthy of The Sullivan's acclaim.

And she'd have one already prepared for Chef Oscar Granger, award-winning, albeit exacting, baker, head of the pastry kitchen.

He'd take one look—and then one taste and...

Well, her big sacrifice of moving thirteen hundred miles from home, hours and hours of training, and even the scrutiny of her resort boss, Daniel Sullivan, would be worth it.

Not an apprentice anymore, but a full-on bakery chef, in one of the best pastry kitchens in Orlando, with multiple convection and deck ovens and space for roll-in ovens when needed, plus a stove, a long wooden island for bread making, a marble one for tabling chocolate, three massive refrigerators, a proofing case, two mixers, and every other tool a pastry chef could desire.

Take that, Declan-the-Jerk Kelley.

Blinking away the exhaustion that kept sneaking up on her, Lily took a swig of her coffee, now cold, and leaned down to take one final look over her confections at eye level. Ten gorgeous chocolates seemed to wink back at her from their placement on a simple white plate with a golden caramel spiral. She inhaled the sweet, rich chocolate aroma.

Mmm. Yes. Genius.

Grabbing her pen, she added one final word to her recipe card.

Enjoy.

"Lily!"

She jumped, her pen clattering onto the island as she glanced up to find her coworker-slash-friend Kayleigh standing over her, hands on her hips.

Kayleigh sported a frown to go with her stark-white apron and brown hair pulled tight into a bun at the base of her neck. "How long have you been here?"

"Hi." Lily straightened, smiled. "All night. But look what beauty my efforts produced."

"All night? But why?"

"I couldn't exactly create on my wonky stovetop. I needed the chocolate tempering machine—"

"No," Kayleigh said. "Why?" She pointed to the dessert.

Oh. "I just told you. I was creating." Lily rotated the plate. "Oscar can't ignore my suggestions anymore once he tastes these. I've worked here five years, Kayleigh. *Five years* of making the same old boring chocolates."

"And I've been here three. What's your point?"

"It's time for a change."

Kayleigh gave her a look. "Oscar *hates* change."

"He only *thinks* he hates change. But when he tastes these, he'll change—his mind, that is."

"I highly doubt that." Kayleigh lifted an eyebrow and pushed Lily's cup of coffee toward her, as if to indicate she needed to drink more.

Fine, maybe she *was* getting punchy.

Lily drained her cup and tossed it into the garbage. "You'll see. These chocolates will wake him up from the boring dessert world he's been living in. He'll discover there are more ingredients than caramel, walnuts, and peanut butter—though I have nothing against any of them, if jazzed up a bit."

"Oscar likes classic desserts. That's the job, Lily. Besides, since when does the word dessert belong with *boring*?" Kayleigh glanced back at the door. "He's going to be here in ten minutes. And we're supposed to be prepping for the McAllen wedding." She'd donned her pastry hat. "What kind of bride doesn't want a cake?"

"I think it's fun—a dozen different desserts and chocolates for the dessert table instead. Which is why I made these."

Kayleigh shook her head. "You know Oscar's never going to accept one of your suggestions, right?"

"You don't know that. Last month, Carlos suggested we add sprinkles to the strawberry Pop-Tart fudge for that kid's birthday bash we catered, and Oscar agreed to try it."

"But that was *Carlos*."

"Yeah, the Golden Boy." She finger-quoted the words.

"The man has zero imagination. Sprinkles? For a ten-year-old boy? How about the sparklers I suggested?"

"Carlos is smarter than you think. He's already created a five-year plan to own his own shop. *He's* going places."

Lily blinked at her. "And what, I'm stuck in a vat of cooling chocolate hardening around my feet? Seriously. Did you not see these chocolates?" She held up the plate. "*Perfection.*"

But Kayleigh wasn't looking at her. In fact, she pushed past her and peered into the tempering machine. "Lily, you need to clean this. You know Oscar insists on a spotless kitchen at the start of the day."

Oh. "I guess I got too involved with finishing the chocolates." She hurried toward the tempering machine, grabbed a ten-pound mold, and flipped the switch to empty what was left of the chocolate from last night's batch into it. The chocolate pumped out steadily at first, then slower, filling the air with the sugar-laden smell of melted chocolate.

"I'll get these." Kayleigh walked Lily's spatula and a few other tools to the sink and began washing them.

"Thank you." The chocolate stream ended, and Lily moved the chocolate mold to the counter. Then she removed the auger from the machine and placed it in the right side of the sink. "I'll wash that in a minute."

"I don't mind."

Lily stopped at the exasperation in Kayleigh's tone. "Clearly you do."

Kayleigh picked up the mold, started scrubbing. "You just always do this."

"Do what?"

"Lose track of time, get your head stuck in the clouds, forget about what you're *supposed* to be doing."

Her words struck something deep inside Lily—and a memory surfaced from long ago. Another voice, much angrier, more masculine, saying similar things. She pushed the thought aside. No. She was different now.

But Kayleigh's words still stabbed at her. And maybe she hadn't changed that much because shoot, it ignited all her defenses.

"What I'm *supposed* to be doing here is becoming a better chocolatier. Learning from one of the greats. But how can we become great, how can we push ourselves to become better, if we aren't allowed to experiment, to create? That's the best part of this whole job."

Kayleigh dropped the clean mold into the rinse sink, looked at her, suds on her arms. "The best part of this job is keeping it. We've got an amazing opportunity here."

"I know that."

"Especially after the pandemic." Kayleigh dove again into the sudsy water, this time with the auger. "You're lucky you had a connection with Mr. Sullivan. I waited two years, and called every week, hoping they'd take my apprentice application."

No, she was lucky that her childhood friend Dani Sullivan had talked up Lily to her father, Daniel, who had grown up eating the Hart Family Fudge.

No, lucky might be her family's shop *not* dying after the pandemic.

Maybe she didn't believe in luck, really. Just...reality.

Tempered occasionally with a good dessert. Like Mr. Sullivan said, desserts brought people together.

She wanted to believe that with everything inside her.

"Listen, I'm grateful that Oscar hired me."

"Are you?" More suds went flying as Kayleigh dropped the auger into the rinse sink. "Because you seem intent on throwing that opportunity away."

Okay, ouch. "I just think this job should be, I don't know, fun. Creative." She scraped the remaining chocolate down the drain.

Kayleigh sighed. "I'm sorry, Lily. I shouldn't have said that. You've clearly got a lot of talent. I just think you should be careful. Stay focused. I won't always be here to clean up your messes."

Lily's head shot up. Never mind the *clean up your messes* part. "Are you *leaving*?"

Kayleigh grabbed a towel. Turned, her mouth tight.

Oh no.

Finally, "Oscar recommended me for a job as Assistant Master Chocolatier at a new hotel in Nashville."

A beat. Then, somehow, "Wow. Congratulations," emerged from her mouth. Nah, she could do better. Kayleigh was her *friend*. "That sounds like an amazing opportunity. But I'll miss you."

Kayleigh lifted a shoulder. "They wanted someone with a degree. Otherwise, I'm sure Oscar would have recommended you, since you've been here longer than me."

She didn't bother to argue that an associate's degree was a degree. But Lily knew what Kayleigh meant. They wanted a bachelor's degree, and Kayleigh had graduated top of her class with a bachelor's in Chocolates and Confectionery Arts Entrepreneurship from the Sunshine State Culinary Institute.

The same program Lily had failed out of five years ago. So yeah, there was that.

"Lily…" Kayleigh took a step toward her.

Lily held up her hand. "I'm fine. It's fine. And great for you. Seriously. You deserve it." She gave Kayleigh a quick hug. "And to celebrate—here." She moved to her plate of chocolates, pulling one off and holding it out to Kayleigh's hands. "You can be the first to try them."

"You haven't tried one yet?"

"Don't need to. I did several small batches that weren't right, but I just have a feeling about this batch."

"You and your feelings." Kayleigh huffed out a laugh. "Honestly, they're usually right. At least where chocolate's concerned."

"Thank you." Lily took a bow, then grinned and held up a second chocolate. "Here's to new beginnings."

Kayleigh's eyes shimmered with unshed tears, a rare sight. "That means a lot, Lily. And I know you'll get your big break someday."

The sentiment warmed Lily's heart. "If this chocolate is as amazing as I think it is, maybe sooner rather than later."

"I hope so." Then Kayleigh took a bite of the chocolate. Her eyes closed and she tilted her head toward the ceiling. Then groaned. "Okay, I think I just got seven cavities. That's delicious."

Lily pumped her fist and then took her own bite. Flavor exploded on her tongue—unique, immersive.

And yes, perfect.

The door slammed open behind her. "Good morning," a baritone rang out.

Carlos stood on the other side of the island, staring at the kitchen behind Lily, his bushy black eyebrows bunched together. He made a huffing noise and shook his head. Gave a small grin. "You are in so much trouble, Hart."

What—?

But behind him, through the door walked Oscar, a tall fifty-something with a handlebar mustache and piercing brown eyes.

His gaze landed on the tempering machine, still crusted with chocolate on the inside.

He looked at her. "Tell me." And then he pointed at the machine.

"I'm sorry, sir. I was just getting the machine cleaned."

"You mean the machine I assigned you to clean last night?"

Lily darted a glance at Kayleigh, whose eyes widened.

"Um, yes. Well, actually, I did clean it but then took the initiative to create some new chocolates for tonight. I worked all night on a new recipe for a bergamot chocolate crunch. That's not the name—I haven't come up with the name yet, actually, but—"

"Ms. Hart—"

Nope, she couldn't stop now. "Try one, sir. I think this could be our next big thing. I even wrote down the recipe so we could mass produce it for tonight's wedding if you like it."

"Tonight's menu is already set."

"Sir, if you'll just try one, I think—"

He held up a hand. "I don't pay you to think. I pay you to do what I assign you. And you clearly haven't done that."

"No, but if you'll just try—"

"This isn't the first time, either. You know what's holding you back? Discipline. You're impulsive and flighty. Not dependable."

She stilled, the words pinning her in place. No, that wasn't...she wasn't—

"If you could just taste—"

"I don't need to."

And then he walked over to her plate of chocolates, picked it up, and...

Dumped it in the trash.

She stared at the mess, then back at him. "Have you lost your mind? That—those took me all night!"

And maybe something just snapped inside her. "They were delicious. Artwork. Pomp and circumstance. It's a medley of flavors, a symphony for the mouth. And you just dumped them because of what? Pride? Just take a look at the recipe!"

He just stared at her, nostrils flaring.

Okay, so maybe...um. She cut her voice low. "I'm sorry, I'm not trying to insult you or your work, but—"

"That's enough, Ms. Hart." He snatched the recipe card from her hand, glancing at it, then back to her. "The thing you don't seem to understand is that this is *my* kitchen. My kitchen, my rules, my recipes. When you have your own kitchen—and honestly, Ms. Hart, I *very much doubt* you'll ever reach that level of success—*you* can decide what to make. Until then…"

He ripped the recipe in half, then again, and again. Then he added the papers to the chocolate, spilled in with the other debris from last night's dinner.

She barely had a voice. "Why did you do that?" She took a breath, found more of it. "I've given you five years of my life. I've catered to your every stupid whim, spent countless hours doing tedious work, cleaning and sanitizing, and—this is how you treat me?"

She might be shouting now, so she schooled her voice. Hated the tears that rimmed her eyes. "That was mine. You had no right."

"Correction," he snapped, stepping up to her. "You used company resources to create it, so it was actually *mine*. And I decided I didn't want it." Oscar slid the garbage receptacle back into place. "Just like you, Ms. Hart. I don't want you."

She blinked. "What?"

"I don't want you here anymore. As of this moment, you are no longer an employee of The Sullivan."

Lily just stared at him, the words not quite landing. The silence buzzed loudly in her ears.

What—?

No, no, no. This is not how things were supposed to go. Lily pressed her lips together and blinked her eyes rapidly. She would *not* cry. Crying hadn't stopped her grandpa's disappointment in her. Hadn't stopped the Kelleys from accusing her, or Declan from turning away from her. Hadn't stopped Professor Hamilton from failing her.

Oscar folded his arms over his chest. "Did you not hear me? You're fired, Ms. Hart. And I won't be giving you a reference, so don't even ask." He pointed toward the door. "Your chocolate-making days are over."

Declan Kelley stepped off the Chicago "L" train—and straight into his new life.

Adjusting his tie, he made his way down the platform, relishing the tug of the crowd flowing around him. Everyone had somewhere to be, something to do.

Including, finally, him.

At seven thirty, the July humidity lay on his skin, his shirt sticky under his three-piece suit. But not even the oppressive heat could steal the pep in Declan's step as he approached the skyscraper on The Loop where McGentry Food Company occupied the top four stories. Was his corner office visible from way down here? His neck craned upward, taking in the building's seemingly endless rows of windows glinting off the rising sun—a gorgeous sight, given how cloudy the summer had been so far.

If Declan believed in omens of good luck, he might think the appearance of the sun on his first day as McGentry's business operations manager portended good things.

But Declan just believed in the value of hard work. And goodness knew he'd worked his tail off—both in his career so far, and all throughout his MBA program—to get to this place. Add to that six months of job searching...

But that was then, this was now, and hello to a perfect future.

Cold air blasted him as he stepped inside, blowing so hard he smoothed his hand along his hair, but his new gel had seemed to hold things steady up top. Being inside muted the din of honking taxis but enveloped him into a sea of people in suits, many talking on their Bluetooth devices, dressy shoes echoing against the travertine and through the stories-tall lobby. Declan flashed his shiny new-as-of-yesterday badge at a security guard, who waved him in, and headed toward the bank of six elevators.

His phone vibrated. He pulled it out—Brandon, his cousin. Probably just calling to wish him good luck, but the doors to the elevator opened, so he declined the call and got on with a handful of others.

He'd text him back later.

Scanning his badge, Declan hit the button for the eighty-first floor.

Eighty-first. Which meant a view of the Windy City. *Looks like we made it.* A tune sang in his head as he flashed a grin at the pretty brunette in a pencil skirt across from him. She smiled back.

Oh—he didn't want to get too friendly. He pulled out his phone, swiping open his email as an excuse to look somewhere else. Not that he wanted to be rude, but after Kim, the last thing on his mind was dating.

His phone vibrated in his hand. Brandon again. Weird. His cousin wasn't the type to call twice.

Not unless something was wrong.

He glanced up at the numbers. Only at floor eighteen, with clearly five more to go.

Declan answered, pitched his voice low. "What's up,

Brandon?" He put a hand to his other ear, bent his head to capture his voice.

"Did I catch you at a bad time?"

"I'm on an elevator—"

"Right. Sorry." Wind blew across Brandon's receiver. Probably his tour-guide cousin was standing on a cliff somewhere in Arizona, overlooking a different kind of view. "And now you're the jerk talking in the lift."

"Yep."

The elevator stopped and opened. Two of the businessmen stepped out, one glancing over his shoulder at Declan with a frown. Yeah, yeah, he knew it was rude. Declan raised his hand in apology but the guy was already walking down the thick-carpeted hallway.

A sigh came over the phone, and he forgot about the men. "What's going on?"

"It's Grandma."

Sweet Grandma Kelley, who had been frailer and frailer every time Declan had visited home. Who never had a cross word to say to anyone, even though the Kelleys (except for maybe his Aunt Jill) weren't generally known for their ability to win friends.

"What about Grandma?"

"She had a small...episode last night."

"What do you mean, *episode*? Like a heart attack? A stroke?" He glanced at the brunette. She'd turned, staring at the numbers, as if trying not to listen.

"She fainted and they're still running tests to verify what happened. But she's stable now."

"Good. Stable's good." He blew out a breath. "Is she

at the Jonathon Island clinic or did they take her to the mainland?"

"She's at the Port Joseph Hospital, but they said given the fact she's eighty-three, they'll keep her overnight for observation. Sorry I didn't call you sooner. We didn't want to call until we had good news. I know how much she means to you—to all of us—and didn't want you to worry."

Oops, he hadn't realized he was pacing until the door opened and another man got out, and the woman took another step away from him.

He retreated to the corner, facing the wall, and fought to keep his voice low. "I appreciate the call, but you definitely should have told me sooner."

He'd never be ready to lose Grandma, but especially not now—before he'd figured out some way to restore his family's faith in him.

But this job...maybe it was a start.

"So she's okay?"

"She's okay. Physically, at least."

Declan stilled. "What do you mean?"

"Apparently the reason she had the episode in the first place is because the county is foreclosing on her home."

Foreclosing—it took a second. "What?" Declan schooled his voice as the elevator stopped again. He glanced, and the woman got out, leaving him, blessedly, alone. "Why would they do that? The house has been in the family for more than a hundred years. It's on the same road as all of us. All the kids. Aw, we should have never let her live alone."

"We? Dude, you haven't lived here for ten years—since graduation."

"I know, I know—sorry, it's just…"

Brandon's voice softened. "I get it. You never really leave the island."

Huh. But he was trying to, wasn't he?

"Apparently, she owes ten years' worth of back taxes… ever since Grandpa died," Brandon said. "And she didn't tell anyone, despite multiple warnings from the county. Now, it's too late."

Declan swore under his breath just as the elevator opened again. Oops, his floor.

He stood there, not moving.

This was his fault, wasn't it?

The doors started to close, but he stuck his foot into them. "Why didn't she ask Dad for help figuring out her taxes?" Frank Kelley, Grandma's oldest son, was a CPA and handled all of the accounting and marketing for the three family businesses.

"He asked the same thing. Apparently she didn't want to be a bother."

"Aw, Grandma."

A female receptionist greeted visitors from behind a sleek black desk, the logo of the McGentry Food Company behind her. She sent Declan a friendly smile, wiggling her fingers at him while she spoke into her fancy headset.

Shoot. He took his foot out of the door. It closed.

Declan leaned against the back wall. "Surely someone in the family has the money to bail her out of this."

"It's a lot of money, Dec."

"I get it—I'd do it myself, but most of my savings went to paying down my student loans and living while trying to land this job."

"I get it too. We all want to help. It's Grandma. But everyone's strapped—money is tied up in businesses and home and debt. They don't have enough pooled between them. And you know what the pandemic did to us. Every restaurant is leveraged, just trying to stay afloat. Mom with Good Day Coffee, and Uncle Patrick with Kelley's Bar & Grill, and your mom with Martha's on Main. And it doesn't help that the competition has rolled into town with the one-dollar houses—"

"The what?"

"It's a marketing thing—the town has been giving away houses for a buck for businesses that move to the island."

"Seriously?"

Someone had called the elevator, and it began to move.

"You do know they're restoring the Grand Sullivan Hotel, right?"

"I feel like Mom mentioned that, but kind of zoned out when she was talking. Shoot. I have to go, bro." The doors opened on the floor below, and Declan got out into a hallway of law offices. He followed the signs to the stairs. "Thanks for letting me know about Grandma, and please keep me posted. Are you on island right now?"

"I'm at the hospital in Port Joseph at the moment, but yeah, visiting my mom for a while. But Dec—"

"Declan, is that you?"

Oh, great. He opened the door to the stairwell. "Hi,

Mom." Clearly she'd stolen Brandon's phone from his hands. "I heard about Grandma. I'll be praying for her, all right?"

"Yes, it's just awful." But Martha Kelley's voice didn't sound tearful or weepy. It sounded…well, the same it always did. No nonsense. Commanding. There was a reason she'd assimilated so well into the Kelley restaurant dynasty on the island, running the café herself after she and Dad had gotten married, changing its name from Kelley's Diner to Martha's on Main. Nobody could say no to her. "You need to come home right away."

He stood in the cold hallway and rubbed the vein between his eyes—the one that always throbbed when he spoke with Mom. "I'm starting my new job today, remember?"

"Right." She sighed. "If they're a good company, they'll understand that family comes first."

Ha. And the words were right there, on his lips—then why didn't she get along with her own brother-in-law? Then again, if anyone outside the family ever spoke ill of Patrick, she chewed that person out. Apparently, only a Kelley could insult a Kelley and get away with it.

"Listen, Mom. Brandon said Grandma's doing okay. Maybe I can come visit this weekend, once she's out of the hospital." He did the mental math—he'd have to leave early on Friday to beat the traffic out of town for the Fourth of July weekend. Six hours to the ferry in Port Joseph, and then another hour to the island.

"You should be here. Now."

He sighed. "Mom, I appreciate your desire for our family to be together at a time like this—"

"What I *appreciate* is that shrewd brain of yours. You've got financial savvy, and we need that now to save Grandma's house."

"Me? What about Dad? He's the accountant."

"And he's good at what he does, but I need someone who can think outside the box."

Voices lifted in the hallway. Declan caught sight of several businessmen and women stepping off the elevators. He glanced at his watch, frowned. People were starting to arrive for work, and he was going to be late for his eight a.m. with his new boss. What kind of impression would *that* make?

"Send me all the information and documents, and I'll work on a solution from here." He started up the stairs.

"Declan James Kelley, this needs to be your main focus. Put that big MBA brain of yours to use."

"I'm trying," he muttered.

"What's that?"

"Nothing." Another glance at his watch. "Mom, seriously, I'll call you back in a bit. I promise, I'll think of something."

"It's so sad. Grandpa never forgot to pay his mortgage. Grandma's been lost without Grandpa."

And there it was. The reason he'd mostly stayed off island for the last decade except for holidays and a few weeks in the summers between classes.

Because the guilt would always be there, would always be a part of him, something he'd never forget. And if he did, his family was right there, more than happy to remind him of what he owed them.

What he owed Grandma.

Blowing out a frustrated breath, he squeezed his eyes shut for a moment. "I'll do my best to come."

Another sigh. "The family needs you, Declan. We can't lose that house."

She made it sound like they were in the mafia. Sheesh.

"Mom. I can't request a leave of absence on my *first day of work*."

"I know." Her voice shook.

"No, I don't think you do. If I do this—there's no guarantee my job will be here waiting for me when I return. And it took me six months to find *this* one."

"I know." A big sob. "It's fine. I just...we need you, Declan."

Oh, shoot, those were the words, weren't they? He closed his eyes, pinching the bridge of his nose. "Calm down, Mom." He sighed, and the words just spilled out. "I won't let you down."

Because it had only taken one selfish decision to let down the entire family ten years ago. One mistake that had changed everything. That had made him the family pariah.

And the consequences of that error in judgment had been fatal.

"I'll be there as soon as I can."

He barely heard her thank him as he hung up.

Then he sighed and stared up. So much for his first day of triumph.

Bonus Epilogue

Thank you for reading *Meet Me on Lilac Lane*. We hope you loved this story. Find out what happens next for Mia and Cody with a Bonus Epilogue, a special gift, available only to our newsletter subscribers.

This Bonus Epilogue will not be released on any retailer platform, so scan the QR code to get your free gift. You acknowledge you are becoming a subscriber to the newsletters of Andrea Christenson and Sunrise Publishing. Unsubscribe at any time.

Thank You

Thank you so much for reading *Meet Me on Lilac Lane*. We hope you enjoyed the story. If you did, would you be willing to do us a favor and leave a review? It doesn't have to be long—just a few words to help other readers know what they're getting. (But no spoilers! We don't want to wreck the fun!) Thank you again for reading!

We'd love to hear from you- not only about this story, but about any characters or stories you'd like to read in the future. Contact us at www.sunrisepublishing.com/contact.

Acknowledgments

Writing a book is only possible with a cohort of people dedicated to making it happen. I love my team and I'm grateful for each of them.

Many thanks to everyone at Sunrise who loved Cody and Mia's story enough to help me figure out the sticky spots, iron out any wrinkles, and generally make the book beautiful.

A huge shoutout to my writing besties. I would be lost without Michelle Aleckson and Rachel Russell cheering me on. Let's keep swimming, ladies!

I'd be remiss if I didn't mention Grace Sperry. Every time I see you, your enthusiasm makes me smile. You are an energy giver. You're my favorite, but don't tell anyone.

And, of course, the deepest and widest and highest thank yous belong to my family. Eric, Macy, and Anna, I'm glad you are mine. Thanks for supporting my dreams even if it means I don't always make supper and sometimes stare at you like I'm listening but really I'm miles away thinking about what my made-up friends are doing at that moment. You're also my favorites. Don't tell Grace.

"Now to him who is able to do far more abundantly than all that we ask or think, according to the power at work within us, to him be glory in the church and in Christ Jesus throughout all generations, forever and ever. Amen." Ephesians 3:20-21

Andrea Christenson lives in Plymouth, MN, with her husband and two daughters. She is a lifelong lover of books, and at an early age, realized reading great stories wasn't enough; Andrea wanted to create them. She began to write her own fairytales, and as she matured into her teenage years, her stories did too. No longer did her pages only include princes and princesses, but mirrored real-life situations featuring her friends and their love interests.

Today, Andrea writes contemporary Christian romance that is meaningful, engaging, clean, wholesome, and theologically sound. She brings a depth of biblical understanding and practical application to her writing with a degree in biblical studies, over 15 years as a pastor's wife, and over 20 years of experience in youth, children, and women's ministries. Her stories contain elements of real life, true love, and authentic faith.

Andrea writes clean, faith-filled, family-honoring stories that can be trusted to entertain the heart, engage the mind, and edify the soul.

"We love because he first loved us" - 1 John 4:19.

Visit her at www.andreachristenson.com.

Jonathon Island

Where faith, family, and romance meet small-town, beachside charm. Whether you spend a weekend at The Grand, take a stroll down Lilac Lane, or cozy up in the Christmas Cottage, you'll fall in love with this heart-warming contemporary romance series, full of second chances and unforgettable love stories!

Check out the full series at sunrisepublishing.com.

We solve the problem of what we read next.

Available on Amazon

It's time to come *Home* to *Heritage*

"A heartwarming and inspiring story of second chances, renewed faith, and the enduring power of love."

—SUSAN MAY WARREN

USA Today bestselling author

We solve the problem of what we read next.

Available on Amazon

MAGNOLIA BAY

Where southern charm and romance intertwine...

"Heartwarming, genuine, and utterly captivating."

–SUSAN MAY WARREN
USA Today bestselling author

We solve the problem of what we read next.   Available on Amazon

YOU MAY ALSO LIKE...

When a blizzard strikes Deep Haven and Megan is overrun with catastrophes, it takes a former Ranger to step in and help. But the more he comes to her rescue, the sooner she'll move out... Come home to Deep Haven in this magical tale about the one who got away... and came back.

***Still the One* by Susan May Warren and Rachel D. Russell**

Working together to keep Fox Bakery from going under, Robin and Sammy find that something more than friendship is simmering between them. But will Robin follow her old dreams back to the glamor of Paris, or will she discover how sweet it is to be loved in Deep Haven?

***How Sweet It Is* by Andrea Christenson**

Back in Hearts Bend for the first time in ten years and thrown together at Haven's Bakery, Chloe and Sam have a second chance at first love. The more time Sam spends selling pastries, the more he sees a new future. But where does Chloe's heart belong? Can they find the recipe for leaving regrets behind and start something new?

One Fine Day* by Rachel Hauck and *Carrie Padgett

We solve the problem of what we read next.　　　Available on Amazon

SUNRISE PUBLISHING

**WHERE EVERY STORY IS A FRIEND,
AND EVERY CHAPTER IS A NEW JOURNEY...**

Subscribe to our newsletter for the latest news, weekly giveaways, exclusive author interviews, and more!

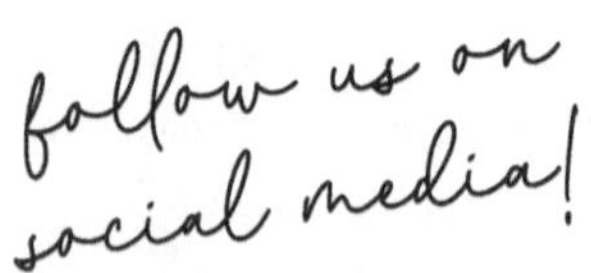

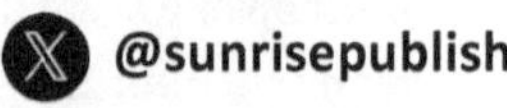

Shop paperbacks, ebooks, audiobooks, and more at
SUNRISEPUBLISHING.MYSHOPIFY.COM

www.ingramcontent.com/pod-product-compliance
Lightning Source LLC
Chambersburg PA
CBHW061109310726
48974CB00002B/460